Praise

Mo(ther) Na(ture)

"...compelling pacing and evocative writing...an inspiring message wrapped in an enthralling tale." - *Jackson Anhalt, author of From the 911 Files*

"A love letter not just to the human race, but to the ties that bind us to each other...infinitely relatable." -Robin Jeffery, author of *The Cadence Turning Mysteries*

"A story of love—sisterly love, young romance, and passion for nature in our big, beautiful world. I was captivated from start to finish." —*PJ Beaven, author* of *ZooFit Safari*

From A Youth A Fountain Did Flow

"...never dull...a neat twist on the concepts of the fountain of youth and reincarnation." -*Kirkus Reviews.*

"A fast-paced, intriguing, richly written puzzle box of a book. Every twist and turn left me breathless." —*Aaron Michael Ritchey, award-winning author of The Sages of the Underpass and The Cunning Man series.*

"A captivating tale about witches and demons and a battle as old as time. It is a story of love, loss, and being captured by purpose...I highly recommend it!" —*Cheree Alsop, best-selling author of The Silver Series.*

A Tear In Time

"A mind-bending journey through time and space, a quest to find and save one's self, a tale of heart break and the complexity of love, this book explores it all. A must read." *—Lorinda Boyer, author of Straight Enough*

"This book is exuberant with its gleeful use of time travel, lizard monsters, interdimensional galactic politics, visitors from the future. A cheerful, ghostly sidekick cracking wise. Telekinetic powers. The story, in the end, is an examination of family memories. Highly recommend." *—Peter Gorman, podcast Gorman on Gore*

"I was glued" *—Jackson Anhalt, author of From The 911 Files*

In Orion's Hands

"Never before have I been so emotionally ripped to shreds and then built back up in one read. Glaringly honest, painfully real and yet so full of hope. A must read." *—Lorinda Boyer, author of Straight Enough*

MIRANDA LEVI

AUTHOR OF "FROM A YOUTH A FOUNTAIN DID FLOW"
& "A TEAR IN TIME"

Mo(ther)
Na(ture)

Additional Books by Miranda Levi

The Fountain of Youth Series
From A Youth A Fountain Did Flow
The Sea Withdrew (Spring 2024)

The Traveler's Journals
A Tear In Time

Poetry
In Orion's Hands: a collection of poetry

Mo(ther) Na(ture)

MIRANDA LEVI

Rainbow Quartz Publishing
RQPublishing.com

Copyright © 2023 by Miranda Levi
COVER ART BY
IG: mirandalevi_author
www.MirandaLevi.com
www. RQPublishing.com
ISBN: 978-1-961714-01-4

DEDICATION

At its heart, this book is about sisters. Which is fitting, considering I wrote it for my sister, Melanie.

To all the sisters out there, this book is for you.

1

MONA

Humans blow hard.

I'm talking big, ugly chunks.

They're pimples.

That's not quite right, though. Even pimples have a cure. The only treatment that comes to mind for humans is eradication.

I suppose that's not too far off. Teenagers essentially eradicate pimples the first time they use a *Clear Skin* spray. It would stand to reason that by curating a storm, which acted like *Clear Skin*, it might eradicate all human life from Earth.

I'll unleash seven levels of hell, wipe the planet of human chaos, and delete them from the system forever.

"What in the stars above do you think you're doing?" Penny says.

With a swish of my fingers, I clear the holographic storm system from the room, "Good morning to you too."

"That was Earth," Penny says.

"Wow, congratulations. You can read a map," I say, decidedly unimpressed.

"Mona," she says.

"Penelo-peee," I mock.

Penny puts her hands on her hips and stares me down. I know she won't give in, and there's no point in waiting her out.

"It's not like I was going to kill them *all*." I wasted too much time backing up their internet to cause a functional extinction event. Damn, my stupid love of raccoon videos.

"You rolled your eyes just then," Penny says, pointing to her pair of sapphires. "Look at me right here and say you weren't going to mutilate them." Her piercing stare makes me wish she shot actual daggers instead of mental ones.

"Geeze, Penny. It's not like I try to kill off the human race every day or something." Just every other day, but I can't say that. "What gives?"

"That was a bit snarky, even for you," Penny says.

I take a deep breath and muster my most innocent expression, "I wasn't going to mutilate anything. Besides, maiming is a product of your bipeds."

"Historically speaking, you're a big, fat liar."

"I'm not fat!" What I am, is going to pull her ginger hair until she screams. I go for her, but she puts up a hand to stop me.

"I didn't mean," Penny rubs her eyes and takes a forced breath through gritted teeth. "Look, I worked hard on humans. I don't want you to ruin it, okay."

"Oh, so now I ruin things? Everything Mona touches turns to dust?" I spit my words at her.

"We had an agreement. I want you to hold up your end," Penny says.

My part in making humans was one of the worst mistakes I've ever made. As a result, I'm never going to get into university, and I blame Penny ten thousand percent.

I scoff at her. "Is that what you're saying? An agreement. You act as though I had nothing to do with making them. I worked hard on humans too. But sometimes, you have to move on. Cut your losses. Our agreement ended when your humans started killing my project and my future. Not to mention the mass extinction of thousands of species," I say.

"So, it's okay for you to have a successful project and commit genocide? You're such a damn gaslighting narcissist, Mona. The hypocrisy never ends with you, does it?"

Penny never gives me a chance to explain.

"You'd save yourself and throw me under the bus?"

"What bus?" I ask.

"You know what bus. The metaphorical bus!" Penny is waving her hands at me.

"Can you please stop? That's another human phrase, and I don't appreciate it. I would never throw you under anything," I say. "Besides, your way too heavy for me to throw around anywhere."

"Who's calling who fat now?" Penny's face has turned scarlet.

"Doesn't feel great, does it?"

Penny is tightlipped.

I know she cares about humans, but I don't think I'll ever understand why. Penny designed them to look like us. In fact, they're primitive versions of our species. They develop emotions, although they are not advanced enough to control them, let alone remove them. The technology is simply not there yet.

Instead, these beasts are destructive to the point of demise. Why would she let humans go on this long? It's beyond my understanding.

The Bio-Matrix makes them real, but it shouldn't prevent us from doing what's best for the world. Humans aren't the only "real" things out there. They're not even the only "real" things on the planet. Earth is just as real as humans. She's bigger and supports more life than them too.

All humans seem to do is destroy. At least Earth provides.

I take a deep breath. I'm never trying to be mean to Penny. I'm just trying to make a point.

"I never said it was okay for you to fail, Pen. I never even implied as much. I'm simply pointing out that when you came to me about putting talkies on my peaceful life-breathing planet, you called them an *experiment*. You said, *do it for the art Mona*. You said, *let's turn a monkey into a man*. And I thought, okay, you're my sister. Why not give you a little slice of Earth to work with? It's a big planet," I say. "It seemed like the right thing to do. Mom is always lecturing me, begging me to *give your twin some room to work*. So, I agreed."

Penny rolls her eyes at me, "That's not what happened, and you know it."

"Then, they just TOOK OVER. Isn't it better to have something rather than end with nothing? I can't sit by and watch the destruction of everything I worked hard to create."

"Why can't you take a little ownership, Mona?" You wanted to know if they could think and feel as much as I did. And guess what? They can. You can't just flood them away whenever you don't get your way. That's so childish."

"I only did that once, and it's not like it worked anyway," I say more to myself than her.

Penny found out about my eradication proclamation. Instead of trying to stop me, she warned those loci and big shocker. Some survived. They started worshiping her, too, absolutely beyond my understanding.

Humans are like cockroaches. They fight and climb up out of the pits of the void to live another day.

They never die.

They survive.

No matter what happens, they survive.

No.

That's not fair. Cockroaches are far too high of a compliment for humans.

"Earth is central to my educational goals, Penny. You know this. I'm never going to get into university without an entrance project. Earth is that project. Why would I give up my future for humans?" If Penny would only listen once in a while, we wouldn't have to have this conversation repeatedly. "I just wish you could see it from my point of view this once."

"They're sentient. Don't you have any other projects to play with? The all-mighty Mona doesn't have four backup plans?" Penny asks.

"I'm not playing around. You're missing the point entirely. I could say the same thing about your pets. You have plenty of different species to *play* with, so why do you have to have humans too? I don't believe for a moment that humans are your only entrance project. You want to talk about hypocrisy? Take a look in the mirror." You can put them somewhere else," I run my fingers through my curly brown hair, untangling the mess I haven't had time to do anything with.

"That's not the way it works, Mona. Ever heard of science? Supporting this specific life takes a particular type of celestial body. Unfortunately, when we started this entrance project, you weren't willing to make me a second version of Earth," Penny says.

She grabs the hairwand from our shared space and waves it over my head. In one whoosh, I have perfectly detangled, commercial-ready curls.

"My hair was fine," I say, waving her away. "Why does your project rely on my ability to do half of it for you? That's not an entrance project of your own. That's you being an opportunist."

"I'm not an opportunist. You're playing favorites!"

"It's not always about playing favorites, Penny. What would be the point if I made every planet with Earth's unique environmental features? How would my project be unique? If I made you a copy of Earth, what would make my project special to the admissions committee? It's like you've never heard of a little word called *irreplaceable*. I'm trying to get into the ivy league, not some state school. I don't want to be like these losers living through trashy uploads. I don't need to live a thousand lives. I just want to live one. This one. I want to create the uploads, Penny. I thought we both did."

"We did. We do," she says, and it's so quiet I almost don't hear her. "But there's a lot of life you're missing. It doesn't have to be go-go-go all the time. You'd know that by now if you tried even a single lifetime upload."

No way. I'm not about to live some menial life for eighty or ninety years and lose motivation. Uploading for a long weekend is one thing, but a lifetime? I can't even wrap my head around it.

On the other hand, I know what I want.

Penny doesn't. I can't blame her for not having a life plan. Everyone can't know what they want to be in the third grade.

Time for a change of subject. "Have you thought any more about upgrading to the SoTo chip? I'm telling you. It's the only way to upload. Especially since you're completely on board with the whole living other lives bit. No more gross sweaty suits or those icky patches that pull out your hair. It taps right into your nervous system and optic network."

"And then, you'll never have to feel anything again," Penny says.

"What's that supposed to mean? On the contrary, I *feel* everything," I say. "When I upload to Zion, my hair is wet after swimming in the fire lakes. The feel of the flames dancing and licking my skin is as real as it gets. Food's the same way." I suppose on the downside when I tripped and landed face-first into a gravel pit, it hurt. I was tender for the whole weekend. But I don't say that part out loud.

"Exactly, uploads are the ultimate defiance of death. Can't you see Mona? You can live a hundred lives and never age. So why don't you take your time and upload for a few years? Perfect what it means to upload to Earth. I'm not saying you have to do it for a lifetime. Just settle in and learn a few things. Enjoy life."

"I enjoy life just fine. Besides, why wouldn't you want all those lives you live to be as real as you could make them? The SoTo Chip is the only way to live. I'm telling you, Pen, I know what I'm talking about."

"You're missing the point," Penny says.

"I guess I am because I don't understand what you're talking about," I say.

"You're not the same person. The SoTo chip has side effects. One of them is your sheer lack of empathy. I wouldn't do that to myself. The Mona I know would care about exterminating an entire planet," Penny says.

"Exactly, I care about the planet. I care about Earth. I love it when you make my points for me." I can't help the smile playing on my lips.

Penny crosses her arms, "You're such a spoiled brat. You've always got to have your way, don't you? I bet you couldn't survive one day on Earth. You'd be too afraid." Penny averts her eyes while playing with the hem of her dress.

"I'm only afraid you'd lose the bet. Then, I'd be stuck dealing with a sad, miserable, dejected Penny," I say.

"You don't even know what that means Mo-Nah."

"I'll take your bet Penelop-pee. Let's make it more interesting, though," I say.

Penny cocks her head. "Oh? What did you have in mind?"

I scratch my chin. "I'll go to Earth. I'll even stay a week. Two, if it shuts you up. I'll live amongst their ginormous Earthen crypts they call houses. But when I get back, your humans are gone. Done. Zip. Zilch. You rehouse them, or I will delete them all. I don't care what you do with them, but they don't get to live on Earth or any of my planets, for that matter. Maybe it's time you stepped up your game and made some planets of your own."

"Oh yea, 'cause that's so possible to do on command. You know that's not how it works. You studied nature, and I studied humanoid animation. There's no clear-cut crossover between the two," Penny says.

"Then maybe you should respect the planets more. Instead of housing your destructo-monsters on them!"

"We agreed to work together," Penny says. She waves away her statement. "Fine, you go to Earth. But let's not pick some arbitrary number of days. What would be the point in that?"

"I don't know. What's the point in any of this? Please, why don't you enlighten me," I make a show giving her the floor.

"You could just hunker down in a hidey hole for seven or eight days and walk away. What would that teach you? You're offering to live in a human's shoes for a while. So that's what I want you to do," Penny crosses her arms. She's sizing me up, going in for the kill. "I believe once you've experienced human emotions the *human way*, you might be ready. When you've felt what they feel and walked in their shoes, then and only then can you come back and decide what to do with the human race. If that takes you a day, fine. But if that takes you a year, so be it."

I snort, "I'll be *ready*. Oh, honey, I'm going to kill them all. I'm ready to do that now." I smile wickedly at her, "Walk in a human's shoes. As if. What can they offer me that I don't already have? Look around, Penny. It's not like we're living the life of poverty here."

"They're sentient beings."

"You say that as if I'm meant to care."

"I'll file a motion, and they'll be protected under the Biomatrix Sentience Act."

"Not before I press delete, not before I ruin all the backup files, and you are left without proof or protection for your pets."

"A threat Mona?"

"Never, it's a promise," I say.

"You're clearly not ready to hear it yet," Penny sighs. "Here's the thing. If you play fair, I won't remove them. You can delete them all if you want to. But only after you've experienced all eight basic human emotions. You do that first, and I won't stand in your way."

"So, I can brew the storm of the century, and you won't try to stop me? Maybe I'll send smoke through the trees like in that Shyamalan movie. I'll say, that's one human with the right ideas."

"See, you can relate to them. Or one of them—sort of."

Penny is reaching, but I don't mind. The thing is, I love to watch her squirm. I love when she admits I'm right and she's wrong. And what I love even more than that is knowing I'll enjoy eradicating Earth of every irritating, uncivilized, putrid human being.

I push my hair out of my face and cross my arms, "Okay, I'll bite. I'll stay on Earth until I've experienced all eight little human emotions. But, like, wow. Eight is such a big number. What will I ever do with myself?"

"Yes, we'll see, dear sister. We will see," Penny says.

She thinks if she can make me human, I'll have some crazy crisis of conscience and save them all. Doesn't she get it? I'm two nano-seconds away from deleting them. I'll have fun causing the San Andreas fault to quake while hitting Japan with another Tsunami. I'll flood the lands and strike the human race down one by one with bolts of lightning. After all, I've always preferred playing with my food before eating.

How bad could living on Earth be? What would a few Earthen days be in the long run anyway? It's been a while since I've visited. I used to think of Earth as a refuge. I could upload for thirty seconds and spend the night. Take a two-minute vacation swimming in the Great Coral Reef before a test, and it's like I've been on a two-week vacation.

Time moves as fast or slow as I want on Earth—the perks of being the creator. Unlike traditional uploads, living the length of a lifetime virtually might be equivalent to one or two whole days in real time. When you combine that with a nutrition patch, there's no actual harm done to my physical body. While on Earth, it can move as slowly or as fast as I want.

Unfortunately, I agreed not to intervene through uploads after Penny created her hairless apes. In her words, *so things can develop organically.*

Ha!

Organic, my ass. Like, I don't see her uploading. To be fair, it's not like I had the best luck with any species I created. I can admit that dinosaurs weren't my highest quality design. They didn't do much but fight over food. It was an eat, sleep, and defecate scenario.

Dinosaurs were a massive learning curve. But when the time came for me to move on and better the whole of the world, I wiped them out.

That's what any good creator would do.

According to the *Creator's Handbook*, you must be willing to make hard decisions.

POW!

With one perfectly aimed asteroid, I liberated Earth and started fresh.

Almost.

Penny wanted humans. She insisted upon them.

The whole thing quickly turned into a science experiment gone wrong. But I can't stand by any longer watching Earth's destruction at the hands of monsters. Especially those who believed they were above caring for the planet. It has supported their survival for tens of thousands of years! How absolutely conceited are they?

Self-righteous, entitled, ignorant beasts.

At one point, I even created a tiny disease-transferring parasite. Humans call it all kinds of things, muskiet, hyttynen, mug, kounoupi, yatoosh, and mosquito, to name a few. It was just too bad that this strategy was taking longer to execute than I'd expected it to.

Bad math was at fault.

But I won't tell my professor that last part. I approximated precisely how long it would take for a blood-sucking bug to kill off the human population. Only I was wrong.

I'll never let bad math stand in my way again.

What was once an untouched oasis is now something humans call a landfill. Holes in the ground were playing peek-a-boo with garbage while trying to win the laziest sandcastle award is an acceptable dismissal of their waste. The oceans are polluted with plastic and oil spills. Sea life has never attacked a human without provocation. In my not-so-humble opinion, they've had ample provocation.

Note to self, consider letting sea life attack humans.

The Plastic War.

Revenge of the Seals.

The Ocean's Vengeance.

Plastic.

Ugh.

At the rate they're going, there will be more garbage than ocean in a few short years. Humans are vile. Filthy, disgusting, bawdy, scalawags...

"You're muttering again," Penny says, interrupting my thoughts.

I let out an exaggerated sigh and pretend to close my eyes in defeat., "Fine. You win. When are we doing this? Can we get it over with? I have things to do, places to go, people to kill."

"You don't need beauty sleep before tackling the beast? I'm surprised," Penny says.

"Oh please, you're the one with the beauty issues. I don't understand you. You'll wear blood-red lipstick but refuse the SoTo Chip. You spend hours picking out your clothes, designing your hair color, and you've got new modifications every other day," I say. "I guess I just prefer the all-natural look. And every moment I stay here gives humans a larger window to trash Earth" I throw my hands up. "Curse the rivers of Sion. Who knows, if I wait much longer, there might only be radiation-marred heaps when I arrive. That would take centuries to heal."

"So, what you're saying is you'll go? Now?" Penny asks.

I want to pull her hair again.

"Let's just do this and get it over with."

"Pinky swear?" Penny reaches her pinky finger to me.

I blow out a breath and lock my pinkie with hers. "I pinky promise I won't destroy anything until after I've won this bet." We both kiss our thumbs, and the pact is made.

Penny swishes her long red hair out of her face. "Your wish is my command," she snaps her fingers and is suddenly gone with an explosion of glitter and pink smoke.

2

PENNY

My lips aren't blood red. They're *Happy or Bust* red.

I don't modify my coloring *that* much. Besides, what harm does a little eyeliner do?

Exactly none.

It makes my eyes pop. Eyeliner doesn't cause a loss of empathy. But that damn SoTo Chip does.

Not that Mona sees it.

If she can't see it, I'll make her see it. Even if it means losing everything. As often as I'd rather waterboard her than listen to her crazy ramblings, she is still my sister.

So, what's the best place to send a selfish, un-empathic, human-hating chick?

So many choices and so little time.

Ultimately, I throw a mental dart and land on Bellingham, Washington. It's a relatively Earth friendly town in northwest America. Statistically speaking, my location algorithm suggests Bellingham as one of the best places for Mona to interact with people who care about her planet as much as she does—folks who might care about her too.

It's an important decision, and I'm not about to let this opportunity pass. I've been planning this fight. I gathered all the data before deciding to poke Monasorus-Rex. If humans are going to have a fighting chance at survival, they need me at my best.

For humanity's sake, I hope I'm right.

If I'm being candid, a small part of me wants to send her to the worst slums imaginable. Let her struggle.

After a small internal war rages in my gut, I decide the end result is what matters most. For this reason, Bellingham wins. It's most beneficial to everyone if Mona comes around a little on the whole *human* topic. But it has to be at her own pace.

Her choice.

As much as I'd like to torture the woman who created the concept, it will never work that way.

3

MONA

Coughing and covered in pink glitter from Penny's theatrics, my eyes open to a new world.

It's my world, or something that once resembled it. The last time I uploaded to Earth's network, everything around me sang harmoniously—a symphony with all my creations in tune. The sheer number of hours I've spent creating this planet is uncountable. I don't want to think about how many years it's been. I've known this is what I wanted to do from a young age.

My heart breaks. Have I wasted my life? Have I ruined things by letting Penny have a say?

The trees aren't singing.

According to my onboard guidance mapping system, I'm standing in the middle of a tree sanctuary.

The quiet is deafening.

What a ghastly idea, saplings needing protection from humans. There's a stillness only disrupted by metallic monstrosities conjured by the human brain.

Damn you, Penny.

This is all your fault.

I hadn't thought going to Earth would make me angrier at her, but it does.

First things first. I adjust my onboard settings. The SoTo chip, short for somatosensory chip, provides me with an onboard display. I can bring up new information on anything with only a thought. The screen layers over top of whatever input my eyes process. Be it upload or real world. This gives me access to edit mode, so I can make little changes here or there as I see fit. I can even create something from thin air as needed.

Okay, the settings are configured.

I blink away the majority of the overlay, leaving only a small set of icons until I get a good look at where I am.

Holy rivers of Sion.

This tree sanctuary is a joke. I bring up a species listing and am appalled to see such small numbers. No more than one or two of any tree type. Where a thousand thick groves once stood lay only a mere hundred saplings now.

"You, poor things," I coo, touching my trees, calling them by names. "Georgiana, Fredricka, Ashby, you poor things, what can I do? Who would do this?" Bastard humans, that's who.

I make my way through the trees, and wildlife peeks from every corner. I bend down and pet a squirrel. A raven lands on my arm. None of my creations shy away from me. Instead, it's as though they each seek me out. At least there's this. At least in this horror-plagued place, my designs don't run from their maker.

A corkscrew willow wraps its long vines around me, and the air carries a question with a whisper from her to my ear, "Mother, is that you?"

"Yes," I say. "My darlings, I'm here now. But what have they done to you?"

"Oh, Mother Nature," she starts, but I cut her off.

"Let me just stop you there. It's Mona. That whole Mother Nature bit was a joke. A poor one that's gone rather droll now," I caress my handiwork, sending waves of radiating life force through her trunk and to the tips of her leaves. They shudder and groan with deep satisfaction. "I'm sure you can understand how I feel. Mother Nature feels too egomaniacal. If you could pass it along, that would be grand." I send one more tree-shaking vibration. "I'd like this to be the only conversation I must have about it." I sigh with relief and smile, glad to get that minor correction out of the way.

"Mona?" comes an easy, undemanding voice. I look down and see a white-tailed rabbit standing on its back legs.

"Yes, my darling?"

The rabbit lowers himself and hops away.

"Just checking, I see," I sigh and head deeper into the park.

4

PENNY

A group of early morning joggers descends a narrow cement bridge. I may not have a SoTo chip to upload seamlessly, but my readouts are clear enough. Mona is verging on disgust.

I've spent the last four years cultivating a program that reads human emotions—allowing me to break down the science of humanity's big questions.

It is absolutely fascinating.

Mona looks at the humans wearing neon-colored spandex and a shiver of revulsion moves through her. She's never experienced the physical reactions of a human body before. Mona's logs show that her only previous uploads have been something that flies, swims in the ocean, or the occasional Jade Vine. Never has she uploaded as anything other than something she alone created.

Figures.

Revulsion creates a tidal wave and rips through her stomach. Bile rises in her throat. The mere idea of encountering an actual human makes her physically sick beyond reproach.

Oh man, this is too good. I can't help the smile I know is playing on my lips. I don't care. Watching Mona squirm might be worth all of it.

Okay, fine.

Maybe not all of it.

But I'm still allowed to enjoy this. It doesn't take away this fantastic moment.

Mona backs into the trees and off the path as the Joggers gain on her, shielding herself from view. I can see it now.

What if one of them accidentally or purposefully touched her?

Gasp!

She might, like, catch a disease. She's fretting about spending her days lying in some contaminated hospital bed, frothing at the mouth.

Oh, Mona, you don't hide your emotions well.

She returns to the joggers, clutches her stomach, and bends at the waist.

I snap my fingers, and everything around her freezes.

Mona takes a couple of slow deep breaths and looks around. The Joggers are midstride, taunting her, threatening to reach out and contaminate her.

"Oh see, that was way too easy," I try to maintain my giggle but fail. "You'll have this in no time at all." I give Mona a wink and lean against a willow tree.

"What's with all the glitter? It's like a freaking sparkle party up in here. You're adding to the pollution problem Penny," Mona says, seething.

"What? It's just a little human craft time herpes to welcome you back to Earth. What's the big deal? You're always such a spoilsport." I roll my eyes and snap my fingers. The remaining glitter disappears with a whoosh.

"I'm not a spoilsport," Mona says. Her emerald eyes look through me to that damn SoTo screen. She's still brushing the non-existent glitter off herself. "What are you doing here?

Have you come to award me my prize? Do I get to kill them already?" Mona glowers at me. Then her face becomes calm, almost serene.

"Would you stop it," I know she's just thinking mean thoughts.

"Floods, earthquakes, and eruptions. Eradication, eradication, eradication," she gives a serpent's smile.

"Funny..." I say. "You've just embodied your first emotion, loathing. Not so bad, eh? The utter revolution and rejection of something so profound that your body reacts without your permission. That is the ultimate manifestation of loathing and disgust, Mona. Bravo. Just think, only a few more pesky little emotions to go. If I'm being honest, I hoped it would take you longer." If she can't see how wrong she is, Mona has damned the world to the same fate as those poor Jurassic beasts.

"Is that what that was? Blah! I guess it was an appropriate feeling considering the subject. If you could keep your hominids away from me and stop pressing pause on all this," Mona says, motioning around her. "Then I could finish up and get back in time to human bomb the world."

"The phrase doesn't work that way. It's called a bug bomb. With humans, it's called genocide," I say. "Either way, it's not appropriate."

"Whatever. Genocide it is, then. Political correctness is the least of my concerns," Mona says.

"Besides, that's not part of the deal, Mona. You've got to experience human emotions, which means you've got to live like a human. Interact with them. No hiding out, remember? Why don't you try being nice for a change? There's an old human saying, you will catch more flies with honey than vinegar."

"I don't need to catch flies and I don't need your advice," she says.

"Prove it. Look, there's one right behind you. It's even an adorable miniature guy. Shouldn't be too scary," I say. Then, before she could make a rebuttal, I set time moving in motion again. I don't tell Mona that I coached the little boy over.

He needs a friend as much as Mona does.

5

MONA

A young voice catches me by surprise.

"Are you okay, lady?" it's a small human with dark fur and a caramel-colored meat sack. He's watching me.

"What do you want?" I say, sidestepping further from the thing. It's just breathing room, though. I enjoy my space.

I'm not afraid of him.

No. Not fear.

I'm crazy powerful. There is nothing a human can do that I can't protect myself from. With a blink of my eyes, I could collapse the whole planet in on itself. What I create in the AI Mainframe, I can remove from the AI Mainframe. I made this entire world.

It's only a bio-matrix. There is nothing to fear.

The tension brought about by the joggers starts to ease from my neck and shoulders. I look back at where Penny stood; she's gone. The world is moving, and Penny is still selfish.

"Hello?" the tiny human says.

I grunt at him.

"I umm... It's just that you looked like you'd seen a dead body or something really gross," he says. The boy wrinkles his nose and reminds me of a baby goat.

Damnit Penny.

It should not be endearing. On the contrary, I shudder at such a crazy thought. It's like Penny is invading my brain, coaxing me to think inappropriate, dare I say, *kind* things.

She's sending the young one to trick me. It's just downright despicable. Penny knows I have a soft spot for baby animals.

Such a bitch.

"You've seen dead humans?" I ask, incredulous. This babe has probably never seen such a gleeful event.

"Eww, gross. I'm only a kid." The boy rolls his eyes and then narrows them at me. "But have you?"

He's a bit young to be so morbid. Maybe they start this way? It wouldn't surprise me. Humans are basically born assassins. It's part of their genetic makeup. If I could only prove as much, Penny would have no choice but to let me kill them all.

"Sure, I've even slain a few," I say.

"Ha! Whatever, you're not a good liar," he says.

"What's your name?" I give him a proper once over. He's shorter than me and is relatively young, with blue eyes.

The young boy takes a step back. "I'm not supposed to talk to strangers."

"Too late," I say.

He looks me up and down and comes to some conclusion. "You smell like fresh-cut grass, and your eyes are the same color as the Thuja tree at my friend's house. You look pretty normal to me."

"Well, appearances can be deceiving. Don't let me fool you," I say.

"You sort of remind me of my mom. Is that weird for me to say?" he shrugs to himself. "I'm Oliver. Oliver Harvey," he reaches his hand out toward me.

I look at the tiny hand, but I'm not sure what he expects me to do with it. After a brief moment, I deduce it must be some form of a human greeting. So, I mirror his motions without contacting him, lest I be contaminated. "Hi Oliver, Oliver Harvey, I'm Mona."

"You're so weird." Oliver claps my hand before I can pull away and giggles. "I like it."

It's everything in me not to recoil from the boy. I let go and wiped my hand along the side of my shirt.

Oliver kicks the ground a little, lost in thought. "So, do you want to, like, go get ice cream or something?"

"Ice cream? That sounds cold. Don't larger ones usually accompany small humans? Or do I have that wrong? It's not like I was paying close attention. Young animals often wander off alone. Although most of those become food," I say, more to myself than Oliver.

"Well, yeah. My brother's over there." Oliver points to a building just outside the park's boundaries where a row of structures lines the street. According to my onboard heat sensors, there's a lot of lethargic movement inside the building.

I wonder for a moment if Zombies are real. I'm pretty sure Penny nixed that idea. Not for lack of trying on my part.

"Why aren't you around other humans? I don't understand why they let you alone. You seem too small to be in the wild."

"Dad let me stay home from summer day camp today because I wasn't feeling well. But then he got called into work.

So, I was with my brother, but then he got called into work too. Mr. Cain's sink broke, and he's got to fix it. I got bored waiting and decided to explore the…." Oliver's eyes grow two sizes more prominent, and he whispers the last two words, "Forbidden Forest."

"What's the Forbidden Forest? Are you telling me you're diseased?" I say, taking a significant step backward. Penny is going to pay for this.

"Harry Potter! Duh…"

"What's a Harry Potter? Is that like a furry human or something?"

Oliver giggles, "No, Harry Potter is a book. It's about a boy who's a secret wizard. He goes to a magic school, and there's the Forbidden Forest, where no one's supposed to go because there are monsters!"

"Oh. Okay then," I say. "What's a wizard?"

"Like magic, you know?"

"I don't," I confess.

Oliver raises an eyebrow, skeptical of me. "What's diseased?" he says, only he pronounces it "dee-zeez."

"Diseased Oliver, diseased," I say, enunciating the word for him. "Do you have the plague? How about typhoid? Smallpox? Viral hemorrhage fever? Is it measles? By the three suns of Zolach," I can feel a tightness in my chest. "You have malaria, don't you? Are we all going to die? Is it yellow fever? Just tell me, Oliver. Spit. It. Out," I say, flaring my arms in Oliver's direction. I've gone from zero to sixty in three point two seconds, but I can't help it.

Oliver doesn't say anything at first. I think he's confused by my sudden outburst. "My dad said it's just a cold. Dad said I was fine." His cheeks turn pink, and tears well in his eyes.

"Are you going to leak? Please don't do that. It's so gross. I'm—" For the love of Zion, what am I trying to say? I take a deep breath. "Oliver Harvey, Olli? I'm… sorry."

Oliver perks his head up and bites his lip. "My big brother calls me Olli too."

"I see. Do you mind if I call you Olli as well?" I ask.

"I guess that would be okay," Oliver says.

"I'm here on a mission, Olli, and I just can't afford to catch some human malady," I smile a big toothy grin at him. "I need to be in tip-top condition if I'm going to win. Do you know what it means to *win*?"

Oliver's head is still hanging low. "You talk funny, but I'm not dumb," Oliver says.

"That may be. What's this ice cream you mentioned?" I ask.

"You don't know what ice cream is? Do you live in a rock?" Oliver says.

"Why would I live in a rock? Do you live in a rock? How do you get inside? Wouldn't that be cold? Unless it were a heated lava-based rock, but then you would boil. Your human shell would melt. Do you mean like a mountainside or a cave?" I'm so confused by human shelter choices. Rocks? Of all things.

"I don't know," Oliver shrugs. "But you're the one who doesn't know what ice cream is."

Time to concede. "Okay, let's go find this frozen water cream, and you can show me all the excitement." At least this human seems mildly tame. Besides, Penny will never let me avoid human interaction forever. If this is what she wants, then this is what she'll get.

I can play along.

I might even have enough self-control not to delete him from the system.

I'll show Penny I can human just as well as a human does.

Oliver smiles, and I notice he's missing a lower canine tooth. How weird. Maybe he's deformed. Some abnormality of his generation. All those toxic pollutants humans put into Earth, even hurting their young in the process.

No wonder his father makes him stay home. It must be embarrassing for everyone to look at him.

Ah, well, it's not as though it will be of any consequence soon.

6

MONA

Oliver and I leave the park side by side.

Penny never specified exactly where on Earth I would serve my penance. That is how I see this visit, penance—a life sentence for getting caught.

If I only brewed that storm a little quicker. Cast some lighting down before watching raccoon videos and backing up the internet. Or even if I deleted everything and wiped the drives, none of this might be happening.

I'm a good creator and an even better coder. There is no reason any of this should still be here. It's plain wrong timing.

Penny has always got to muddle things up.

I wish I were an only child.

"Where exactly are we going, Olli?" I ask.

Oliver points forward along the path.

"How many cycles are you?" I ask.

"Cycles? Like a bicycle? How many bicycles do I own? One. What a silly question. My turn. Where are you from, Mona? How many bicycles do you own?" he says.

Oliver is jumping over every crack in the sidewalk, walking on tiptoe at times to avoid landing on one. He's humming a rhyme as he moves. "You know what would be cool, to own a bike of every color, shape, and size. Then, I could start my own circus. I could call it The Terrifying Traveling Cyclists Who Defy Gravity. Or something like that."

"You're only one? How is that possible?" I say. "I thought humans developed much slower. You must be some sort of savant."

"I'm not one. I'm eight, almost nine." Oliver holds out his eight fingers. "I only have one bicycle."

"Oh, I see. Eight. What's a bicycle?" I say. So many new things that I wonder briefly if I should be taking notes and then decide it won't matter in the grand scheme of things.

Oliver shakes his head. "All adults know what a bicycle is. I might be young, but I can tell when someone tries to pull one over on me. How old are you?"

I think about this before answering. The SoTo tells me that Oliver's heart has begun to race rapidly.

"I'm sorry," he says. "I forgot what my brother says about asking a girl her age. It's rude."

This makes me smile. "How old do I look?"

Oliver shrugs, "I dunno. Maybe fifty?"

"I look fifty?" I say, flabbergasted.

"Maybe like fifteen, then?" he says.

I let out a short chuckle. "So, you have no idea?"

"I asked, didn't I?" he says, and I nod my agreement.

"They don't even have a number for how old I am in human years," I say.

"Sure, they do. I know how to count. I'm pretty smart for my age," Oliver says.

"Well, your number system stops at what? Centillion, I think? Let's say, in Earthen years, I reached Centillion before Earth was even conceived."

Oliver's mouth drops open. "Yeah, right. How old are you really?"

"Why would I make that up?" I ask.

"The Earth is only four and a half billion years old. So, there's no way you're more than a Cent-trillion years old. That's impossible," Oliver says.

"How do you know that?" I ask.

"I'm into space and stuff. I love the planets and our solar systems. I want a telescope, but Dad thinks I'm too young. Or maybe he can't afford it," Oliver shrugs. "Either way, I'm going to show him how responsible I am, and maybe he'll buy one for my birthday."

"When's your birthday?"

"August 17th, just a few more days. Not that I'm counting," Oliver tries to appear nonchalant about it, but I can tell he's excited. His heart has begun to beat faster again.

"For the record, nothing is impossible, Olli. Some things are a little less probable than other things." I consider what to tell him before deciding on the truth. "Let's just say if I were a human, I'd be somewhere around the proximity of seventeen verging on eighteen human years old. Would that suffice your curiosity?"

"So, are you or aren't you, Cent-trillions years old?" Oliver asks.

This makes me chuckle again. "Yes, I am Cen-till-ions of years old, but if that's too big of a number, then we can pretend I'm much younger. I look it, don't I?"

Oliver shrugs. "Maybe you can meet my brother. He just turned eighteen."

"Maybe, if I can't avoid it," I say. "So where is this frozen water? The temperature is too high. Thanks to global warming, it's even hotter than it should be. It shouldn't be a hard concept to understand, but it seems lost on all of you." I feel my face crumple along with my soul.

"I know. I keep telling my brother that we have to do our part and recycle more. Like, everything is recyclable or can be reused. Dad calls me the Recycle Authoritarian. I don't know what that means, though."

I stop, dumbfounded. I didn't expect the little human to agree with me. Let alone have the word *recycle* in his vocabulary.

"What? I know what global warming is. I do go to school, you know. I'm not an idiot," Oliver says.

"I never said you were."

"You thought it, though. It's okay. Most do. Thanks for not saying it out loud. I have feelings just like everyone else," he says.

"Don't let others bind you into a box Oliver. Your little life is short. Don't waste time trying to fit in. Just surprise them all and be amazing just the way you are. And always put Earth first." I shake my head and set my shoulders, remembering why I'm on Earth.

It isn't to comfort a human child.

It's to save my project, get into university, become a famous world builder, and eradicate humans once and for all.

Oliver Harvey is trying to do his part to save Earth too. Even if it is small, I should appreciate the effort.

I should.

Mo(ther) Na(ture)

But I probably won't.

7

PENNY

Two senior women stand, engaged in conversation on the corner of Donovan Avenue and 4th Street. The first dons a bright-colored shawl and a white pantsuit. The second is wearing a gray and black floor-length dress.

Paired next to one another, the women add to the common misconception that opposites attract. Opposite magnets attracted one another, but birds of a feather romantically flock together.

Agnes Witherbee looks up and down the street. Dementia took most of her short-term memory six years ago, leaving her lost in the present moment—the folds of her charcoal frock sway in the light breeze. Agnes sways with it.

"We live over there," Cora Nightingale says to her best friend of seventy years. Dementia activated in Cora's genetic makeup shortly after Agnes's decline.

"Are you sure?" Agnes looks up and down the street again.

"Yes, I used to have ice cream cones over there." Cora points to Dean's Soda Shop, outfitted in red brick, advertising *open since 1923*.

"That sounds yummy," Agnes says.

Cora nods her head in agreement, "Yes, it does." She wraps herself in her oversized ornate rainbow shawl.

"Well, how much do you think they are?" Agnes asks, running a few fingers through her short silver curls and tugging at the pearl earring on her left earlobe.

"I think you can get a cone for a dollar," Cora says, a grin peeking out the edge of her lips.

"That's a pretty good price. But I left my money at home Cora, and I think we're lost." Worry shadows Agnes's face.

Cora's eyes, a soft twinkling gray, smile, "I know where we live. It's right over there." She points to a sign which reads Summer Grove Retirement Community, her smile as bright as her pixie white hair. When she remembers something, her eyes shine as lively as the colors she wore.

"Are you sure?" Agnes asks.

"Yes, I used to have ice cream cones over there," Cora says again, pointing to Dean's Soda Shop.

"Oh, that sounds yummy. How much do you think they are?" Agnes asks.

"I think you can get a cone for a dollar," Cora says.

"That's a pretty good price. But I left my money at home and think we're lost." Agnes looks up and down the street again, with no signs of recognition.

This conversation repeats for the third time as I watch invisible to all, but most importantly, without notice of the approaching Mona and Oliver.

8

MONA

Oliver and I are watching two elderly women have the same conversation repeatedly.

"I always feel sad for them," Oliver says.

"How so?" I ask.

Oliver shuffles his feet. "I don't want to get old and forget things. I don't like to think about getting old at all. It means having wrinkles and funny old people smell. Dad says it's the moth's balls."

"The moth's balls do it, eh?"

Oliver looks up. "I'm not even sure what they are. Why do old people keep them around?" He let a breath out. "Are they balls made of moths? Or are they a moth's like balls?"

I can't stifle a snort. "I'm not sure, Olli. But if I ever find out, I'll let you know."

"Why do old people always say that youth is wasted on the young?" he asks.

"I guess you'll find out someday if you become old," I say.

"Yea. Maybe."

Neither of the older women realizes Oliver and I have approached. Are they absolutely binary?

I can't help but watch the conversational cycle with fascination. My mouth curves upwards. Is it a glitch in the program? Why are they repeating the same conversation on a seemingly endless loop? Well, whatever is happening, it's semi-entertaining. Despite her persistent arguing, this proves that humans aren't as intelligent as Penny claims.

"Hi, Mrs. Witherbee. Hi, Mrs. Nightingale," Oliver says.

"Hello there, young sir," the one wearing bright colors replies. "What are you doing out here all alone? Where is your brother?"

"He's inside working. We were just on our way to get ice cream," Oliver says.

The one wearing funeral clothes turns to Oliver. "Where's your brother? Young boys shouldn't be wandering the streets alone, you know."

"I know, Mrs. Witherbee, but I'm not alone. I'm here with Mona," he says.

"Who's Mona?" The old woman covers the nape of her dress with her cardigan.

"I'm Mona," I say.

"Oh, I thought you were lost," the first says.

"Me too. Doesn't she look lost?" the second says.

"Not exactly," I say. "Who are you?" Oliver can keep them straight, but I'm struggling.

"Agnes, and this is Cora," the one in black says.

"Do you live around here?" Cora asks.

"I don't remember where we live. I think we're lost." Agnes looks around for something she can recognize. "We live right over there," Cora points.

"Are you sure?" Agnes asks.

"Yeah, I used to get ice cream right there." Cora and Agnes fall right into step despite our interruption.

I can barely keep the bubbling laughter inside. "I think maybe you've tapped into the glitch or have one of your own. May I?"

"Who are you?" Agnes takes a step back.

"I'm Mona. I'm a friend of Oliver's. But we've established that now, haven't we? Just sit tight, okay."

"Oh, Oliver, you must know his brother then? Isn't he the sweetest boy?" Cora says.

"How long have you been standing there, Oliver? Is she lost?" Agnes says.

"I can't keep doing this. I don't know why the AI Mainframe is doing this to you. Or maybe this was Penny's doing? She's always buggering things up. Here, hold on a second."

Before either woman can move, I touch them on the temple. Actual contact with a human is unsophisticated, in this case, unavoidable if I want to fix Oliver's friends.

Without hesitation, Penny would be proud.

Penny can suck it.

My onboard readouts on the women show an abundance of chemicals and pollutants. Damn, humans are killing themselves.

Over what, evolution?

I start by moving the chemical blockage from each woman's brain without damaging either. There would be shouting to the stars above if I accidentally harmed one. Penny would never let it go.

The dark matter moves through their bodies, and when it is ready to eject, I let go of the women. "That should do it. Now spit that out, please," I say.

Agnes gags and sputters on a dark, sludge-like substance. She wipes the drool from her chin. Cora clears her throat with one guttural growl before spitting the dark mucus out like a sports ball player.

"What the hell did you do to me?" Cora places one hand on her hip.

"That was ghastly, Mona. Why did you do that? Mona... Your name is Mona? Cora, her name is Mona." Agnes's eyes change from a foggy gray to a more bottomless, vibrant ocean cerulean.

"And you're Oliver and your dad. He's a good ol' piece of man meat." Cora clears her throat and flushes pink. "I mean, umm. He's a gentleman," she snickers, clapping her knee as she winks at me. "Your brother works here. Oh, Agnes!"

Oliver rolls his eyes at Cora. His cheeks turn rosy.

"I don't think I've felt this vibrant in years. What did you do to me, Mona?" Agnes looks into my eyes. I know she's sizing me up.

I also don't care much.

"I just cleared a little blockage. If you humans stopped polluting my Earth, this wouldn't be an issue. I can promise you that," I say, probably a bit gruffer than Penny would approve.

Cora and Agnes settle into their thoughts. Memories long ago locked away by time and poison.

I stand up straight, shoulders back, proud of myself for fixing Penny's pets. More to the point, for finding a flaw in Penny's argument.

Sure, humans have emotions but come on, what's the point if they lose their faculties?

"Cora… I think William's— I think he's gone. When did he?" Agnes shakes her head.

My monitor reads a heart rate increase. Tears well in her eyes, and her breathing becomes more ragged.

"Aggy, please don't cry," Cora reaches out to her trembling friend and holds her, "It was years ago. It's going to be okay, honey."

9

PENNY

Summarizing a human existence is as easy as teleporting to Zion. I enjoy reading about their lives. Miniature biographies I gobble down in seconds by downloading the information. I may not have a SoTo chip, but I can accomplish the same thing.

Speaking of.

I'm glad I remembered to disable Mona's ability to scan people for their stories. She'd never have to interact if I'd forgotten. Or worse, she'd start saying things that would send the humans into a panic. They'd think she was a psychic or mind reader.

Not good.

But my attention is somewhere else now. Two beautiful people are hurting all over again because of Mona. Sometimes it's not about pollutants, Mona. Sometimes they forget because it's the only way to save the mind. It's a kindness she'll never understand.

Sigh.

Cora and Agnes are sweet. They're close as sisters, true soulmates if ever there was such a thing. They shared everything. From makeup to their wedding days. Inseparable even after dementia took the best parts of their lives.

Cora and Agnes opted for a double wedding in 1959 before their boyfriends were sent to Vietnam. The heat of the moment took over, and at seventeen, each girl wed. Cora to her high school sweetheart Ralph. Agnes to a young army recruit she fell in love with over the summer named William.

Agnes rocked an inconsolable Cora the following year when two Army Officers showed up at her front door. Ralph's body never returned from the war leaving, Cora to bury an empty casket. William and Agnes went on to have three daughters and a son they named in honor of Ralph.

Cora lived like she might die in her sleep, never making it to morning. She never settled down again, unable to give her heart to just one person. The only man who owned it whole took it to the grave. Instead, she visited ninety-one countries, lived on four continents, and fell in love every chance she got. Cora was a Yes Girl, always up for an adventure. Cora landed back on Agnes's doorstep when the nights got lonely or a craving for the familiar tugged at her chest.

As time progressed and she got older, Cora found herself with Agnes more and more. After William's passing, the two moved into Summer Grove. Agnes's memories were going, and it seemed only a matter of time before Cora's would also fade. Summer Grove offered them time together.

The only thing either of them wanted.

Agnes's tear-stained face crumples into her hands. She relives the pain of losing her mate again, fresh as the first dark day.

"It just happened— I know— I just—can't." Agnes's voice catches in her throat, the words unable to leave her lips.

"Why are you leaking? What's going on here?" Mona says, personally affronted by the sudden negative outburst from the wrinkled human, no doubt.

Ugh.

"When William passed, Agnes was already losing her short-term memory. She would forget within an hour sometimes, but always by the next morning. Eventually, telling her he'd gone to the store was easier. Only William's been at the store for the last five years," Cora looks up at Mona.

"Ouch," Mona says.

Oliver is stunned by the exchange. I don't think he understands the gravity of what's happening. But he knows it's big.

Mona takes a step backward, and the world around her freezes.

10

MONA

All I need is a few minutes of quiet. A few moments free of emotionally antiquated humans.

"You're not allowed to press pause, Mona. I'm allowed to press pause. You're not. Me. I'm allowed to. Not you. Have you got it? You're supposed to be experiencing it all as a *human*," Penny, whose voice elevates to an undocumented octave, flicks her hair over her shoulder.

I think I see smoke coming out of her ears.

It's too many humans too fast. I don't care about the women's bodily fluids or well-being. What I care about is having a few minutes free from the insanity.

"I am being human," I groan. "You don't have to get all uppity. Okay? I'm just not sure I understand what's going on. She should be happy about memories returning; instead, she's leaking everywhere. Isn't it better to have memories of something than none at all?"

"I guess that's something you'll have to decide for yourself," Penny says. "No more pause button. How is it remotely fair? You stop living a human life as you see fit? Pause, pause, pause. No." Penny is shaking her head furiously. "They don't get to use the pause button, so neither should you."

The way Penny sees it, I'm breaking the rules because it suits me. Of course, she could force me into default, but I know she won't.

Penny might rub it in my face if she was more of a stickler for the rules.

She is not, though.

At the end of it, Penny wants me to like humans the way she does.

Silly Penny.

Doesn't she know? I'm already planning their demise.

"No more pausing," she says.

"Fine," I say and move time forward again before Penny can start to lecture me. The world moves in synch yet again. And yet again, I'm forced face to face with overemotional humans.

Great.

With closed eyes, I sigh, secretly hoping it's all a bad dream.

All I have to do is wake up and be home again.

Oliver clears his throat.

"So," I take a deep breath, "Oliver and I were thinking of grabbing some frozen water. What did you call it? Ice cream?" I grit my teeth.

Oliver nods.

"Although I still don't understand the appeal," I say.

Doing something is way more complicated than thinking about doing something. I hate Penny.

"Would you—uh," being nice takes far too much energy. "Would you two care to join us?"

"Are you okay?" Cora asks.

"Me? I'm not the one leaking. I'm quite fine," I say through a clenched jaw.

"Your smile, it doesn't reach your eyes, Mona. You're a bit. What's the polite way of saying this?" Cora searches for the right word. "Awkward. Mona, you're a bit awkward."

"That's polite?" I ask.

"Well, no. But I'm too old to be polite all the time. We get to a certain age and, excuse my French, but we stop giving a shit," Cora laughs.

"I don't think that's French. But sure, I guess." Something in the older woman's tone strikes me as odd. "Can you pull yourself together for a little while?"

Agnes looks at Cora, who nods back at her. "Ice cream would be nice right now."

"She has a point. Ice cream is good wallow food, honey." Cora is rubbing Agnes's back. "Besides, didn't we stand here for a good hour talking about it?"

Agnes gives Cora a faint smile.

"Shall we?" I start toward Dean's Ice Cream and Soda Shop. I clench my teeth and try not to think about walking inside of one of their corpse ridden structures.

Don't let Penny win.

Hand in hand, Cora and Agnes follow behind, with Oliver in tow.

All the touching seems so unsanitary.

I don't understand any of it. But whatever gets this day moving is a positive thing.

I guess.

Keeping a wide berth between myself and the others, we enter Dean's.

Never have I ever stepped foot into a human store. Let alone an *ice cream* parlor. Contrary to the outdoors, inside the building, I can taste the sugar in the air without placing a single bite on my tongue. The fluorescent lights are harsh on my infantile eyes. Or maybe they're brutal, period. I don't know how they stand this. I'm unsure how to process the sugar air, and being boxed in such proximity to other humans adds to my convictions.

Penny's wrong. Life is clearly better outside in nature instead of cooped up inside manufactured monstrosities.

Is it all necessary? Buildings, ice cream, and buying things. What's the purpose? Whatever happened to peace on earth and loincloths? Being one with nature.

Oliver looks up at me, "Can I?"

"Can you what?" I say.

"May I?" corrects Oliver.

"I'm not some grammatical authoritarian," I say.

"You know," Oliver waves his head toward the ice cream. "Can I get some?" his words a rush.

"I don't see why not. Weren't you the one who brought me here? I thought that was the point," I say.

Oliver jumps from toe-to-toe with a giant ear-to-ear grin until he reaches the flavor case. A tall, slender man behind the counter with skin the color of maple syrup leans over to take his order.

Something Cora said is nagging at the back of my mind. "What did you mean when you implied, I would understand what it's like to be old? Specifically speaking, what makes you say that?"

"Awkward dear, awkward," Cora's eyes twinkle up at me. I'm several inches taller than her. "Well, not to be rude, darling, but you're no spring chicken."

"Right. Hmm. Well, like, what exactly gives you that impression? Can you be clearer with your words?"

"Honey, do I need to spell it out for you?" Cora looks at me blank-faced. "I can see I do. You've got to be at least near my age, give or take a decade. Seventy? Seventy-five?" Cora is whispering.

I struggle not to roll my eyes at her. Lowering her voice so that I'll come closer to hear her and risk contamination.

Rude.

Cora can't even focus on me long enough to hold a conversation. She's too busy ogling the man behind the counter. She pulls at her neckline and swishes her hair. I get the feeling she's been successful at mating.

Interesting.

What I can't get over, though, is the age thing. I mean, I guess I expected Penny to age me appropriately. Not by my mental capacity over these humans. I suppose it's not meant as an insult, but still.

Odd, Penny. What kind of game is she playing?

I look down at my hands, but they don't appear aged. I try to pull up any stats with SoTo, but I'm not getting anything. Penny must have limited my software access.

Bitch.

"I see. Yes, well," I smile and step away.

"Mona, look! I got Bubblegum, Cake Batter, and Chunky Monkey. I hope that's okay?" Oliver is bursting with excitement.

"Oh sure, that sounds interesting," I say. "Do you eat monkeys in your ice cream normally? I'm not okay with it if that's the case. If you only knew how cannibalistic it was, I don't suppose you'd be so eager."

Oliver giggles over his bowl, "Chunky Monkey doesn't have monkeys in it. That would be gross. It's just the name."

"I'll take your word for it," I say.

11

PENNY

Dean Pronaoi, the IV, has worked at Dean's Soda Shop for the last forty-three years. It's his family's business. The original Dean was his great-grandfather, and he takes pride in what that means. Although the costume gets old, the smile on every child's face is worth it.

Life is about the little things. I like that about Dean. I like his love for making people happy.

Maybe I should feel guilty about watching Mona.

But I don't.

"What can I get you, dear?" Dean says when Mona approaches the counter.

"Well, if you would explain what you're selling, then I can tell you what I want," she says. She makes me want to slow time again so I can tell her not to be such a robot to everyone she meets.

First impressions matter.

"We have nineteen flavors of ice cream. You can choose between a cone, cup, waffle bowl, or sundae. Or, if you prefer, we also sell it in a pint or a quart. We even have *pink sprinkles*," Dean gives Mona a wink.

He believes all little girls loved pink sprinkles—a proven ice cream fact. Too bad Mona's not a little girl.

I almost laugh but manage to contain myself.

Mona looks to Cora and Agnes for guidance. Oh, this is too good. Serves her right.

"You can't seriously tell me you've never eaten ice cream?" Agnes says. Her tears are drying, and the distraction seems a welcome one.

Mona shrugs. "Let's say I've never had this before, for argument's sake. What should I get?"

Agnes and Cora look at each other in mock thought. Then in unison, "Chocolate."

"It's a good place to gather your flavor baseline from," Dean says, providing Mona with a small spoonful of a dark brown cold substance. "Just tell me what you think, and we'll go from there."

Mona hesitantly reaches for the spoon. She even manages to avoid physical contact with Dean. Still not wanting to touch anyone. She smells the sweet cream before popping it into her mouth.

Mona closes her eyes and sees fireworks as if for the first time. Her tongue is flavor bombed with an intense, succulent, rich, smack. It sends shivers down her body from the top of her head to the tips of her toes. She stands perfectly quiet, trying to savor the mouthful. She keeps her eyes closed to enjoy it without distraction for a little longer.

I can't let this go on.

The reality is that my readouts on Mona skyrocket through the roof when she tastes chocolate. I make time slow to a near standstill before becoming visible to her.

"Who would have guessed? Mona gets to experience amazement and loathing within an hour of each other?" I say.

"Why do you always have to ruin a good moment?" she asks, eyes still closed. "I was just starting to find a reason not to destroy them, but you've ruined it. Oh well, death it is."

I lean close to whisper in Mona's ear, "You did not, and besides, that's what sisters are for." I give her my best smile.

Before I could stop her, Mona's made everything move again, cutting me off.

Whatever.

I could care less.

"I'd like more, please," Mona says, handing the spoon back to Dean.

"How many scoops would you like?"

Mona eyes Oliver. "How many scoops did you get?"

"Three," Oliver smirks.

"I'd like four," Mona says, never to be outdone. "And whatever these three are having as well. I'll pay for it all."

There are few things Mona understands about humans. Unfortunately, economics wasn't one of them. This is too bad, considering it's one of the many reasons Earth is hurting so much.

The fact that Mona even has a basic idea about buy and sell concepts is surprising to me.

I hate admitting it, but Mona has a point. Humans fight over money and any resource that might grant them more. The whole economic system causes humans to kill one another. Destroying each other over things like oil is crazy.

Oil!

Liquefied dead plants and animals.

Yum.

Flaming stars, even I can think of better things to fight over.

I suppose Mona and I might agree on two things now. I hate to admit it, but ice cream would be first on that list.

Cora and Agnes order much smaller portions, only a scoop each of chocolate.

Mona slips into a chocolate coma. Bite after delicious bite. She seems to be nearly praying with pleasure, sun rays dance on her cheeks, and a smile peeks at the edge of her lips.

"So, did I hear you correctly? Are you buying today? How sweet of you. Is it your grandmother's birthday?" Dean's patronizing smile grates on Mona's nerves.

Instant karma for being such a pain in my ass.

"Grandmother? As if she's part of my ancestry." Mona reaches into the pocket of her jeans and pulls out a single one-thousand-dollar bill, and hands it to Dean.

"Aren't you cute? But your total comes to nineteen fifty-three in *American dollars*, sweetheart, not monopoly money."

"Right. Too big, then?" Mona puts the large and, from this eye, extremely extinct denomination back in her pocket. She pulls out a twenty-dollar bill next. "Is this better?"

I wonder momentarily if the man would regret not taking her money if he'd known it was actual currency.

Dated.

But still.

I shake my head of these thoughts.

Dean shows off a mouth full of pearly whites. "Thank you, sweetheart."

"No need to be condescending. It takes away from what might otherwise be considered a pleasurable experience. Good chocolate, though," Mona says. She tips her bowl to Dean, turns her back, and walks out of the ice cream parlor.

12

MONA

Outside of Dean's Ice Cream and Soda Shop, the sun peeks through the gray scape. I'm seeing the world through fuzzy, chocolate-coated spectacles. Honestly, I'm not sure if the cocoa brown ice cream afflicts me so or if it is something to do with being back on Earth. After all this time, Earth has always been my favorite project.

Well, Earth and Four-Riatla. But Earth is just ever so slightly more beautiful.

Till the talkies came, anyway.

Speaking of the talkies, one is approaching with vigor. I fight back the urge to run.

No.

Not run.

I'm not afraid. But one can never be too safe with a rabid human. A frown paints his olive brow. His tall stature and robust features are less inviting as a result. Although how inviting they might be without the frown is still debatable.

"What do you think you're doing, Oliver? I've been looking for you everywhere. You had me worried sick. You've made me sound like Dad. Great." The man-child removes his purple ball cap, stained in sweat and grime, and wipes his forehead with the back of his arm.

"Noah," Oliver drags out his name like I do Penny's. "I was getting ice cream with Mona, Mrs. Witherbee, and Mrs.

Nightingale. So I am perfectly safe." Oliver's face softens, and I know he's not angry with this Noah person.

Oliver's adult has an accent that I can't place. It was different from the older women and even Oliver's own. Some of his words are drawn out and sharper.

Meh.

Maybe he's witless. It would explain why he left the young one in the wild.

Alone.

"You should have texted me. Why do you have a phone?" Noah asks.

"So, I can text you or call you and tell you I'm safe," Oliver says monotone. This is not the first conversation they've had on the topic.

I find myself sizing up Oliver's human. He has shaggy dark hair as rich as obsidian. A shadow of a beard highlights his jawline. Looking into his liquid blue eyes, I feel a sudden warmth slither through me. A shiver runs down my back, and my legs take on a jiggly feeling I'm not accustomed to. It's not too unlike eating ice cream, only warmer and gooier.

I shake my head to clear it of the fuzzy human thoughts. I wonder briefly if Penny's done something to me.

This stranger might as well be one more face in a sea of bodies. Oliver's Noah was no exception to the human's must-die rule. Plus, he's already rubbed me the wrong way. I'm not too fond of the way he chastised Oliver. People shouldn't treat others like property. He should stay with him if he wants to know where Oliver is.

Idiots.

Stars above. I haven't developed a soft spot where the kid is concerned.

Right?

Well, I'd never be caught dead admitting it aloud. What am I even thinking?

People shouldn't treat others like property?

Ha!

As though I care what happened to these amoebas.

They are all property. Penny's annoying property.

I rub my eyes and shake my head, trying to free myself of these thoughts. Emotions bounce in every direction. Although I'd never tell Penny in a million years, maneuvering the ever-changing winds is proving more challenging than I anticipated.

The stranger licks his lips and tilts his head to me. "Hi, I'm Noah. Noah Harvey. I'm Oliver's older brother." Noah wipes his hand on the side of his jeans before reaching it to me. "I mean, obviously," he smiles, a large pearly white toothy grin.

I look at Noah's hand for a long dragging moment. His nails are thick with dirt, and the lines of his hands are rough with use.

The last *Noah* I encountered built an arc and saved the human race. The whole thing ruined my plans to free Earth of the talkies. I should have gone with a meteor. Why fix what's not broken? Sometimes the tried-and-true methods are just the best ones.

Blood sloshes in my ears. I close my eyes, trying to make it all go away.

I'm just being irrational. It's these uncontrolled adolescent emotions. Penny must have done something to my SoTo chip.

She's wrong about it shutting down emotions. But I'd be lying if I didn't admit it helped keep things in perspective.

Human emotions suck.

Stupid damned human emotions I could shut off with a flick of a switch if I wanted to. It's tempting to mess with the settings or stop my upload completely. I don't have to do this to myself.

The only thing stopping me is Penny's incessant voice, mentally mocking me for the rest of time. More than that, I'm not ready to lose the bet.

The damned bet.

Is it such a horrible thing that I want more out of life than this? I'm simply not willing to give up so easily.

When I open my eyes, Noah still holds his hand out, and a smile plays on his lips.

"Mona," I say, reaching out and taking Noah's hand. He is strong, solid, and offers a firm grip until a spark bites the inside of my palm. I let go, dropping my hand to my side.

"Oh ouch, that was crazy static. I'm so sorry. Are you okay?" Noah rubs the inside of his hand. His brow furrows, and he reaches for me again.

I take a step back. "Um, yea. I'm okay. Thanks."

Static?

Was he trying to shock me to death?

Doesn't he know who I am?

If I had a plastic fork and some almond milk, I would make him scream until he begged me to delete him from this life once and for all.

The sudden thought of Oliver being deleted leaves me cold.

"Don't you usually have today off work, Noah?" Cora asks.

"Yes, I do, but—" Noah pauses. A question in his eyes. "Cora?"

"Yes, Noah?" Cora gives him a wicked, knowing grin.

"You remember my name? How are you feeling today?" Noah asks.

"Thanks to Mona, I feel better than I've felt in years," Cora smiles affectionately.

My cheeks grow hot, which is so odd. I look for the sun and find it's not directly overhead, beating down on me.

"I didn't really do anything. You two just had a little blockage. That is all." If they wanted to know how the coding works on humans, I'd explain it, but I'm willing to bet the programming would go over their simple human brains.

Perhaps they should remain naive.

"I wish I still had a blockage," Agnes says, wiping a tear-stained cheek.

"What's wrong, Aggie? Are you okay?" Noah envelops his arms around the frail and timeworn woman.

In Noah's arms, Agnes has the feebleness of a child. She leans into him and weeps.

"Let's get you home, Aggie. Maybe you'll feel better after some hot tea and a nap. Does that sound okay?"

Agnes nods.

Noah leads her into the retirement home, stopping after he reaches the top steps. "Oliver, I'll be back shortly. Please stay with Cora. Mona, it was nice meeting you. Maybe we can do it again soon." Noah winks at me.

Did he wink?

He winked.

He winked!

Winked.

Winked is a funny word.

Noah glances back before entering the retirement community. My coiled midnight hair dances in the slight breeze. I know he's admiring it. I think of the firmness in his touch and the spark of lighting we captured between our palms.

He smiles at me before going inside.

I roll my eyes.

"So that was your adult?" I say.

"Well, that's my brother. I forgot to text him. I should have remembered." Oliver throws his head back. "I'll be better next time. At least it wasn't dad."

"Don't beat yourself up too bad, Olli. You are a human, after all. It's not like you're built to be perfect all the time. Your kind are prone to making mistakes. It's in your nature to grow with those errors in judgment. You will improve it in your next life," I nod. I'm confident his next life would be less fraught with antiquated social mistakes.

"Yea, it's fine," Oliver says. "I'll text him next time."

"What is a text?" asks Cora, trying to follow the conversation but clearly failing.

"Technology, Cora. Technology. It's taken a life of its own since you've been trapped inside of that head of yours. I can barely stand the slow pace of it all, personally. I'm like, move it along already," I say.

Cora nods. "Right, sure."

I straighten and brush a wrinkle out of my shirt. "So, what do you do around here for fun? Like, if you only had one day to live, what would you do?" I take another bite of my ice cream. It's melty and nearly gone, but still incredibly delightful.

"Mona, are you, are you okay? Should we worry?" Cora's face grows dark with unease. "You're not thinking of hurting yourself, are you?"

"No. Nothing like that. Just curious, you know. What ifs, I guess," I say.

"Oh. Well, in that case. I guess I'd want to spend it with my friends and family. I'd want to do exactly what I'd do any other day," Cora says.

"Not me. I'd want to go to Disneyland. Oh, and I'd want to eat a box of Bertie Botts and try all the flavors. Probably a chocolate frog too. I hear they have Ear Wax, Earthworms, and Dirt. Even Rotten Eggs. So gross!" Oliver is tumbling into a fit of laughter. "I'd like to see the real places from the books I read. I wish I could go to space and be among the stars. If I only had one day, I'd want to do that."

"I'm not sure I understand the appeal of a chocolate frog or Earthworms. I mean, don't get me wrong, I understand the circle of life. I mean, I designed it. I suppose outside of your odd eating habits, nothing in your fantasy is too weird," I say, however disgusting it sounds.

Oliver is still giggling. "That's the point, Mona, it's every jellybean flavor, duh. Every flavor doesn't mean only the good flavors. It means every flavor. Kind of like life, got to take the good with the bad."

"So, you would eat the worst possible food flavors and visit fanciful places. Cora would go about business as usual. Let's pretend for a minute you met someone who's never been on Earth before," I say.

Oliver's eyes grow large, "Like an alien? I've always wanted to meet an alien."

"Sure, an alien. Whatever," I say flatly. Cora rolls her eyes exaggeratedly. Humans are so obsessed with the idea of aliens. "What would you have them do? What would you show them? You know, to, like, get an idea of what it's like to be human."

"Can you truly experience being a human without living like a human? Are you talking about a last day, Mona? Or are you talking about being human? Those are two different things," Cora says.

"I don't see how," I say, straightening.

"Oh, Mona. What a life you must lead. You can do many things, see all the wonders of this world, and jump off a cliff with only a bungee tied to your ankles. Both of which are exhilarating, I might add." Cora sighs. "I should know. But none of that comes close to opening your heart to the people in your life. That's what makes us so special, our ability to love." Cora reaches out and touches my chest with the palm of her hand.

I let her, wondering briefly if she knows who I really am. "I don't see how love matters," I say. "But, I appreciate the input."

"Anytime. If your hypothetical changes course, don't hesitate to come by again. I'd love to indulge in a little gossip. And science," Cora says, clearing her voice. "So come on by. For the science, of course."

"Right. Science. I'll keep it in mind."

13

PENNY

The thought of losing the entire human race on a bet is not enjoyable. But sometimes, you have to take a leap of faith. Jump with both feet into the deep end, hoping it isn't all for nothing.

From time to time, I read the souls of those who've passed on. I read those feelings and memories on the young soul of a woman who had just died. The woman took a running jump off of a waterfall. She went head first and cracked her skull on a reef. She bled out in the open water, eventually consumed by ocean life.

Dust to dust and all that.

The running jump didn't work well for her, but I still appreciate the analogy. Faith is an interesting and singularly human concept.

I like to believe humans have the potential for great things. Kind souls too. But in the heart of all their emotions, a war rages on. A battle for what is right and what is wrong. Good and evil, darkness and light, the good and bad wolf, serial killer, and saint.

This battle with a hundred names makes humans genuinely unique. Humans want to do what's right. But, sometimes, they don't know the difference.

Do you kill one person to save twenty? Or is it a *no man's left behind* scenario, where five die to save one? Do you live in a beautiful house with an ugly view or an ugly house with a beautiful view? The correct answers are no easier to hear than they are to decide upon. And more than anything else, I love watching humans squirm over their choices.

Reality TV is popular for a reason.

That is what they are all doing on Earth. They are learning to listen to the battle, to control the darkness and the light. To embrace both and find peace within themselves and love for others. While train wrecks are hard to look away from, other moments warm my heart. Once upon a time, they even thawed it. Changing me from an ice princess into the caring creator I like to think I am today.

The problem is that sometimes what feels right isn't, and sometimes when it doesn't feel right, it is. I can read the confusion in the hearts of men. I ache, wanting to make it all better with the snap of a finger.

Mona will never see that.

No matter how much I want it, I can't improve things. Especially for a grade. What kind of admissions project would that be?

Not an honest one.

After all, it is part of my agreement with Mona. It's not only Mona who can't interfere with humans. I'm not supposed to, either. The deal was that we could upload from time to time to observe, much like I'm watching Mona. But neither of us could make significant changes without consulting the other first.

Free will and all.

Not that it's stopped either of us.

Not that either of us will admit it to the other.

Letting humans grow independently while cycling through life and developing control over their emotions is impressive. It's also what is going to get me into university.

The thing is, Mona doesn't understand any of it. It's not like she's taking the time to learn. Instead, she sees one bad seed and assumes the whole batch is trash. But that's why I'm here.

Right?

To change her mind.

To help guide her.

Or, in extreme cases, such as these, clamp open her mouth and shove the good down her throat forcefully.

No backup plan exists if shit hits the figurative fan. The actuality of life on Earth is this: If Mona fails to see the beauty in civilization, then the whole human race is condemned.

Condemnation might seem to imply that humans have a bit of notice or a chance to change or save themselves. Unfortunately, neither is further from the truth. It isn't like the films humans make, where they band together and stop an asteroid from killing everything on Earth. Or fighting off an alien attack which causes them to bond, realizing all their petty fighting was pointless.

Sometimes I wish it were all that simple. "Listen up, little humans. All you have to do is save Earth. It's not a hard concept, children," I say to no one. I run a hand through my long copper hair. "Mona won't find glee in your death if you only equated saving Earth with your survival."

Which it does. Only humans don't see it that way.

Yet.

Maybe.

They all have free will for a reason. I just hope it isn't their undoing.

It's too dark and gloomy to think about. I'm an optimist at heart. I prefer to be hopeful and look at the positive side of things—puppies, rainbows, and everything that sparkles.

It's not denial.

It is more akin to acceptance. Besides, it might all work out in the end. With a nudge, here and there, that is.

Probably.

Hopefully.

Humans are a funny little species. Constantly worried aliens will invade, or the ocean will rise and wipe them out when the reality is much grimmer.

Well, there was that one time when Mona nearly did flood them all away. And there were a few hurricanes that were also her fault. To be fair, so were the China floods, the Spanish flu, the Tangshan earthquake, Black Plague, Smallpox, Covid-19, and even the Bhola Cyclone.

I'm also confident Mona is behind Jar Jar Binks, but I can't prove it. Mona doesn't have an excellent track record.

Destroying the human race, or any race, is as simple as pressing the delete button. I finger and caress a big red button Mona personally programmed and hand labeled, *For a good time*. If I pressed the button, humans would cease to exist, lost in the dark void of nothing. They would be filed away with every other failed attempt at creating a sustainable, peaceful, and productive life.

As it stands now, humans are recycled. Their essences are used repeatedly, giving them ample opportunity to grow as a species. That one was Mona's idea, ironically enough. She was on board the first time around before the SoTo chip and her lack of empathy. Mona wanted to allow humans to live many lives of all genders with different cultural backgrounds. She wanted them to grow and live in harmony with the Earth, experiencing everything they possibly could.

She wanted one love.

For obvious reasons, new souls are constantly presented to the pool of newborns. After all, if everyone grew simultaneously and there weren't youthful souls in the mix, the elders might not have had the opportunity to share their wisdom. Plus, the truth is, humans reproduce like rabbits.

There are some noticeable glitches in the program.

It started with a small percentage of people who would remember their former lives. Children have always been particularly susceptible to the glitch. It isn't uncommon for a soul who's had a violent death to scar the memories of a young body.

Once, I saw a child wake up crying every night for a month. He kept saying, "He killed me. He killed me on the cliffside with the knife." The mother cradled her child and explained he was safe and that it was all a bad dream. With a bit of research, it was easy for me to track the boy's soul. He indeed died on a cliffside after being stabbed with a knife during a war.

Crazy, right? It's the glitch.

War is a little tidbit I hoped Mona would overlook.

Or not notice, maybe.

Even in adults, though, triggers from a former life sometimes breach the current one, causing paranoia and an array of other psychosis. Humans call it mental health problems, but I know it's just the glitch.

It was never in the original plan. Someone tapping into the archives via one of the many programming glitches might teach others how to do it. Or hone their access paths. We did weigh the pros and cons of fixing the glitches.

At first, that is.

We made a list of everything.

In the end, we decided to leave it. The number of people who could tap into the glitch was so finite compared to the numbers on Earth. Besides, I argued it offered a little extra color to the world and might further enhance human lives. Plus, the added bonus of shaking things up once in a while.

It's not like Mona seems to care either way. Programming errors are always my fault. We might not be in this situation if she had been willing to take responsibility for her actions.

Watching humans grow and evolve has been the serenest science experiment of my life. If only Mona could choose to understand instead of choosing to be a stubborn mule about everything.

I mean, I get it. Okay, I'm not dense. I just don't like it. For being such a talented creator of life, Mona could be less selfish. She never puts my needs, or the needs of humans, above her own. Would it kill her to do that occasionally? To think of something or someone other than herself for a change?

Watching Mona refuse to try sucks. It was a wonder anyone took the time to stop and converse with her at all.

Uploading to experience life in a new world should be seen as an adventure, not a punishment. It's the kind of poetry I can live by.

Mona wouldn't know poetry if it hit her in the back of her head. She'd never give it a chance. The day Mona reads a poem is the day I turn into a pig and sprout wings. Humans can create beautiful art with their words and their hands.

I feel weepy at the thought of Mona never experiencing these things. Life without them is not nearly as beautiful. I'm fortunate to know such beauty intimately. Is it wrong to want the same for my sister?

If Mona would only let her guard down for a few minutes. That's all it would take. But suppose she experienced making a friend, falling in love, or simply feeling life's rush. Maybe humans would have a shot at living longer than it takes to press delete.

But how?

Mona felt loathing and amazement quickly, but those are guileless emotions—something any simpleton can achieve. Real emotions like ecstasy, grief, and trust are things she'll struggle with.

But what's a little push?

I know what being human means. Admittedly, I plug in as often as Mona isn't looking. I've walked among them. Ate their food, breathed their air, and even got a tattoo or ten.

Two of them stand out in my memories. The first was a unicorn bust with a rainbow mane on my chest. It was a nod to one of the many magical creatures I tried to sneak on Earth, which Mona eventually found and removed. The second was an Indian elephant inside of a palm-shaped Hamsa, a nod to a past love from long ago.

My most recent human life got a little wild. Not that I would brag about it, but I did single-handedly start the punk revolution. Of course, if Mona found out, she'd probably consider it too much meddling in human affairs.

Of course, that was basically last month. Not the best life I've ever lived, but it was a damn good one—sixty-two years of head-banging defiance of *the man*.

Being human is complex. It's like a drug I can't get enough of. At the end of it all, I still want more. I want to be human again and again and again—all the time. I want to experience all of it. I want the chance to feel every right moment until I burst, and then I want to feel all the wrongs.

But was it wrong?

Even the bad moments are worth living for. Is loving someone wrong? Even if you're not supposed to love anyone?

No, a love affair wasn't wrong.

Love is never wrong.

I know the rules. I'm careful. Never giving away my secrets. Never letting anyone know I'm not human. Coding sparingly. Being human.

Until I'd been caught.

Once.

One time was all it took.

I will never forget the softness of his face or the ease with which he held me. A shiver runs down my spine, and I feel a tug at my chest. Thinking of him always makes my body quiver.

I'd been coming to Earth when Mona was in class or gone for some training course she signed up for—always keeping my distance when she was looking.

That's when it happened. I met a man who challenged all my views on what it means to be human.

His name was Kalidasa, and he was one of the greatest poets the world has ever seen. He moved me to tears with his words.

Words!

Who would have thought a human's words could cause such strong emotions?

He changed everything.

He humbled me.

He changed me.

Kalidasa taught me about life, human emotions, and what it means to love within the bounds of a single poem. He taught me more than I could have learned in a hundred other lives. I was a machine with a mechanical heart, pumping blood, cold as ice.

He was human.

On cool nights, Kalidasa would stay up, sketching charcoal images of my naked body, sleeping by firelight. Before he rose every morning, I would trace the lines of his figure in the sky, painting the sunrise in radiant hues just for him. I committed every moment with Kalidasa to memory.

I wanted it to last forever.

I wanted him to last it with me.

We'd been lovers for two years when I became pregnant. What we might bring into the world scared me more than I could admit. Without Mona to confide in, I didn't know what to do. I concealed the pregnancy. Never getting the chance to tell Kalidasa what our love created.

We lived together until, by a cruel twist of fate, he died at the hands of someone who'd meant to harm me. I was only three months pregnant and now forever alone. Why didn't I stop the killer? Why didn't I see it all coming? Why couldn't I have changed just this one thing?

I couldn't do any of it without disrupting the whole of human life. It was the one thing I promised Mona I wouldn't do.

It's the one thing I'll regret forever.

Mona can't delete humans.

She'd delete my family.

I consider all of the facts. Is it wrong to interfere?

I don't know.

But I do it anyway.

14

MONA

Crashing hard from my first sugar high, I feel like I can't stand still for more than thirty seconds. Got to keep moving, got to stay awake, got to bounce, bounce, bounce.

If these human meat sacks are everything Penny makes them out to be, going for a run will be a piece of cake. I might as well push this body to its limits.

Admittedly I don't go outside much, and I've never gone running a day in my life. I don't see the point unless something or someone was chasing me. Besides, it's not a necessity for anything outside of travel. Even then, that's what uploading is for. You can have a fully toned body with *Body Toning Spray*. You can find almost anything you could ever dream of wanting in a spray.

Fat Remover Spray.
Hair Color Spray.
Mermaid Tail Spray.
Heal Spray.
Private Bubble Spray.

The last is one of my favorites. Humans have no idea what they're missing.

In theory, if this body is so great, it should be able to shake its physical reaction to the ice cream.

"Thanks for sharing this cold, delicious cream experience with me. It won't be soon forgotten," I say.

"Ice cream," Oliver says.

"What did I say?" I ask.

"Cream," Oliver says.

"Yes, icy cream," I tease.

"Ice cream," Oliver annunciates each syllable.

"Same difference," I say. "I think climax in a bowl would be a more appropriate name."

Cora smiles, "Yes, I'm inclined to agree with you."

"What's a climax?" Oliver asks.

Cora's face goes three shades of red. "Nothing, dear. Don't worry your pretty little head about it."

I'm ready to explain it to him, but Cora tells me no.

"Thanks for buying it. I can't believe I got three scoops," Oliver starts to giggle.

"I don't care if you turn into ice cream, Olli. It can't be much worse than being human," I say.

"I'm not going to turn into ice cream. That's just silly," Oliver says.

"It was wonderful getting to know you, Mona. I hope you'll come around again," Cora says.

"It was not horrible meeting you either, Cora. I'm…well," I pause, looking for the right words. "I hope Agnes sorts her emotions out." It seems like the right thing to say.

"Yes, dear. I hope so too. She'll bounce back. Aggy has always been a fighter," Cora says.

"Give her my best wishes to move on from the loss of her long-time decaying husband," I say.

Cora doesn't respond right away. "Are you sure you're going to run? It doesn't seem safe. What if you break a hip? Or trip?"

"There are worse things I could do. But I appreciate the sentiment all the same," I say.

"You know us oldies got to stick together. That's how we stay goodies," Cora says. "I'd hate to visit you in the infirmary. The food there is utterly distasteful. You won't like it."

"You'd visit me in the hospital?" I ask.

"Of course," Cora says. "That's what friends do," Her gracious smile meets her sparkling eyes.

A weird thing happens at this moment. Something I can only explain as a glitch. My stomach flutters like a bird flapping wings inside my belly—such an odd feeling. I look down at my stomach, then push the thoughts aside and press on.

"Thank you, Cora, but I'll be quite fine. Besides, I've got to try out the legs at some point," I say.

"Why? Were they broken?" Cora waves the question away. "Never mind. If you insist on going at it, then speed walk. It's just as good for your cardiovascular system and easier on the joints. Doctor's orders."

"She's not old," Oliver chimes in. "If she falls, she'll just brush off the dirt and go again."

"I'm okay, truly." I reach out to touch Cora's arm but think better of it and pull back. "Well, goodbye."

"Maybe you could come to my birthday?" Oliver says.

"Sure. I mean—umm, maybe?" The chocolate high is causing my rational brain to be clouded and confused. It is the only logical explanation. Artificial chemicals must be a compromising agent in ice cream. It isn't as if I'm planning on sticking around or anything.

No way.

I'm here to feel these stupid emotions and then move on.

I set out down the jogging path, away from Summer Grove Retirement Community. Still, far from thrilled with the paved ground, it takes several paces before I move from foot to foot. An obstinate jog at first. Eventually, though, I find a rhythmic run and hit my stride.

If I wanted to change things around here, I could do it with a thought. Since that would be cheating, I won't.

Well... Not exactly.

With every new stride on this horrible, paved path, cracks began to form under my feet. The asphalt vibrates to dust as I lift off. Leaving behind flush greens and fresh sprouted flowers in my wake. Every stride leaves behind newly untouched ground.

"What do you think you're doing?" Penny apparates on the jogging path.

Nearly tripping over top of her, I fling myself around my sister and fall to the ground. "What the hell Penny?" I rub at my freshly skinned knee. "That hurts. Damn SoTo."

"It's supposed to. Your skin is the largest organ and it's quite likely to lose battles like knee verses pavement."

"I thought we were done with this," I say. "What do you want?"

"You can't destroy the world around you," Penny's hands are on her hips, judging.

"What are you talking about?"

"Do you think people won't notice you've disintegrated the pathways?"

"I'm putting it back to normal."

"That was normal," Penny says. "It's their normal."

"Black tar on Earth is not *normal*," I say. "Lush greens are normal. I'm simply resetting the status quo."

"Let me make this abundantly clear. You can't interfere with their lives, even like this. It's part of our agreement. Unless you're willing to give up already?" The smile spreading across Penny's face is fuel to the fire.

"Give up? Since when do I give up anything?" I say.

"Put it back."

"Make me."

"Ugh! You're so difficult," Penny waves a hand and sparkles out of existence.

In few swipes of my screen the unsightly asphalt is back. *Normal* is overrated.

Sweat beads down my forehead, armpits, and in the small of my back. Jogging is messier than I expected. The change in my body temperature and the sudden aroma wafting around my nose brings me to an abrupt stop.

"I thought touching one of them was bad, but this is much worse. Why do they exert themselves at all?" I lift an arm and smell myself for good measure. "So, gross." The endorphins are pleasant enough, but still. The smell doesn't seem to weigh evenly enough on my mental scale.

"Mona? Is that you?"

I look around for the cause of the buzzing. When I find it, I can't help but smile. "Oh, hello, my lovely. I'm glad you got the memo, as the Earthlings say."

"Oh yes, of course. I heard from River, a turtle, a few beats north, who heard it from Nova, the local ally cat. They share a watering hole. Nova heard it from an orchid in an apartment on Cleveland Street that likes to be called Boss. I'm unsure where he gets his news, but it travels fast. I'd guess it's making its way across the globe as we speak."

Pleased with myself, I can feel a real grin forming. I wouldn't need to have a thousand conversations about why Mother Nature was so passé, and Mona is my preferred name. I'm so proud of this little bee. This tiny conception is also one of my most remarkable ones.

I have a soft spot for the underdog despite what Penny might think. The honeybee is so slight, with only a single stinger for protection–using it would be the ultimate sacrifice. Without this little creation, most of the Earth would die off. Pollination is a trickier idea, but I'm a professional.

No, I'm an artist.

Earth is my canvas.

Everything lives in harmony.

Correction, *used* to live in harmony. It *should* live in harmony.

This little bee's life is no exception.

"Mona, would you like to come inside? I know Queen Leslie would welcome you with open wings. For you are the Queen of my Queen," the fluttering bee says.

While it's a sweet thought, I can't quite wrap my head around the invitation—an offer *into* the hive. Of course, I know what the inside of a hive looks like, and there is the draw of individual and unique qualities to consider.

And yet, "That is such a kind offer, soldier. But I have a question for you first."

"Yes, my Mona, anything," the bee says.

"Answer me this, how do you see me?"

"What do you mean?" the bee asks. "I see you the same way as a hatchling sees its Queen. With love and admiration."

"Let's stick to the basics here, my good soldier."

And cut the brown-nosing is what I'd like to add, but I refrain. Penny doesn't think I have a kind bone in my body. What does she know?

"What do I look like?"

"Well, my Queen—Mona, you are more beautiful than Queen Leslie, and she is the loveliest bee in the whole hive. I don't know how it is possible, but you are even grander."

Despite myself, heat rises in my cheeks. "But I fear I am too large for your hive."

"The bigger, the better. More of you to worship, my Queen."

Realization dawns.

I'm being played.

I press pause. I no longer give a single Orian tail what she thinks.

"Penny," I roar from a guttural place. "Is this some game to you? Not just a human body, eh? So much for a fair bet."

The silence strikes me.

Damn her.

"I don't know what you're playing at Penny, but I'm not falling for it."

"I'm not playing at anything," Penny says, showing herself.

"A bee? I thought I was supposed to be human."

"You're supposed to be, but clearly, you're still using tech. I can't help it if people—err, wildlife sees you the way you intended. As Mother Nature."

"Don't call me that," I spit my words.

"It's who you are to them," Penny says.

"So, I'm supposed to be a honeybee and a human?" I say, crossing my arms.

"You're not supposed to be anything. You *are* Mother Nature. I can't help what you are any more than you can change who I am. We set precedence when we created them," she says. "You and I both know that doesn't change easily. But for the most part, people see you as you."

"For the most part?" I know she's lying.

Penny raises a brow, "It's not like you're giving me a lot to work with."

"How about human?" I say.

Penny presses a couple of unseen buttons in the air. "Done."

"How old?" I ask.

"Ugh. Fine." Penny makes a few more unseen strokes. "Seventeen. Will your actual age do, or would you prefer that I age you up a bit?"

"Seventeen. Fine," I say.

"Good," Penny huffs.

"Goodbye."

"Ugh," Penny snaps, her fingers disappearing once more.

I take a succession of slow meditating breaths. Listening to my heart thudding into my ears doesn't help.

Stupid little human heart.

Despite my agreement with Penny, the temptation to delete the world is all-consuming. It would be no significant loss. Everything would end without suffering, a kindness compared to the sheer destruction I'd rather cause. Humans wouldn't know anything had happened.

It would be as though they simply never existed.

Damnit.

I'm a woman of my word.

But I don't have to be.

The undeniable pull of going to university rears its ugly head. I'm not ready to renege on my agreements. Yet. I need my project to be intact from beginning to end. I don't want to imagine explaining why I deleted half of it to the board. Why I deleted Penny's half. Even if I managed to cover it up and feel confident I could, I'd still have to explain why it's missing intelligent life. I need my project to be worthy of admission.

Damn, the rings of Saturn.

I shift my attention to the bee who needs to get on with his pollination, "You are too sweet, my young soldier. I must not intrude on your home. I am on a mission, and I should stay on task. As I'm sure, you can understand."

"Of course, my Queen Mona. If there is anything we can do for you, buzz the word."

Reaching out, I gently stroke the bee with one finger. "May you never want for pollen or nectar, may your queen always have royal jelly, and may the stomachs of your young never want for honey."

With a final goodbye, the bee leaves me to my jog.

15

PENNY

The rate at which the asphalt pathway breaks under Mona's feet directly correlates with the attention she gains from human bystanders.

At first, she pretends not to notice the crumbling blacktop.

This much is clear as day.

"Penny can suck a dragon's toe," Mona seethes between gasps for air.

Stupid.

Like I'd ever create another dragon.

Humans stop and point at Mona in high-pitched voices.

Mona seems to grow increasingly uneasy. Dare I say, even a little jumpy.

Mona stops. The pathway no longer breaking apart at her feet.

Suddenly, Mona sprints into the line of trees, shielding herself from the view of prying human eyes. She's breathing heavily. My readouts show it is primarily due to exhaustion. However, her fear of humans has climbed to an outrageously irrational level. The gathering of folk in the park is getting to her.

What if these people touched her, spread disease, or forced her to experience more "anthropological bullshit," which she'd "rather avoid."

Serves her right.

My data outputs say the run took most of the energy Mona has. She musters a little more and pulls herself up into the branches of one of the trees—a Yew. Mona maneuvers strategically. With every step, she tests her weight, moving through the canopy covering a large park area.

I hope her muscles burn with the exertion.

"Watch out below!" a young bird chirps before diving from the top of a tree.

"It's too sunny. Can't we get a little rain?" another complains. "I need a bath."

"La, la, la, la la!" four sing in unison.

The fluttering of daily life from Mona's avian creations calms her racing heart. I watch it steadily decrease to a regular pulse rate.

"Mona, what are you doing among my branches? Do you need sanctuary?" an Acer asks. Despite her sheer lack of empathy, her creations are loyal to a fault.

Fault being the keyword.

Mona's pace slows to a stop. She reaches out, steadying herself against the tree trunk. "I'm not sure what I require right now," she says.

"The human world is quite different from the world you remember. So much has changed," the Acer says.

"It's not their world. It's mine." Mona closes her eyes and rubs her forehead. "I'm sorry dear one. I didn't mean to lash out at you. I'm struggling with this human body," Mona motions to herself, disgust pinging my screen again.

"Tell me, Mona, what do I need to thrive?" the Acer is old enough to carry the wisdom of human ways.

"You require a process called photosynthesis, which only occurs—"

"Mona," the Acer interrupts, "What do I require to thrive on the most rudimentary level?"

Mona is visibly annoyed by the interruption and shrugs, "On the most rudimentary level, you require water, sunlight, sugar, and oxygen."

"You are not so different than I am in your human shell. You require the same things, food, water, sunlight, and proper rest."

Mona groans. "My dear Acer, can you point me toward a good watering hole?"

I wish I could replay the moment when Mona smells herself. I'd turn it into a gif.

"This body requires a bath," Mona says. "The smell it's excreting is rather sharp on my nose. I need water too. My mouth has taken on a cottony-like feel."

"Just around the bend, you will find the first of many waterfalls."

"Thank you, Acer. I appreciate your kindness. It won't be forgotten," she says.

Before Mona leaves, she turns back once more. I can't decide if she's mentally taking a picture of the Acer or if she's picturing the effects of a nuclear bomb on her creation and calculating the cost versus the gain. Either way, she takes a deep breath and walks away.

16

MONA

The watering hole is not what I expect. The pool is expansive and surrounded by a canopy of trees and shrubbery, but the glistening water gives the area a false sense of being. I take a step backward, framing the near-perfect view. I was so positive humans eradicated any sense of beauty from Earth. Inside the inlet is a small waterfall cascading into a pool of liquid clarity. However, in the middle of the water was all that was wrong with this planet.

Humans.

Wearing minimal amounts of cloth on their bodies, less than a dozen are wading in and out of the water. Fabric doesn't bother me one way or the other. For the most part, clothing can be a bit restrictive.

But to each their own.

Two humans climb the surrounding rock face. One jumps off the precipice feet first into the water below. Five more are wading in the shallows. One lays out bathing in the sunlight.

To human contact or to bury myself in avoidance for as long as possible. That is the question.

I won't get out of interacting for the long haul if Penny has her way. The question boils down to whether the water is contaminated or not. For all I know, humans defecate in the same place they bathe.

How barbaric.

I take a deep breath to ready myself. I mean, what's the worst that could happen? If I know the worst-case scenario, I can be prepared for almost anything. Right?

Suppose I do catch something from one of these mangy humans. Would it be enough to break my agreement with Penny?

Not that I would ever renege on a deal. But let's say, hypothetically speaking, I was incapable of finishing life on Earth. Wouldn't it stand to reason I'd win the bet? I could finally give Earth the fighting chance she needs to survive. I could get into an Ivy League University.

Maybe it's a sacrifice I'll have to make.

Now or never.

I close my eyes, hoping to block out the faces below.

It doesn't work.

Their human bodies are burned into the inside of my eyelids. One more deep breath and I take a running start straight off the cliff side, diving headfirst into the liquid escape. The frigid water shocks my system. I hold my breath until my lungs burn from oxygen deprivation.

When I breach the surface, I am startled backward and into the water once again. I surface a second time, more mentally and physically prepared for the beasty.

I form fists in the water.

"Hi there. I didn't mean to startle you," it says.

I'm met face-to-face with a girl.

I think.

"Are you okay? I didn't mean to run into you. I'm so sorry," the girl offers me her hand.

"I'm fine," I say, unable to fathom why I might take it. "You didn't startle me. I slipped. That's all. I unclench my fists and brush my long dark mane out of my face.

"My name is Rhett, well, it's Margrhrett Mati, but no one but my mother calls me that."

Rhett's shoulder-length dark hair hides rainbow tresses that match her swimming suit flawlessly. She has soft brown eyes and creamy brown skin. She gives me the impression of Asian descent. Although I never paid much attention when it came to Penny's humanized geography.

"Did you fall in? Or?" Rhett says.

"What do you mean? I intentionally jumped in the water. Did *you* fall in?" I ask.

Rhett giggles. "I didn't mean," Rhett stifles yet another giggle. "No, I didn't, but I'm also wearing a swimsuit, honey. I only ask because you're still wearing shoes. Come on. I'll help you lay out your clothes. It's still nice enough out they might dry."

"Mona. My name is Mona."

Rhett leads me to the edge. "It's nice to meet you, Mona. I've never seen you around here. Are you from these parts, or are you looking at colleges?"

"Not exactly," I say.

"Not exactly from around here or not exactly visiting schools?" Rhett asks.

"I'm visiting the area. The college I want to attend is not around here," I say, trying to leave the contempt out of my voice.

"Well, I'm a local if you need anything. I come here pretty regularly, especially on hot days like today," Rhett says.

"This is a hot day?" The SoTo chip means regulating my internal body core as I see fit is as easy as clicking a button, making me impervious to the weather. Despite the upgrade, it didn't feel more than seventy-two or seventy-three degrees tops.

"Well, you know how it goes in Washington. As soon as we reach fifty degrees, everyone is in flip-flops and shorts. So yeah, relatively speaking, it's a nice day." Rhett's smile holds something familiar and warm.

I slip my shirt, pants, and shoes off, leaving me in nothing more than a bra and underwear. I start to slip these off as well, but Rhett stops me.

"Umm," Rhett says.

"Yes?" I pause, glancing in Rhett's direction.

"Ah, maybe you should leave those on. I'd say go for it if it was night or private property. But we're in the middle of a park, and it's not even two," she says.

"Right. Okay," I stand there awkwardly.

"So, what brings you to my little slice of life?" Rhett says. She hangs the last of my clothes on a nearby tree in full view of the sun. We slip back into the crisp water.

"Research," I say.

"For school? Are you going to attend Western? No, wait, you answered that already."

"No. It's more of a personal interest in the human experience. I'm researching what it means to be human," I say.

"Ah, wow. You seem a bit young to be an actual reporter. Blogger?" she says.

"Something like that. It's more of a family bet. If I win, I will inherit the ability to make big changes to the family business. If I lose, my sister gets the controlling shares," I say, not exactly lying.

"Oh, wow. The family business can be such a drag. I hear running a business can be stressful in and of itself, but the added stress of family can make it much more difficult to separate work from home life. But I'm sure you know all about that," Rhett says.

Surprised, I find myself agreeing with her. "Yes, she doesn't understand the permanent damage inflicted on the organization if it continues down its current path. It's time for a change. I could make some big changes. I'm ready for that."

Rhett mulls this over. "Change can be hard. It doesn't come easily to everyone. Take your time with her. I'm sure she'll come around to see your side of things. Especially if it matters as much as you say it does."

An agreeing smile finds me, but it is more than that. It's a smile that tells the truth of things. Penny will have to come around to see things my way. Eventually, she'll have no choice.

Basking in the sun and floating on my back is a gratifying feeling. Maybe I don't get out much.

Whatever.

Rhett and I spend a long time this way.

Relaxing.

Others come and go from the watering hole, but I remain relatively unbothered.

"I think it's about time to get out. The sun has shifted," Rhett says.

"Yes, I concur. It's uncomfortable when the sun is not high in the sky. Rhett?" I say, rolling her name over my tongue for the first time.

"Hmm?"

"I was wondering if you could point me in the direction of your local resources. I have some studying, and I should probably tackle that research," I say. I plan to learn what I need to so I can go home.

"Sure, the library is probably your best bet. It arguably has the best resources and book selection plus the interwebs," Rhett says. "And you should never discount the amount of information librarians know. Bottomless pits of knowledge. But they're not going to be open much longer. I think they close at six, and by my guess, we're coming up on five or six now."

"The library," I say, committing it to memory. I'm tempted to pull up directions using my SoTo chip, but I refrain. "If they are unavailable today, I'll find it first thing in the morning."

"What are your plans for the evening?" Rhett asks.

"I don't really have any." In fact, I'd been so confident I'd win by the end of the day that I hadn't thought out what to do with my time beyond trying to *feel*.

"Where are you staying?" Rhett glances at me sideways as we pull ourselves out of the water onto the bank of rocks.

"I'm not," I sigh. "I didn't think this trip through. I assumed I would have more time in the day to finish my research. I was wrong. I haven't decided what to do yet."

"You haven't decided? You're a kick, Mona," Rhett says. "What about your folks? Aren't they going to be mad?"

What is that supposed to mean?

Does she want to kick me?

Internally, I cringe—not for the first time today. "No, they don't know I'm here. It was an impulsive decision. They think I'm with my sister." Not a lie, not the whole truth.

"Yea, I've been there. Rents. Right?" Rhett says.

"Ha, yea," I might not know what *rents* is, but I feel confident we're agreeing.

Mostly.

"Well, I'm meeting some friends at the Horsehide if you're interested in going. I'd love it if you'd join us. There's some local music, and they make a decent burger," Rhett says.

"Why would I go to a Horsehide?" I ask. "I mean, I enjoy the company of horses, but it seems like an odd place to get food. Please don't tell me you eat horses. I'm not okay with that here, especially when plenty of alternatives exist."

"Gods, no. The Horsehide is a restaurant and bar. They're open till like three am. It's cool," Rhett says.

"A Horsehide that doubles as a restaurant," I say, trying to wrap my head around the new image this conjures.

"No, Horsehide is just the name," Rhett clarifies.

"Oh, I see. Maybe next time," I say.

Penny's face pops into my mind, her voice internally mocking me. Telling me I'll never win the stupid bet.

"Why do you want to spend time with me?" I ask.

"Well," Rhett's thoughtful for a moment. "You don't have to. It just seemed we got along. I could always use a new friend. You don't seem to know many people. Figured what was the harm?"

"Okay," I say. "Sure. I don't have any other plans. Thank you."

"For what?" Rhett asks.

"The invitation."

Rhett waves away my words, "Psh, thanks for coming. I didn't really want to go out alone."

"I thought you said you were meeting friends?" I eye Rhett skeptically.

Humans lie.

"Well, it's not cool to walk in alone," Rhett gives me a wink. "But a friend of mine is a waiter, and another bartends. So, yea. I'm meeting up with some friends, but when they get busy, I have to fend off the barflies all on my lonesome."

"Ah, I guess that makes sense. Are flies a problem in this bar?" The word *bar* is foreign on my tongue. "I could help remove them to a safer location if needed."

Rhett bursts into laughter. "No, not like actual flies. A barfly is someone who is more than a regular at a bar. They practically live there. Spend their whole paychecks on booze or food and their free time hitting on women a fraction of their age. Obnoxious is more like it. You think they'd take a hint. Pedos."

I nod, but I'm still not sure I actually understand.

Before Rhett notices, I dry my clothes with a flick of a button on my screen. I slip into them, and no one is the wiser.

"Should I meet you there? Or?" I ask.

"How about I drive? I live a couple of miles from the place. Do you have something to change into?" Rhett says.

I look at my clothes. Should I have conjured a new set? "I didn't really plan this out. As I said, it was only supposed to take a day. But then, life."

"No worries, I've got something that will fit you. You can borrow an outfit of mine," Rhett says.

As we leave the tree sanctuary, a sign reads *Whatcom Falls Park*, over a quaint bridge covered in moss, to a small paved lot with metal and plastic human movers parked in various colors, shapes, and sizes.

"That bug is mine," Rhett points to a lime green machine.

"You own bugs? That seems a bit odd. Which ones?"

I puzzle over why a human would want to own bugs. They domesticated cats, dogs, several reptiles, and even some less domestic beasts in the animal world. But bugs?

A sudden image of Rhett in a fly costume comes to mind. Little wings carrying all five and a half feet, one hundred-twenty pounds of her around the park. The image nearly makes me giggle.

Nearly.

"No, I drive a *bug*," Rhett points again, but this time I picture an oversized cockroach wearing a harness. Rhett's laughing. "I'm sorry, but it's just hard to believe you don't know what a bug is. Where did you say you were from?" she asks.

"Not from around here, that's for sure," I say.

Rhett unlocks the doors to her machine, but I don't get in. I've never been inside a moving coffin before. Is it even safe? I try breathing out my reservations, but as much as I hate to admit it, I don't want to die, not even in this upload. I open the door, and it gives a low rumble creak. At least I'll get to delete everything if this goes south. A small comfort in a world where everything seems out to get me.

17

MONA

We arrived at Rhett's apartment safely, much to my own surprise. "That was hands down the longest ten minutes of my life," I say.

"Well, you looked like you were hyperventilating before I had the chance to leave the parking lot," Rhett tries not to laugh at me even though I know she wants to.

"I managed to calm down, but you're right. That was far more terrifying than I'd anticipated," I say. "I've never ridden in such a crazy machine before."

Rhett looks at me incredulously. "How did you get here?"

"What do you mean? You drove us," I say.

"I mean to Bellingham," Rhett says.

"Oh," I say, realizing what she meant too late. "My sister brought me," I say feebly.

"Did she drug you to get you here?" Rhett asks.

"Something like that," I say.

Two flights of stairs, and we've entered the second-story dwelling where Rhett lives. I look around, assessing my surroundings. It's not quite what I expected. Somewhere in the back of my mind, I was anticipating mud on the walls and fecal matter piled in the corners. But that's not the case at all. This is the first time I've been inside a human habitat, and it's hard to deny my fascination.

Warmth radiates from the space, both in color and heat. A large painting is hung over an ornate brick fireplace. Two people embracing, limbs tangled in bright blue and deep purples. The contrast grabs my attention, holding it.

"Isn't it beautiful?" Rhett interrupts my thoughts.

"Mmmm. Yes, the colors are fascinating," I say. I don't know what the purple and blue blobs are supposed to be, but I'll withhold judgment for the time being.

The kitchen overlooks the living room. There's a bar with stools attached to an island. At first, it seems to be the only formal dining area. Still far better than I expected to find. For all I know, humans eat from slop piles.

Rhett walked through a set of doors opening the way to a more formal dining area.

"I know it's small, but it's home," Rhett says. "Come on, I'll show you around."

We walk as Rhett points out little things like the shine her mother uses, the bathroom in case I need to relieve this body, and her bedroom. I follow Rhett into a brightly lit room. Her bed was covered in an eggplant purple blanket.

Hesitantly I reach out to feel the bed; to my surprise, it's soft. I sit down.

"Let's see. I have all kinds of stuff. Mom's always trying to get me to donate the things I don't wear. But the struggle is real." Rhett pulls out a modest but sparkling chocolate-colored tunic, a deep burgundy plunging neckline top, and a teal dress with fringe far too short to be considered clothing. "If I had gotten rid of all this stuff, I'd have nothing to share. So I consider it a win."

I'm unsure how well I'm hiding my disdain for her clothes.

"Any of these tickle your fancy?" Rhett asks. She goes back to digging through her closet. Tossing garment after garment at me. The flowing materials make a rainbow in the closet. Seeming to morph from one color to the next.

"Here, these colors complement your skin tone. What do you think?" Rhett says.

I think I'm living Penny's dream—drowning in clothing choices. If I was at home, all I'd have to click is the button for today's clothing. I don't like options that have no impact on my daily routine. An abundance of clothing choices is simply wasteful. I don't say anything because I need to make a friend.

Has it only been a few hours here?

With a cursory glance, I find a color I don't hate. "I guess the maroon top."

"Good choice! This is one of my favorites. It stays relatively humble, but then the light hits it, and POW! Sparkles right in the kisser."

"Pow?" I slither out of my clothes and slip the long top on.

"Here, what about these jeans?" Rhett tosses them to me.

"Umm, are you aware they have holes in them?" I say, wondering if she's giving me her garbage.

"They're stressed on purpose. It's the style," Rhett says. "What size feet do you have?"

"I'm not sure," I say, holding out my foot for her to examine before slipping on her discarded and used jeans. At least they smell clean. It seems unlikely I'll catch anything.

"Girl, you live under a rock," Rhett says, reaching for a pair of shoes. "Here, try these on. I'm sure they'll fit you."

I inspect the pair of black wedges. I'm still unsure why I can't wear the shoes I came here with, but I refrain from sighing and slip them on.

All of this dressing up is a Penny thing. I have a moment of wonder, did Penny put Rhett up to this?

Nah.

If she interfered like that, her bet would be void. I don't think she'd risk it.

It's not like I hate glitz and glam. It just feels so fake. Like I'm not allowed to just be who I am. Dressing up equates to a façade.

I just want to be me.

"I feel like a fish out of water," I say. "If my sister would wear it, I usually don't."

The top Rhett gave me doesn't fit right. It's too tight around my breasts and too loose around my stomach. But, with the slip of a finger, I am able to code the top to fit my body flawlessly.

"Wow, that looks stunning on you," Rhett says. "You can keep it. It's never looked that good on me.

"You really think so?" I ask as I feel the rough fabric. It's not as soft as the bedding but not intolerable. I turn a circle.

"I do. You said your sister's name is Penny?"

"Yes."

"Don't let her limit your choices. At some point, you'll have to realize that just because someone else likes something first, it doesn't mean you can't like it too." Rhett smiles. "I'm just saying, you look beautiful. Whatever makes you feel beautiful is good, regardless of your sister."

Rhett sits down and pats the spot on the bed next to her. She's got a seaweed plaid bag in her hands. "Now for a little war paint."

"You expect me to go to war wearing this?" I say, glancing at the shoes.

Rhett is laughing.

I sit down and start to remove the shoes.

"No, no," Rhett is still laughing. "You really crack me up, Mona. The shoes are fine."

I put them back on.

"Here, close your eyes. Let me give you a little somethin' somethin' on those peepers. It will bring out the color of your eyes and make your cheeks rosy."

I couldn't help but stare at her. What is a peeper, and why do I want roses for cheeks?

The distrust must be radiating off me because Rhett speaks up again. "Close your eyes. I'm not going to hurt you. You can't tell me with a straight face you've never worn eyeshadow.

"Would you believe me if I said I'd never even put makeup on a day in my life?"

Rhett shakes her head, "Are you a cult survivor? You can tell me if you are."

"I don't think so?"

"At this point, lady, not much would surprise me."

Rhett tried to convince me to let her drive us to the bar. Obviously, I was having none of it.

"It's only a couple of miles away. Besides, didn't you tell me it was close to your apartment in the first place?" I say.

"Well, yes. But then I'll have to carry my bag and anything else I might need. I can't just lock it in the car and run out to grab whatever I need from there," Rhett says exasperatedly. "I'd need to carry my jacket, purse, makeup, extra shoes, and whatever else I need. I promise there's a method to my madness Mona."

"You don't need all the stuff," I say. "That's all it is, right? Stuff?" Why do humans pack around so much stuff every single day? What is the point?

"It's not just stuff," Rhett says.

"It's so much crap. None of it is necessary to go out with. Or is your ability to enjoy yourself strictly tied to the number of things you bring with you?" I ask.

"It's also a status thing. A car is an important part of being a successful teenager," Rhett says.

I raise an eyebrow but don't say anything.

"Clearly, this is lost on you," Rhett sighs.

We leave her apartment, and to my surprise, she leaves her excess of things behind, only grabbing her driver's license, some cash, and a lip gloss.

Nothing seemed important enough to bring with me. But it wasn't like I came here with anything. Besides, if Rhett is correct and I fail to understand the importance of such possessions, I could always conjure them at will.

As we approached the Horsehide, I took note of the line of humans waiting to get in. Groups of them buzz around the outside of the building. They're dressed in various colors and come in all shapes and sizes.

I force down the mounting bile and breathe away the fit of nausea.

They're only humans.

The rest of the street seems bereft of life. The whole town seems to have closed down. The buildings are dark, and there's a limited presence on the roadways.

"What's up? You okay?" Rhett asks. She's stopped walking. "Are you coming?"

"Hmm?" I guess I stopped walking too. I clear my throat. "It's the mob of humans. It creates an anxiety bubble in my stomach, and I can't always shake the panicky feeling." The words leave my mouth before I realize I've said them out loud.

I pick up my pace and catch up to Rhett.

"Don't worry, we won't have to wait in line. I know the doorman," Rhett winks at me.

"I'm not exactly jumping at the chance to be swallowed alive by this parade of humans." Why would I want to jump the line and become a sacrifice for the offering? "I don't mind waiting."

"Nonsense," Rhett says. She approaches the doorman. "Hey Mak, what's shaking, baby?

The human Mak leans in and wraps his arms around Rhett and doesn't let go before he puts his mouth on her cheek. I breathe through the bile that threatens to surface.

"I haven't seen you in; what's it been? A week? It feels like ages, girl," Mak says.

Rhett giggles as Mak holds her at arm's length. "That long, eh?" she says. "I must be losing my touch." Rhett turns to me, "This here's Mona. She's a friend." Rhett blinks an eye at me.

"Do you have something in your eye?" I ask.

Rhett's smile widens like it's eating her face. "No honey, why would you think that?"

"Never mind," I say. I still don't understand what's going on. Or why she keeps blinking one eye at me. Is it a wink? Why would she do that?

Mak lets go of Rhett and opens the conversational circle to me. "Hey, Mona, it's nice to meet you."

He reaches his hand out and grabs my own before I can stop him. This Mak guy has the audacity to bring my hand to his lips. He presses them against my hand and drops it quickly back to my side.

The smile on my face wavers.

"Man, you're a sultry one with a sort of serial killer vibe, aren't you?" Mak says.

I don't know if this is an insult or a compliment. So, I just keep smiling. While he's a good foot taller than me and about three times as broad, I'm confident I can take him. I can and will attack any human who stands in the way of winning.

Deep breath. Don't let him ruin the game plan. He's not worth it.

Mak holds his thumb and first finger apart, making some sort of secret symbol. "I need to see some ID, hon. I trust you, Rhett, but if the boss comes 'round and she ain't got one," Mak tisked. "I'm up shit creek. You know what I'm sayin'?"

"No worries, Mak, we're just going to eat tonight," Rhett says.

"What's ID? I forgot to ask you earlier," I say.

"Girl, you look as empty as my pockets," Mak says.

Rhett leans in and whispers, "Identification, like a driver's license."

"No offense, doll, but you could be on barely legal, and I'm not chancing it," Mak says.

Rhett hauls back and punches Mak in the arm.

"Ouch! What was that for?" Mak is laughing while rubbing his arm.

"You know exactly what that was for," Rhett says.

Before I can decide precisely what they're talking about, a man that makes Mak look like a toy plaything comes outside to relieve him for his dinner break.

"Mmm, tasty. Damn, you're fine, baby. It's so rare to see a girl as beautiful as you come up in these parts of town."

I stare at the new man. His ebony skin twinkles in the moonlight, and there's something remarkable about how he carries himself. I'm tempted to reach out and touch him, but I refrain.

"The names Dom," he says and reaches for my hand.

This time, I let him take it. I'm not sure why the standard greeting involves mouths on hands. For the first time, I wonder if it's a mating ritual. I will make a mental note to ask the library about this tomorrow.

"Thanks?" I say, regaining my composure. "You're quite interesting yourself."

"Thanks, doll. I got this from here, Mak. You go on now and take your break. I'll handle these ladies," Dom says, grinning ear to ear.

"I'm sure you will," Mak says. He waves goodbye, and I can only assume he's gone out hunting and foraging. I wonder where he'll go.

"Hey, Dom. This is my friend Mona. Mona, this is Dom. He's one of the owners of this beautiful establishment," Rhett says.

She seems to be trying to tell me something without words, but I don't understand her nonverbal communication methods.

"Hello, Dom," I say. I'm tempted to ask him why he's sizing me up like a slab of meat, but I refrain.

"Why don't you two go right in. Seat yourselves. You tell Shae your drinks are on me tonight." Dom licks his lips, "This baby is for you."

Dom hands me a card, and I reluctantly take it.

"I'll be seeing you later," he says.

"She's a bit young, don't you think, Dom?" Rhett patts his arm.

"Legal?" Dom asks.

"As if," Rhett says.

I examine the card, "Umm, thanks," I say and follow Rhett into the dark restaurant.

The space opens up into a number of tightly packed tables. Stools line the length of the bar. Bright accent walls color the room.

"What was that about?" I ask.

"Oh please, Mona. I'm starting to question if you've ever even lived before. He was hitting on you."

I've never been in a fistfight before, so I can't compare a previous experience to this one.

"Please don't tell me you've never, you know." Rhett's eyebrows raise up and down a few times.

"I wish you'd speak more plainly. I'm not versed in body language or human subtleties," I say.

"Okay. Can I ask a question?" Rhett says.

"I believe you just did," I say.

She smiles, "I think you're really cool, Mona. You crack me up as well, and I really enjoy your company. I'm unsure if it's rude to ask, but are you on the spectrum?"

"What spectrum?" I ask. I glance at the card Dom handed me, and for the first time, I realize he's slipped me a murdered tree. It's small, but murder is murder. "Here," I say, shoving the card at Rhett. "I can't stand the idea of murder. I just can't." A shiver runs down my back.

Not the good kind.

"Murder? It's a business card," Rhett says.

"I don't care what it is. Please take it away," I say. I follow Rhett's example and sit on a stool at the cool metallic bar.

Rhett fingers the card, "Not your type? Too old? Dom is super sweet. He's a big teddy bear."

"A big murder card-carrying bear. News flash, bears aren't sweet," I say.

"I'm endlessly fascinated by you, Mona. Do you want something to drink? Rhett asks, "Dom's buying, so I'm ordering."

"Sure. What do they have?" I ask.

Rhett passes me a menu with a long list of sustenance.

"Shae makes the most amazing virgin chocolate milk. And their poutine is to die for. Plus, they have the best apple pie."

"Chocolate, anything sounds really good," I say. My mouth salivates at the mere memory of chocolate.

"It's a girl's best friend. I prefer it to sex sometimes," Rhett says.

I can feel my eyes growing more prominent.

"Well, I guess it depends on the guy," Rhett is laughing, and despite myself, I laugh too.

"What's poutine?" I ask.

"Oh girl, we'll get you all learned up."

"Is this what it's like to be high?" I ask.

Rhett giggles, "It's as close as I've gotten, legally speaking."

"Poutine sounds way dirtier than this, too," I say.

"Don't I know it," Rhett is still laughing. "But it tastes like—"

"Warm liquid bliss. It's savory and salty and—"

"Delicious," Rhett finishes. "We've got to get you out more often.

"Do all the women here think they can get free drinks with their breasts?" I ask. "Look at her. They're practically falling out of her top. It's a barbaric mating ritual."

"I don't know about barbaric, but that's exactly what it is," Rhett says.

The drink in my hand sloshes, "I feel all buzzy."

"I'll let you in on a secret," Rhett leans in conspiratorially.

I tilt into her, spilling some of my drink.

"They're not virgins." Rhett claps her mouth.

"You're drinking virgins?" I set the drink down. "No matter how good it tastes, that's not my thing, girl. I stopped with the human and animal sacrifices ages ago."

"What?" Rhett laughs so hard she nearly tips out of her stool. "It's the chocolate. I read once that it can make you feel high. It's why it's a common substitute for endorphins. Well, chocolate and Kahlua," Rhett says. She places a finger to her lips, "Shhhh."

"Where do you get your information? I don't think that's accurate," I say. I could search with the SoTo, but I refrain. Seems a little pointless at the moment.

"It's common knowledge," Rhett giggles.

"Is that so?" I say. "You humans are non-stop entertainment." Who'd have thought?

"Humans?" Rhett says.

I wave her away with a hand. "You know what I mean."

Maybe it's the chocolate drink. Maybe Penny is right. It's becoming challenging to fault Penny's love for the little bastards.

What am I saying?

Whatever. Don't overthink it. So they're enjoyable to watch. I might not have fought so hard if I knew it could feel like this. I'd have started watching the port screens ages ago.

"Oh, don't look now," Rhett says.

I follow Rhett's eyes.

"I said don't look," Rhett snaps.

I turn back around. "What?"

"Noah Harvey and Coen Kelvin just walked in," Rhett whispers.

"Oh," I say. Pausing to let her words sink in. "Should I know who they are?

"Shh, here they come," Rhett sits up straighter and fluffs her hair.

Mating rituals.

"Hey Coen, how's it going? Rhett says.

"Hey," the guy named Coen says.

"Monosyllabic answers again?" Rhett says.

"What?" Coen says.

"It's Mona, right?" Noah says. "My brother can't stop talking about you."

"That's not too weird. I am me, after all," I say.

Noah sits down at the bar next to me.

"Can I help you with something?" I say.

Noah reaches for some gravy-covered fries and plops them into his mouth. "I love this place." He helps himself to a few more fries before taking my napkin.

"You're welcome," I say.

"So I was thinking, maybe we could swap numbers and hang out sometime," Noah says.

Rhett interjects, "You two know each other?"

"No." I say at the same time Noah says, "Yes."

"We met briefly before my run," I say. "In the morning."

"So, are you free tomorrow? What do you say?" Noah asks.

"No. Ouch," I shoot daggers at Rhett. "Why did you kick me?"

Rhett's smile eats her face, "What she means to say is, we already have plans. But she'll call you."

"Sugar, I think you're a cheap date. Give the girl some poutine and a couple of chocoholics, and she's a goner." Shea slaps the bill down on the table.

"Thanks, Shae," Rhett watches Shae walk away. Before he's rounded the corner, she says, "Did you?"

"Did I what?" Shea saunters back to the bar.

"You're gonna make me say it?" Rhett seems to pout her lips.

"Sure, sure. Dom's covered them. But she was never here. Got it?" Shea nods at me.

"Of course, doll." Rhett blows Shae a kiss.

"You sweet on him?" Coen asks. "I mean, I won't take offense."

Rhett shoves Coen off his stool. "It's noneya."

"What's noneya?" I ask.

"It means it's none of ya business. Well, not yours. His. It's none of his business," Rhett rolls her eyes and grabs the ticket.

"I need to exit my seat now. I should follow Rhett," I say. I'm not sure what the proper protocols are for departing social gatherings.

Noah stands and gives me a bow. "Call me."

I leave him and make my way to Rhett, holding onto the backs of the chairs and booths. My legs and feet don't feel so steady.

"Hey there, lady, are you ready to call it a night?" Rhett asks.

"Is it night? Has it only been one day here? Why does time creep by so slowly here? I could have made a whole universe in the time it took this one day to pass." I shake a finger at Rhett, "That's a slow day. I'm used to it being much faster. Like times a lot." I trip and nearly fall into Rhett's arms. "Oops. Did I tell you about the time I nearly killed that roach, Noah? Sent that guy swimming with the fishes."

Rhett is giggling, but I don't know what's so funny. I'm being serious. "No, I don't think you did," she says.

"Doesn't matter. My sister Penny gave him a heads-up. He lived." Only the word lived seems to stretch on into infinity, sliding off my tongue languidly.

"Noah, as in Noah Harvey?" Rhett asks.

"Who?" I lean my head against the wall. "The line is so long, and I have to urinate."

"Noah, as in the guy who was drooling over you." Rhett takes a step forward in line.

The restaurant is filled to capacity, hopping just as much as the bar we just came from.

"No," I move the hair out of my face. It keeps sticking in all the wrong places. "Okay, Rhett. Rhett... Rrrreee—t. Rhett. Rrrrr—ett. Rhett."

"You're cut off. No more Jesus Juice for you, kid." Rhett helps steady me, but all I want to do is sleep.

"He wasn't all holier than thou, for the record. And he sure as hell wasn't no son of mine. I can't take credit for Jim either. Neither. Either? Neither? Like, like. Liiiiike. You liiiiike Shaeeee. Hey, hey, Shea, hey. You want to know a secret?" I lift a finger to my lips. "Shea," I say, reaching beyond Rhett to clap Shae on the arm.

"Hey, Rhett," Shae smiles. He leads us to the door. "You got to get her out of here."

18

PENNY

Never in all my life did I think I'd get to see Mona intoxicated. The girl can't hold her booze. That part doesn't surprise me at all.

"Mona, you're looking a little green. Are you okay?" Rhett says as she walks Mona to the door of the Horsehide. "You're looking a little bug-eyed. Don't puke. Take a deep, slow breath."

Rhett is holding her own quite well, considering Mona looks like she's about to blow chunks.

"Breathe through it, and don't ralph on me," Rhett says.

"I don't even know what that means. How does one ralph? Or is it, what's a ralph? Ralph. Rrralllffff. Where's my delete button? I'm just seeing two of everything right now. Which one of you, Rhett's, is the real Rhett? Will the real Rhett Rhetty please stand up?"

Mona trips over the threshold, landing squarely on her bottom. She leans onto her back, singing the only human song she remembers. "Will the real Rhett Rhretty please help me up? Help me up? Help me up?"

For her part, Rhett really tries to get her up, but when Mona rolls away giggling, she too falls into fits of laughter.

Mona laughs until everything turns dim, and her memory blackens. Her health stats are clear, if not slightly elevated.

I only waver once, wondering if helping Rhett wrangle Mona would be the kinder option. But then I'd have to explain myself, and honestly, the longer it takes her to figure things out, the more hope there is for humans.

Besides, I think I've witnessed Mona making her first friend.

My heart smiles at the thought.

19

MONA

When I open my eyes, the world around me spins. I try to right myself, but somehow it only makes things worse.

"Chocolate is not a girl's best friend," I mumble to the room.

"It was last night when you were trying to dance on the street lamp and when you shook your ta-tas for Shae in hopes of getting one last chocolate martini out of him," Rhett says. "Mind you, we'd already been escorted out of the restaurant by this point. So I can definitively say that chocoholics were everyone's best friend last night."

"I can hear you. I just can't figure out where your voice is coming from," I groan.

"That's because your eyes are closed."

"I remember going out with you and drinking chocolate. I just assumed it would be a liquified version of the ice cream. Maybe something about the form in which it is consumed changes the effects on the human body?" I make a mental note to investigate this phenomenon when I feel less groggy.

"Yeah, that's called Kahlua. Add that shit to anything, and it changes the effects on the human body. Duh," Rhett says.

I manage to sit upright, still holding my head. My brain is pounding out of my body. It's like someone replaced my head with a shattered port screen. Images shake and blur with every breath.

"Here, drink this," Rhett holds a glass of liquid in one hand and two small tablets in the other. "Swallow these."

"Your voice is so amplified. Much louder than reasonably acceptable. Do you have to scream?" I take the tablets from Rhett. "What is it?"

My eyes are leaking, and my face physically hurts. Whatever was in those drinks felt like being poisoned.

"Water and two Excedrin Migraine. I also suggest the hair of the dog, but I don't think you're quite up for that yet," Rhett says.

"I am not eating dog hair." I take the tablets and the water. "Even I have my limits." I wonder if eating the dog hair would make the room still again and stop the pounding in my head. "How did I?" I take another slow breath, trying to calm the roaring ocean in my stomach. "How did I end up here?"

Rhett sits beside me on the couch with two steaming cups of warm liquid. "Here, now, drink this. Sip it. It's hot."

I put the glass of water on the opaque coffee table and took the mug with two hands. I inhale a thousand aromas. "What do you call this? It's like I can smell the shaded trees of Indonesia." I closed my eyes to enjoy the aroma and take my first sip.

"It's Indonesian coffee, a Sumatra," Rhett seems surprised.

I can smell more than the processed coffee beans, so much more. I can taste every step in the roasting process. My taste buds are dancing and singing.

These small things make me feel an immeasurable amount better.

"You can tell where the coffee's from just by tasting it?" Rhett asks.

"I guess so? I'm honestly not sure. I've never had coffee before."

"Forever an interesting one, aren't you, Mona?" Rhett smiles and drinks her coffee.

"How did we get here?"

"You can thank your good friend Dom for getting you here safely. He was so hurt you didn't keep the business card he gave you, so he wrote his number on the palm of your hand last night. Then, he called us a taxi and personally helped me coax your ass into the cab. Lucky for you, this place has an elevator, or I'd have left your ass on the street to sleep it off."

"Murder card helped us get here?" I ask.

Rhett didn't leave me on the street. This gives me pause. I can't explain it, but I don't think Rhett would have left me, regardless of her words. Perhaps even if her home didn't have an elevator.

I don't know how I feel about all this.

Last night springs to memory in waves. It's all a bit fuzzy, but the overall feeling for the evening is good. It's not negative at all despite the headache.

I chuckle and take another sip of coffee. I feel an unexpected warmth when I think about yesterday.

In the span of a nanosecond, I'm absolutely disgusted with myself.

Warmth?

Uck.

Stars know Penny is watching. The thought that she might have been right about humans is enough to bring reality crashing down.

What in the Rivers of Sion?

What would that mean?

I push the thoughts away. My head is still pounding far too much for any deep ruminations.

Particularly about humans.

I set my shoulders back and made eye contact with Rhett before speaking. "Thank you."

It is all I can muster.

"That's what friends are for." Perhaps it was also all Rhett needed.

"So, what are your plans for the day? Are you going to hit up the library?" Rhett asks.

"Yes, I think it's an appropriate place to start," I say.

Rhett has loaned me a clean pair of jeans and a T-shirt for the day. She put my clothing into the wash. I suppose humans don't have *quick cycle* for their clothes.

Primitives.

"Still set on proving your sister wrong?"

"I just need to find some answers. Maybe it proves her wrong. Maybe it doesn't. I'm on a mission either way." I say.

If I can prove her wrong, I'll stick it to Penny in the worst possible way.

"My legs and head ache so much. Stars above, is it supposed to hurt this much?" Being human is painful.

"I can assure you, this is all a normal reaction to alcohol and exercise," Rhett says.

"I thought running was a good thing?" I say.

"In moderation. You probably just pushed yourself too much," Rhett says. "Drink lots of water today."

"Right."

"So I talked to my mom this morning," Rhett says, handing me beans on toast.

"Thank you."

"She's cosigned my lease, so I felt like I had to check. I'm not sure what your situation is, but you are welcome to stay here as long as needed. I know you didn't anticipate being in town long. It's summer. Classes don't start till fall...." Rhett trails off.

I'm processing her words.

Her kindness.

"It's not charity or anything, just a thought," Rhett says.

"Thank you," I say. Then take a bite of the brunch she's cooked us.

"Okay. Umm, you're welcome," she says.

Rhett gives me hope that there is still good in this world. I'm still not sure there's much worth salvaging, but perhaps I don't understand the depths of humans yet.

20

PENNY

On her way to Shae's, Rhett drives Mona to the local library. Rhett did more than navigate a drunken Mona. She scored a guy's phone number.

Speaking as someone who watched the whole endeavor and knows how exciting new love is, I'm more than impressed with Rhett every day.

Rhett smiles, "I even got Shae's digits."

"When did this happen?" Mona asks.

"It was after you fell over, but before you started shaking your money makers," Rhett says.

I burst out laughing at the memory. Mona decided no *stinking human* would prevent her from getting one more drink. I'd disabled her controls at this point, not wanting her to accidentally delete humans in a drunken fit. Of course, she thought she was more intelligent than the *pin-headed humans*. So she tried to persuade them with mating rituals.

It's the best thing I never knew I needed.

I will never let Mona live it down.

Never.

"Right, I don't need to be reminded of all the messy details," Mona says, rubbing her forehead.

"Are you sure? I'd love to know where you learned the mating rituals of the peacock spider. You were moving like a samba dancer at Carnival," Rhett says.

"I said I do not need the details," Mona says.

"Hey, you asked," Rhett chuckles to herself.

Mona waves Rhett away, ending the teasing.

"So, I was thinking about going shopping later. Whenever you're done studying? If you want to get some new clothes? You know, increase the wardrobe a bit," Rhett says.

"I guess having only the clothes on my back won't work forever."

Ten bucks says Mona was betting on coding herself new clothes. I should block her just to spite.

Breathe it out, Penny, do not stoop to her level.

Be better than Mona.

"So, is that a yes?" Rhett asks.

"Yeah, why not. I hadn't planned on doing any real collecting of goods. Under the circumstances, though, I can't be expected to stay here with only one outfit, right?"

"Exactly. You gotta take care of yourself, boo," Rhett says.

"What Penny doesn't know won't kill her. It might anger her if she knew I was going to dip into reserves for such a frivolous outing. But that's what sisters are for. Right?" Mona says.

Bitch.

She's daring me to out her.

Well, she's got another thing coming if she thinks I'm that easy to roust about.

21

MONA

The Bellingham Public Library is sprawling and predominantly made of glass. I walk around the outside of the building, assessing.

"It doesn't look structurally sound," I say to no one in particular.

Rhett told me to look for the librarian, so that's my plan. If this place has at least one wise person who can address my questions about human emotions sending me on the path back home, then it's a risk I'm willing to take.

In my peripheral, I can see the pause button on the port screen and hover over it mentally. If every new interaction has me clamoring for the keyboard, then Penny wins.

I'm not afraid.

Constant vigilance is required to prevent a premature evacuation of Earthlings.

It doesn't mean I'm afraid.

I glanced at the pause button once more with an affection I'd never admit to Penny for all the rubles of Bellini, and walked in.

Murder.

Mass murder.

I didn't make it five parcins past the sprawling double doors before being confronted by the slain carcasses of thousands and thousands of trees. I started to do the mental math taking into consideration the size of the building, and it could be millions.

"Why?" the words are a whisper.

It is one thing to witness the destruction of the lands and oceans on the port screen at home. It's an entirely different sensation to see it in person.

What is this feeling?

A bubbling burning sensation in my stomach and chest. Like shards of rage flying in every direction. I can't keep it down, and I fear it will burst out of me, release into the world, and come back to haunt me.

Ice slices through my body and settles in my heart.

I bubble with heat from the pits of my stomach to the tips of my fingers.

I could breathe fire and set this place aglow with a dragon's fury.

My fists shake with every step I descend into hell.

Why would someone mutilate my forests?

It's an abomination.

The expectation I perceived involved the library greeting me with intellectually stimulating humans. Instead, I'm accosted with row after row of my creations, torn from their roots and shelved for entertainment.

What kind of sick joke is this supposed to be?

Humans get off on hallucinating by staring at the dead corpses of once beautiful monoliths.

I will never understand.

Observing them in structures was hard enough. I'd taken note of them in Rhett's home and the Horsehide. I was lenient.

Soft.

Mercy doesn't become me.

This isn't a place of knowledge. It's a place of horrors.

A tightness in my chest makes it hard to breathe.

My stomach curls in on itself, and I fear I might lose what little breakfast I'd managed to consume this morning.

I want to scream and cry out, rip pages from the atrocities, and rub the shells of what once was in someone's face. I want to suffocate them with their own sadistic doings.

With shaking hands, on shaking legs, I take one step at a time toward a large section of books labeled *fiction*. I grab a shelf to balance.

Blackness threatens the edge of my vision, and I will the room not to spin.

After a few slow breaths, I'm able to walk the aisles. Each step feels like slogging through mud. I reach out and touch the spines with trembling fingers.

I round a corner and find a stool to collapse on.

Everything in me goes numb.

22

PENNY

I watched my sister from a safe distance, observing as her hands began to shake.

It means Mona was about to explode on the humans around her. I can picture her attacking every last human. Slicing and dicing them with a samurai sword or shooting fireballs from her eyes.

My thoughts race around every potential ending, including Mona grabbing the nearest blunt object and taking out the librarians one by one. Or channeling her inner siren and shattering the glass walls. Calling the winds and touching a tornado down in the middle of what I can only imagine she sees as a graveyard.

The possibilities are an endless cavern of ruthlessness.

I didn't think this bet through the way I should have.

Mona can't live as a human because there are so many things with the potential to set her off.

While a library wouldn't have been at the top of my list of triggers, it doesn't surprise me. Mona just needs to see the good that could come from books.

As long as she never finds out that four billion trees were cut down for the paper industry alone, the library might have a chance of avoiding death by papercuts.

But how could I get her to see this?

If I could just get Mona to open up to me, I might be able to help her.

Mo(ther) Na(ture)

That was it.
Open up.

23

MONA

Several steadying breaths later, I'm able to stand up. I'm ready to retreat.

As much as it pains me to admit, I knew it was time to leave. Time to move along and burn this place to the ground.

I'm nearing the end of the stack when a book falls off the shelf and hits me on the head.

"Ouch!" I rub the spot where the sharp corner connects with the back of my skull. "Damn books."

I glance down at the book, which has fallen open. Surprisingly, I recognized the title *Harry Potter and The Sorcerer's Stone*. The book's cream-colored pages are turned to chapter one, *The Boy Who Lived*.

My eyes catch the words on the page, and for a split moment and I begin to read. Only a couple of lines at first, but when I run out of words, I flip to the next page and continue reading.

I don't know when I picked up the book and cradled it in my arms, but the desperation to know what would happen next was overwhelming.

What happened to the boy who lived? What was really in the Forbidden Forest, and should I be leery of it like Oliver suggested? What exactly does a wizard do? Was it something Penny created?

The moment I flipped one page plagued with words, I was ready to turn to the next. I ingested the story quicker than I could turn the pages.

I want more.

No.

I need more.

"How did you like Harry Potter, Mona?"

A rigidness sets into my bones before I glance over my shoulder.

No one's there.

"Hello?" I say to the empty aisle.

"Down here," a voice whispers.

I hold the book out and flip it over a couple of times in disbelief.

"Hi, Mona. If I might say, it is a little weird to call you Mona. The most recent references list you as Mother Nature," the book says. "I suppose it won't be long till they update it. Only another millennium if we're lucky."

"What in the rivers of Sion is this?" I was not expecting to hear the voice of a fallen tree, and yet, that's exactly what's happening.

My blood, sweat, and tears have transformed into something new. Reborn to live again.

"Don't be distressed on my account," the book says.

"I'm not. I'm just a bit—Well, I don't know. Do you like living as," I look around the library, "paper?" I spit the last word out like the bite of a rotten apple.

"It wasn't my first choice, but I didn't get to choose to be a tree either," he says. "If you could see all the good I get to do, the smiling faces when people see me. No one ever looked at me that way before I became a book. It's a dream."

"I can't begin to fathom any good coming of this," I say, a bit exasperated. "You're nothing but a shell of your former self."

"I don't mean to speak ill, but you're wrong. Were you or weren't you just enjoying Harry's story? Maybe I heard you wrong when you started muttering about finding his way through Forbidden Forest? Or what about when you thought he might lose that chess game, but Ron saved him?"

"Yes, well, that was all Olli's doing." I clear my throat. "I just remembered the name Harry Potter, and I wanted to see if the two were one and the same. That's all."

It's not like I was actually interested in this silly story.

"I won't point out it wouldn't take reading all my pages to learn that."

I have no response. The book is correct. I could have surmised what happened quickly but chose to read the whole thing instead.

"Stories inspire, create vivid images of the unknown, and take the reader anywhere they want to go. You were just at Hogwarts, Mona. You walked next to Harry as he found platform 9 ¾. You ducked when the Troll was trashing the girl's bathroom. Books take us to those special places found amongst our pages. I get to transport every person who picks me up to a place filled with magic. It's incredible."

Tension grows between myself and the book. When I finally decide to speak, it's barely a whisper. "Don't you miss home? The fresh air, the breeze rustling your leaves? Rain in the spring? Any of it?"

The book didn't hesitate in its response. "Did you find the Dark Forest Mona?"

"Yes," I say.

"I get to do more than have my limbs rustled. I'm home to an entire world now. I'm alive in these pages."

"I'm still not okay with this. With any of this." I stand up to leave and start to put the book back in its empty nesting space.

"Wait, please don't leave angry. Why did you come here today? There must have been some reason?"

I nearly forgot why I'd come to the library in the first place. "To find information on human emotions. I was hoping there would be someone who could answer my questions."

"See, you have come to the right place. Non-fiction is on the other side of that barrier to your right. You'll find what you're looking for over there," the book says.

I shelve the book and make my way through the library, avoiding eye contact with every human in this horror house.

My mind hasn't changed.

These emotions are better regulated when I don't want to see it all burn.

For that reason, I'm trying to understand. See things from the other side.

I'm just not so sure I do.

My nerves have about had it, though. Human feelings are starting to wear on me.

At least the murder house is well-labeled. Finding non-fiction was an easy enough task.

24

MONA

It has been three hours since entering the murder house. It's difficult to call this place a library. It feels like a graveyard. All it has to show is the horrors humans have inflicted upon the Earth.

Where should I even start?

Maybe with the mass killings of elephants for their ivory tusks? There were once twenty-six million free-range elephants in Africa, but now their numbers have been slaughtered to five hundred thousand.

All for the sake of ivory.

It's deplorable.

Don't humans know that elephants are a significant part of the ecosystem I have so carefully constructed? Without their tusks, how will other animals find water? Smaller creatures will have no paths, and seeds won't disperse. If they cared to learn, they would find it crucial for pollination among plants and trees.

There will be nothing to create the grasslands which so many other life forms depend on for survival when elephants are gone.

A drop of liquid falls onto the page of my book.

I looked up to find the source, but there was nothing. It takes me a moment to realize it's come from me.

A tear.

Another drop rolls off my cheek, and I wipe away the tears. I refuse to leak when five and a quarter trillion pieces of plastic litter the ocean.

Crying won't solve anything.

Removing the threat to my planet is the only solution. I need to give Earth time to heal.

What more proof does Penny need?

How can I make her understand?

Humans aren't worthy of saving.

Fueled with a new breed of fury, I dig for my book on human emotions. It's hidden under seven other books. I topple the stack, unbothered by the assault on silence I've created.

I will feel each of these emotions.

It will be the last thing I do in this forsaken body.

Then I will revel in pleasure while deleting every last human. They will all pay for crimes they've inflicted.

I memorize Plutchik's wheel of emotions. I scan many books on human feelings, sentiments, and reactions. Still, there are only a few matching Penny's criteria, and they all seem to boil back to the following eight: vigilance, ecstasy, admiration, terror, amazement, grief, loathing, and rage, or various versions of them. Two of which I have already experienced: loathing and amazement.

Thank you very much, chocolate.

The first set has sub-emotions and spin-offs: anger, disgust, sadness, surprise, fear, trust, joy, and anticipation. Then, as if that weren't enough to memorize, even those groups break down again into serenity, acceptance, apprehension, distraction, pensive, boredom, annoyance, and interest. I don't know if things like love, remorse, or awe factor into this game, but at least I've heard of them.

For all I know, Penny could have her own unique list of emotions in hopes of me never figuring it out.

Make no mistake, it won't stop me.

I will adapt and feel them all.

My head is spinning.

If humans are capable of such complex emotions, why do they do so many horrible things?

How can someone walk around without an awareness of their effect on the world around them?

I struggle to wrap my head around all the new information. My skull is starting to throb, and I wonder if the learning process will always feel this way—achy and strung out. I'm unsure if it's caused by the murder house or the lingering effects of liquefied chocolate.

Either way, I need air.

I discard my stacks of books and leave the library with a heavy heart. The weight of twenty-five million elephants lingers on my shoulders.

25

PENNY

I should have pressed pause.

I should have told Mona. She felt rage. But I couldn't bring myself to do it.

Mona isn't someone you want to anger on a regular day. I can't even fathom what poking the bear while she's on Earth would mean. I don't enjoy her when she's angry at home. I don't want to be around her like this.

It's probably better to let her cool off, maybe leave her a nice little note about it after she's calmed down.

With my luck, it will only add gasoline to the fire.

To be entirely fair, I don't need to notify Mona of her emotional state.

Maybe it's a bad idea to continually interrupt her.

It was fun at first. Despite all Mona's flaws, she's still my sister. Teasing her is second nature.

But the more emotions she feels, the less confident I become. Mona is blowing through them quickly, with an unchanged mind.

It's as if being anthropological only solidifies her standpoint on the whole human debate.

That's the last thing I want.

I made the dumb bet because I was confident, she'd feel what it meant to be human and empathize with them. I expected her to come to the dark side.

It's not as if I had much choice in the matter. Or time to think through the ramifications. I was trying to think on my feet.

So much for that.

Mona is going to do worse than simply deleting them.

How can the same blood that runs through my veins match Mona's?

We shared a womb!

We're sisters, for crying out loud, yet I've never felt so different in my whole life.

I rub my face and let out the breath I've been holding. "Why do you have to be so damned difficult?"

"Excuse me?" a teenage girl looks up at me, confusion blanketing her face.

"I'm sorry, not you, dear," I force a smile and walk away, shifting into a different form quicker than a hummingbird's wings.

Why can't Mona think about anyone but herself? Just one damned day.

It's all I want.

Am I really asking that much?

I watch Mona leave the library. I can't pinpoint what it is about her, but something shifted. Maybe it's the light in her eyes or the sway of her head. Something is different.

I just wish I could decide if it's good different or bad different.

26

MONA

I stand in silence outside the Bellingham Public Library, a statue on the lawn.

Time loses all meaning as I watch the world around me. I question everything I've done.

I created monsters.

It's just as much my fault as it was Penny's. Nevertheless, I will take ownership of my mistakes.

Why would any of them want to be here?

What is the point of all of it?

Why continue living on a planet that is dying a little more every minute?

Why live with so much inescapable fatality and destruction?

It's not just the elephants. It's crime, war, and famine. If it's not some big catastrophe killing them, then there is always tripping in the bathtub or walking off a cliff while playing on a handheld computer.

None of it makes any sense.

Are humans really any better than dinosaurs? In fact, dinosaurs were better suited for the Earth than humans ever were. They may have stunted emotional growth, but they weren't killing the planet or causing the mass extinction of thousands of other life forms, not to mention themselves.

Cora and Agnes self-poisoned themselves. They're all the same.

Five minutes or five years could have passed, standing in front of the library. I watch as humans move about their lives.

They take many forms with many colors. Color seems to be the way they express themselves. I wonder what they see when they look at me. How many different manifestations are there?

I guess I'll never really know.

A human with long blond hair pulled into a ponytail is wearing a pink and black spandex jacket and tight black pants. She stops her jog to let a small golden-haired, floppy-eared dog on a lead defecate on the library's lawn. I watch the woman jog in place, annoyed the spaniel chose this spot and moment to relieve itself.

The spaniel turns circles on the lawn. "Was it here? She was here, no, it was here. Yes, right there, no over here. Oh, I know she was here somewhere; I can smell her," the spaniel expresses. After three or four spins, he squats, satisfied he found the exact place to leave a bio-note for his friend.

Humans don't seem to care or notice the intricacy of canine scent and communication. Bio-notes are love letters left behind for another dog to find.

A supremely canine ability.

I smile at the dog, who looks up mid-squat. "Mona!" barks the spaniel, "Did you see Cece come through here? My human didn't leave the house on time, and we missed her today."

I shake my head, careful not to be caught by the human talking to her pet.

Internally, I cringe. Ownership is something I am confident I'll never grasp.

"That's okay. I'll see her tomorrow. Maybe if we're quick enough, we can catch up. I do love me some Cece." The exuberant pooch is excited, and the two continue their jog. Leaving me alone again.

Three humans ride by on two wheels, and more than a few drive on four. Nearby birds croon a song passed down from generation to generation.

No one seems to hear their words or even nod to their soft melody. I let the sparrow's song wash over me. I try to hold on to the happy song. Let it seep into my veins, but it only makes me sad. I'm reminded with every trill humans are too self-absorbed to hear.

Some of them seem happy, while others pass by in angry huffs. I watch the humans walk alone, lost in their own thoughts or engrossed by small devices. They can't look away from them. I even watched one human nearly run directly into a large vehicle when he failed to look up from the handheld device in time.

Perhaps technology is too advanced for human minds.

They walk in pairs, hand-in-hand, spilling soft words to one another, their eyes smiling.

A couple sits side by side on a bench. I imagine what they might be saying. They lean into one another. I scrutinize their faces when they connect at the lips. I examine every movement with the fascination of a scientist.

I think about the spark I felt when Noah's hand touched mine. I wonder what it might be like to mash my lips against his in the same way.

In a human way.

My cheeks flush, and for a tiny moment, I live in those thoughts before letting them go.

I close my eyes and push all my human feelings aside. I step into the vehemence bubbling up from deep inside me.

How could I let myself entertain any ideas of what it might be like to live such a pathetic existence? Thoughts about a human touching me. What it would be like to make my body spark again.

Shameful thoughts.

I could never exist like one of them.

Why would I want to? I am Mother Nature. Goddess over the damned rivers of Sion. I am the reason for all that is and ever will be. It is my responsibility.

All of them.

The creation of this planet, its entire existence, is on me. Every single part of it.

I can't simply remove humans. No matter how much I want to end all the pain and suffering. Penny is correct. It wouldn't be right.

I open the port screen and select the whole of planet Earth.

I don't want to look at it anymore. I don't want to feel the suffering of millions of my species' suffering or witness the constant massacre.

I am done.

My last thoughts are of Rhett, Oliver, Cora, and Noah. "I'm so sorry." It comes out in a small whimper.

I press delete.

27

PENNY

I unplug from my upload, "What in the rivers of Sion do you think you're doing?" I say.

"I'm done," Mona says.

"What do you mean you're done? You don't just get to quit. You don't just get to give up because you're not getting your way. Who are you? A two-headed meepet from Zazerbark? Get over yourself, Mona." I can feel the fire in my voice.

Mona holds her head in her hands.

"The silent treatment won't work on me. I know you better than that," I say, refusing to be deterred.

Mona takes her time. "Sometimes you cut your losses. I'd rather take them all out than continue to watch so many suffer."

"Watch them suffer?" I'm indignant.

"Yes, did I stutter?"

"You can't tell me you've suddenly grown a conscience overnight, Mona."

"Did you know?" Mona searches my eyes.

"Did I know what?"

"Did you know about the genocide of thousands of species? What about their own species? How could you let them get so bloodthirsty?" Mona says. The accusatory tone is evident in her voice.

"How could I?" I say, feeling my anger grow.

"Did you suddenly grow wings? All you're doing is parroting me."

"I did not force them to do anything," I say, trying to remain calm. "I upheld my end of things. Minimal interference."

"So you didn't stop it either?" Mona says.

"It's not like you gave a damn. If you cared about your precious planet so much, why didn't you do something about it earlier?" my voice rises an octave.

"I tried to do something about it. But you stopped me. I tried to rid her of your slaughtering species ages ago. Let me see?" Mona pretends to think hard. "You chose to warn them."

"You can't just erase your problems, Mona. How is anyone ever going to learn that way? Oh, you don't like something? Just throw it out and start fresh. You sound like a spoiled brat. It's no wonder you don't play well with others."

"Sometimes you just have to cut your losses," Mona repeats.

"Really? You managed to spend less than thirty hours on Earth, and you're done. That's it. No more. Forget save the elephants, forget save the ocean, forget Oliver, Rhett, Noah, Agnes, Cora. Forget them all. Delete. Done. You gave up on all of them. You'd rather kill them, than help them," I yell. "You gave up on yourself. I don't recognize this version of you."

"So, you were spying on me? I'm guessing Harry Potter didn't fall off the shelf on its own."

I shake my head. "Don't change the subject. You are so afraid of the unknown, of actually feeling anything, that you'd rather throw it all away before you have the chance to find out what it feels like," I say. "Stone cold."

Mona doesn't answer. Everything is upside down. My world spins off its axis, and I no longer know which way is up.

"What about our bet? You gave up, which means I get the final say. I get to decide what happens to the humans," I say, holding back the tears threatening to spill over.

"I didn't give anything up. I just—" Mona starts to say, but I cut her off.

"You just what, Mona? You just decided all your hard work was for nothing? What about all my work? That doesn't matter, either? You didn't just give up on them. You gave up on me too."

I turn my back on Mona. The sting bore deeper than I imagined it would.

"You know, out of the billions of planets you've created, or even the few thousand I've made, Earth was the only one we shared. Truly shared as sisters. I just can't believe you'd give up on us so easily," I say.

Mona doesn't look at me.

"You didn't just delete Earth, Mona. You deleted us."

"I'm sorry," Mona starts.

"I don't want to hear your excuses. Sorry isn't going to cut it this time. I expected more out of you. The last thing I thought you'd do was give up," I throw my hands up. "The great and powerful Mona, walking away because it was all too hard. Try figuring it out. If you don't understand why, it's worth moving on with every new day, then go back and learn.

That's what you were there for. You couldn't even do that. You're nothing but a coward."

We sit in the ever-growing silence.

Mona shifts back to her command center. "I've never created anything without safety measures in place."

I watch her log back into the system and restore Earth from backup drives.

Mona finds my eyes, "You always have to have the final say, don't you." Mona plugs in and uploads back to Earth.

I press play.

28

MONA

Admittedly, deleting everything wasn't the best move of the century. I don't like fighting with Penny, but it's the principle of the matter.

Standing in front of the library once more, I feel more confident in my human body and my ability to control my new emotions. I've been through the worst of it, or at least I hope so.

My all-consuming anger was the push it took to delete everything. But, even if I hate to admit it, Penny was right. I need to either fulfill the bet or find a different way of managing the negative aspects of being here. If I can't do that, I need to give up and hand the keys to Penny.

Let's be honest. There's no way under these stars I'm going to do that.

I can't pout and throw a fit when I don't get my way anymore. I must knock out these emotions because walking away from Earth altogether is not a viable option.

Unfortunately, neither is deleting it.

Not unless I want to crush my sister. As much as I hate to admit it out loud, I don't want to hurt Penny any more than I already have.

She's still my sister.

My stomach audibly growls. "What in the four winds was that?" I say.

"It sounded like your stomach. It means you're hungry," Penny suddenly stands beside me.

The world around us pauses.

"Okay. I guess I should eat something." I turn and start to walk away.

Penny puts a hand out to stop me.

I spin around, "What? Did you come down here just to rub it in?"

"No," Penny lets out an exasperated breath. "I just wanted to say thank you in person. I know you don't understand exactly how much this means to me," Penny says, "but it does. Thank you. I hope someday you understand the depth of your actions."

"Sure. Whatever. I've got to find some food. Human body and all." I walk off toward downtown with no particular spot in mind.

"Bye," Penny says.

I start to wave a hand but stop, "What does it mean when someone blinks an eye at you?"

"That's called a wink," Penny says. "Sometimes its used when flirting or if someone is sharing an inside joke."

"Thanks," I say and walk away.

I can only think about putting as much space between myself and my sister as possible. Unfortunately, Penny has a knack for hitting my hot buttons.

I want some air, space, and a Penny-free zone.

Penny presses play again and vanishes from eyesight.

29

MONA

The warm, fragrant, nearly tingly smell of spices wafts through the air as I enter the restaurant. I can almost taste the onion, bell peppers, and cayenne dancing in circles around my tongue.

Cajun music plays in the background, and the hubbub of a busy lunch hour fills the room. I've been seated upstairs with a menu. My mouth salivates at the descriptions and the prospect of what's to come.

A waiter approaches me, "What'll it be?"

"What do you recommend, because I'm about ready to order the whole menu."

"Oh, it's all really good. Have you had Cajun before?"

I shake my head no.

"Oh, then you must try the jambalaya, it's the absolute best. And the hush puppies. And well, like I said, it's all delicious," the waiter smiles.

"That's settled then. I'll have a cup of jambalaya, your prawn etouffee, and some hush puppies," I say.

He scribbles down my order, "Got it! Hush puppies are my favorite."

"But they're not actual puppies, right?"

The waiter laughs, "You sure are a cute thing, now, aren't you? I'll put that order in right away. Can I get you anything else while you wait?"

I'm unnerved that he didn't answer my question but decided on some water.

The waiter leaves me alone with my thoughts.

This restaurant is remarkably different than the other places I've visited. However, I'm indifferent to this fact. Perhaps there are different cultures with humans the way some fauna does.

I require some sort of sustenance.

I hope I ordered enough.

I've never ordered a proper meal on my own before.

Rhett has either fed me or ordered for me. I didn't think doing it alone would be nerve-wracking, but it is.

While I wait for my meal to arrive, I can't help but watch those around me. I take in their conversations and their mannerisms. Watching from a scientific place of curiosity, not from the lens of disgust. I don't care what the humans think of me.

Perhaps, it's less about caring and more about physical and emotional burnout. Self-care is important.

Penny might perceive me as a monster, but at least I'm a monster who can self-care. If the humans, or Penny for that matter, think I'm weird, then it's my curse.

From where I sit, I can see every table on the restaurant's second floor. There's a railing to my right side overlooking the tables on the first floor and behind a short bar, where the cooks prepare my meal. It's prime seating for someone trying to understand people. Or at least that's what I'm telling myself.

Across a tight aisle, four teenagers' failed whispers carry and grab my attention.

"You go ask her," the first one says.

"No man… I double dare you to," the second one says.

"Dude! She'll eat you alive," a third boy says.

I'm not sure if their attention is aimed at me, but one of them keeps peeking in my direction. I've made eye contact with him twice, and his face grows scarlet each time.

"Okay, okay. Check it," one of the boys stood up and swaggered toward my table. He leans on the back of a chair across from me.

I tilt my head at him. "Can I help you?"

He makes a clicking noise with his tongue and winks at me. "Hey, Mami. My friends and I were just admiring the view."

I look around, but I can't see out the windows of the restaurant, nor can I understand how this guy is able to. Considering the angle at which his table sits, viewing out the window is even more challenging.

"I meant you," the boy shuffles his foot. When I don't respond, he clears his throat. "So, I am the Juan for you."

"You're what?" I say, mouth agape.

"Juan," he puts his hand on his chest and glances down. "I was wondering if you wanted to join us?" Juan says.

I'm not really in the mood for a tête-à-tête; honestly, I don't know the protocols for sharing food.

I don't want to share.

Maybe that makes me selfish.

It wouldn't be the first time.

I channel my inner Penny, breathe, and softly bat my eyes at him. "I'm sure you'd like that, but I'm way out of your league." I pucker my lips and wink at him.

Old dog, new trick.

"Oh, burn!"

"She just told you!"

"You got owned, man!" The laughter and chuckles from Juan's friends are relentless.

Juan is leaning on the back of a chair, and when he loses his balance, and the chair falls out from under him, I can no longer contain the laughter bubbling up. Juan hits his butt on the ground while his legs flail, nearly tripping the waiter who'd picked that moment to walk up with a tray of food.

Juan's three friends watched this entire interaction with great enthusiasm. They stand over Juan pointing and drawing the attention of the whole restaurant.

"Dammit, Juan, what do you think you're doing? Get up. Get up and sit down." The waiter is growling. "You're going to get me fired. Sit your ass down. Be cool, or I will tell Mom you're making a jackass out of yourself."

I smile at the waiter, who realizes it was my table Juan was at.

"I'm so sorry, miss. Was he bothering you? I'll have him removed," the waiter stumbles over his words and turns three shades of pink. He spins around. "Stop mocking me, Casanova. You think I can't see you?"

Juan climbs over top of his buddies to avoid the waiter's wrath. If I had to guess, I'd say they were siblings.

"It's fine. Really. It's not the end of the world. I've been there. Trust me when I say, if that happens, you'll know," I say. "Gosh, maybe you won't." I smile, showing all my teeth.

The waiter apologizes again and sets my food on the table.

As it turns out, I ordered way more food than I thought I did, and hush puppies are, in fact, made with potatoes, not dogs.

The flavors bombard my senses. The heat and spices were both incredible and slightly overwhelming. I reach for a packet of sugar and pour it onto my tongue, feeling immediate relief from the heat building in my mouth and chest.

I might not know much about human food, but I understand chemistry.

Nine packets of sugar later, I finish my meal and wander downtown. I was offered a box for my leftover food, and took it. Glad it isn't Styrofoam. I give the food to a man sitting on the dirty street corner with a sign that reads, *Hungry, anything helps*. The small act makes me feel better, but the feeling is fleeting.

There are many interesting buildings, which only yesterday I would have demonized.

I'm trying.

Well, trying harder instead of dismissing it all. If Penny can't see that, then that's on her.

I can only try.

I take a corner and find myself in front of a theatre, where a three-man band is creating a tune. It stops me in my tracks.

The melody catches me off guard. Yet, the noise is somehow pleasing to my ears.

But it's more than that.

It's as if it's pleasing to my soul.

Music has been developed on other planets. Even animals sing songs. Although none of it has ever inspired me to move body parts. I feel the pulse vibrating my bones. The beat moves from my ears and buzzes down my shoulders until I bob my head back and forth. My hips sway, and my feet want to jump.

Music is magic.

Thinking back to couples on the dance floor the night before at the restaurant makes me giggle. They moved awkwardly. Too many body parts and not enough room. Rhett had to explain to me that dancing was completely normal. They weren't, in fact, having a fit or needing any medical assistance. Rhett reassured me I wouldn't catch a dancing disease from the patrons.

Of course, I wasn't convinced at the time.

Fifteen or twenty people are mingling around the trio in the street. Some are gyrating to the music while others are clapping to the beat.

It's captivating.

"Do you like Latin music?" I hadn't noticed Noah among the audience members.

"I don't know. Is that what this is?" I say.

Noah's wide eyes give way to his feelings. "How does a person live this long without hearing good Latin music? Doesn't it pull at your soul and dig into your muscles, making you want to shake your hips to the beat while you lose yourself in the melody?"

My mouth goes dry.

I lick my lips.

"I guess I never thought about it that way." I look away, "Or gave it a chance."

Noah smiles and reaches for my hand.

I let him.

Noah pulls me closer to him, placing a hand on my hip. Then, slowly as though I might reach out and bite him, Noah moves my body to the beat of the music in time with his own.

I let him.

30

Penny

Watching my sister dance with someone brings a wave of emotions I wasn't expecting. I know it's not right to be so invasive, but I have to know. It's only a couple of clicks and I've pulled up Noah's thoughts. I click the narration function and listen.

Noah

I've spent my life fantasizing about a moment like this. Meeting a beautiful woman, embracing her, and dancing until were both hot and sweaty. Letting the music pull us together.

Moving to its rhythms without a self-discriminating thought.

A singularly perfect moment, when the world stops moving, and all that's left is us.

My heart pounds into my ears. The thump, thump, thump is almost distracting.

Almost.

It's been three years and most days I think I've made peace with the loss. I don't get out enough, especially as someone so young.

Most days I wondered if I'd ever meet someone with mom's thirst for life.

Someone who'd drop whatever fight we're having to leave it on the dancefloor.

Mo(ther) Na(ture)

Someone who understands that life is short.

Someone willing to embrace all of its adventures and the unknown hand-in-hand.

Someone like her.

- 164 -

31

MONA

Noah's hands burn hot on my hips.

There's part of me that wants to escape. I won't let Penny win.

So I take a deep breath and let myself be.

Be present.

Be kind.

Be human.

I look into Noah's liquid blue eyes. I thought I'd just see him.

Instead, I see eternity.

I see myself.

The Andromeda Galaxy swirls behind his lids, and for a moment, I understand why Penny is fighting me so hard. I forget to breathe, and Noah is so close that I can smell him when I inhale. He smells of fresh cedar, lavender, and musk.

My knees go weak, and I tumble.

Noah catches me.

"You okay?" Noah asks as he searches my eyes.

I grin, "Yeah, I just forgot to breathe."

Noah's smile matches mine as he wraps me in his arms and dips me to the beat of the music.

It's exhilarating.

My heart races out of my chest. Noah brings me up to meet him once more. I bite my lower lip, sending a chill down my spine. He's been on my mind since lightning struck our palms, and now he has me so close.

Every place Noah touches me is on fire, marking my skin. The hair on my arms stands straight up, and I feel a tingling sensation deep within me on a primal level.

Noah is close enough that I can smell his warm, minty breath, and his nose touches mine.

I don't pull away.

I can't move.

He runs a hand through my hair and cups my face. I close my eyes, and his touch sends vibrations down every nerve ending.

Suddenly, his mouth is on mine, and his tongue slowly licks my lips until it finds my own. Fireworks explode behind my eyelids.

Too many new sensations, it's overwhelming.

Let it be.

Noah is a drug, and I'm taking him in, sip by sip.

I pull away, labored breath. I touch my lips to see if they are actually on fire. But they're only warm.

Weird.

I'm unsure if it's from dancing or Noah mashing his face with mine.

"I'd love to see you again," Noah says breathlessly. He reaches out to touch my face but stops short. "You're a fantastic dancer."

"Uhh, huh," I can't seem to combine words.

"Can I give you my number?" Noah says, pulling out a pen and writing it on my wrist.

I try to shake away the daze I feel.

What am I thinking?

I can't do anything with him.

I need to clear my head.

I need space.

"Was that a yes?" Noah says, breaking my thoughts.

"I'm sorry. I've got to go," I say, stepping back.

Nothing that just happened was pretending.

"Wait. Use it, okay?" Noah pleads.

I try to clear my head and gather my thoughts. But I can't deny that what just happened was real.

32

MONA

Before I start leaking, I make it three blocks from Noah.

"What is wrong with me?" I say.

"You're human."

A girl on a bicycle balances in place without falling, cars stop driving, and birds stop singing. The world halts once more.

Penny pressed pause.

"Great." I wipe the tears from my face. "What do you want?"

Penny shakes her head. "Nothing. I just wanted to tell you, you're doing great. And I'm sorry."

"No, you don't have anything to be sorry for. I'm the sphincter in this relationship."

"Asshole."

"What?"

"You mean asshole," Penny says.

"That's what I said."

"No," Penny's laughter seems to thaw the tension between us. "They don't use the proper terminology unless it's a medical condition. You'll catch on."

I shrug.

"It seems as though you already have? You and Noah? I never thought I'd see the day."

"Well, don't. It's impossible. I'm not even one of them. Besides, nothing happened." I shake my head as if I could make what passed disappear from my brain. But I can still feel him on my lips, his hands on me, the heat. I sigh. "Besides, I'm guessing if he knew I'd just deleted the whole of his little world, he'd think differently about me."

I wipe the tears that won't stop falling. "What is this? Why is this happening to me?"

Penny smiles softly. "It's called crying, Mona. You're emotional. When the body doesn't know how to handle a flood of adrenaline, crying is one way it processes the feelings."

"He's human. He means nothing to me."

"Okay. If you say so."

"Penny?"

"Yes, Mona."

"Are they all like this?"

Penny seems to think before she answers.

"Don't lie to me, okay?" I say.

"No, not all of them. But most of them, and those who are, make the rest worth saving."

Penny presses play before disappearing into the background.

Before I have time to catch my breath.

Before I can say anything else.

33

MONA

The clear blue sky is swept away by clouds. Rain starts to fall, suiting my mood just fine. I make my way back to Rhett's apartment, using the walk to sort out some of my feelings.

And by sort, I mean stew.

I never spent much time paying attention to human activities because I've been too preoccupied with all of their destruction. As a result, I didn't notice how they lived, interacted with one another, and formed relationships.

Relationships.

Blah.

When the negative is too much to dwell on, I pretend nothing is happening and throw myself into another project.

There are so many, many projects. Except it eats at me until I can't take it anymore, and I'm ready to explode.

Penny would inevitably find out and put a stop to it. The exploding bits, that is.

The thing is, for all the grief I give Penny, I don't know as much as I think I do. It's hard to admit, even if it's just to myself.

Finally, I reach the stairs of Rhett's apartment. I can only hope Rhett won't send me away because, at this point, I want nothing more than to get away from myself. I'd send myself away without a second thought if I could.

When I enter, Rhett sets her book down, "Did you have much luck at the Library today?"

Rhett beat me home. She is curled up with a book, a teal blanket, and a mug of hot cocoa. Rhett looks comfortable in her own skin, like it fits her.

Like she fits.

I wish I fit like that anywhere.

"I learned more than I anticipated. It was... illuminating. You could say it destroyed my world." I slump into the leather loveseat across from Rhett. I like how there seem to be butt prints worn into each cushion already. The couch seems to swallow me whole. It's a comforting feeling.

"Destroyed? Have you been crying?" Rhett asks.

I reach for my cheeks. They're dry. "What, umm, no?"

"It doesn't take a genius to see something is wrong."

Rhett sets her book and blanket aside. She grabs a coffee mug from the kitchen cupboard and makes me a cup of her mom's secret hot chocolate recipe. Rhett told me that her mom made up containers of it every holiday. She said it was so she could be reminded of her Indian roots whenever she wanted a little mug of home.

I take the mug and sip it. Again, I'm bombarded with sharp flavors. It's another case of sensory overload. Every time I eat or drink anything, my mouth goes on a rampage changing my brain chemistry. How do humans do this every day?

I start to cry.

Again.

"Is it that bad?" Rhett asks.

"No," I chuckle through my tears. "That's just it... it's wonderful. I've never been so lucky before." I wipe my face with the back of my sleeve.

"So, these are happy sniffles? Because they look an awful lot like sad ones."

"I don't know which is which anymore. It all seems to blend." Outside, thunder claps and lightning illuminate the sky for a pulsating moment.

"Do you want to talk about it? I've been told I have big ears, you know."

I give Rhett an appraising glance. "I don't think they're that big. They seem to be symmetrical enough with your head structure."

"The better to hear you with." When I don't get the reference, Rhett rolls her eyes. "Wow, this is bad."

I take another swig of cocoa. It makes my head bubble providing me the courage to tell Rhett about meeting Noah and the spark I felt, clarifying it *was* a literal spark. I make sure to mention his sibling, Oliver.

Conveniently, I leave out the parts about fighting with Penny and deleting the world. I'm not ready to be that honest.

Besides, Penny might not like it if I'm overly direct, giving up all the family secrets. But, even if I were, Rhett would just think I'm crazy... *So, Rhett, I made Earth. And my sister and I created humans as an experiment. Isn't it grand? But I'm not a god or any other weird deity you've made up to make it all the better in your head. In fact, you're all living inside a Bio-Matrixed Earth which I deleted this afternoon because I was feeling overly emotional and angry that Earth is one big trash heap. Cool, right?*

No.

That meek excuse wouldn't work.

Instead, I tell Rhett about dancing and mashing my face with Noah's. Even though I want to keep that bit to myself, I'm unsure how to navigate it alone.

"A kiss," Rhett says.

"What?" I ask.

"Mashing your faces together," Rhett giggles. "You kissed him. You're too cute."

So, we shared a kiss.

"You gave me goosebumps, Mona," Rhett says, rubbing her arms and pulling a blanket closer.

"Is that a good thing?" I ask.

"It's not a bad thing. It wasn't just a kiss, was it?"

"I don't know. How can you tell the difference?"

Rhett smiles, crosses the living room, and sits next to me. "What scares you about him? Did someone hurt you? Like before?"

I never give someone the chance to hurt me.

Why would I?

That would mean giving up control and trusting someone enough to let them hurt me.

How does anyone let that happen?

"It's not like that." I puzzle for a way to explain so that Rhett will understand. "I've spent my whole life working to create stable environments for everyone else. I never thought having relationships mattered very much. I'm not like you."

Rhett's brow furrows.

"That's not what I meant. I'm not used to this," I say, pointing from myself to Rhett. "I don't have these conversations. Because that would mean," I pause, unsure. "I don't know what that would mean."

Rhett reaches out and slowly wraps her arms around me.

I stiffen.

Rhett squeezes tightly, and after a few awkward moments, I relax my rigid posture and melt into her. After a few more minutes, I lay my head on Rhett's shoulder and began to cry.

Rhett holds me.

She doesn't judge me or talk down to me. She just embraces me.

My tears subside shortly, and Rhett brings us a plate of food.

"What are these things? They are so soft and gooey. But also, just the right amount of chewiness," I say.

"Chocolate chip cookies," Rhett says and takes another bite. "It's like you're a foreign exchange student."

I perk up. "Well, I kind of am, I guess."

"What? Where from?" Rhett asks.

"All over, really. We moved around a lot." I get up to get another cup of hot cocoa.

"I think that's great, really. I've always wanted to travel," Rhett says. "Mom and Dad immigrated here from India before I was born. They both traveled before college. I think about it, but I don't know. It's kind of scary, you know? Or maybe you don't?"

"You should travel," I say. "The world is a big place. Promise me you'll leave this town someday and see how mighty Earth really is?" I sit back down and pass a fresh mug to Rhett.

"Thanks. I'll do my best. Do you want to watch a movie?" Rhett says, picking up the remote.

"Not good enough. Promise me," I say.

"What difference does it make if I do?" she asks.

"It makes all the difference. You deserve more than this place. You deserve to see Jiuzhaigou Vally, to hike the Haiku Stairs in Oahu, or swim in the Hinatuan River. You should visit the crooked forest in Poland. It's one of my favorite places. Or the hot springs in Rotorua and the deep-water coral reefs around the Lofoten Islands in Norway."

"I've never even heard of them," Rhett says.

"Grüner Sea? You might know it as the Hochschwab Underwater Park?" I ask.

Rhett shakes her head. "How do you know about all these places?"

"You're missing the point," I sigh and rub my eyes. "There is real magic in this world. You can't be afraid of life."

Rhett takes a shaking breath. "So why are you?"

34

MONA

Rhett left early for work, leaving me fast asleep on her couch.

It was an emotional night, filled with personal revelations and *girl bonding*.

The weird thing, I'm not even disgusted with the intimacy level or the fact that Rhett kept touching me. When she pulled out the nail polish, I had to draw the line. However, I didn't oppose Rhet's use of *Funfrenzy*, a sparkly purple color.

Penny would have loved that.

Sitting on the coffee table is a note. It reads:

> *Mona,*
> *I didn't want to wake you. I'll be home after five. You're a heavy sleeper. Help yourself to whatever suits your fancy. See you later.*
> *— xoxo Rhett.*
> *P.S.*
> *Give him a chance. Life is too short for regrets so live it to the fullest. You said that. Besides, what's the worst that could happen?*

Rhett's scrawl was loopy and somehow familiar. I analyzed the piece of paper. I still don't like that it's made from trees. They could use other more sustainable resources. They have the technology to do so much more, but it seems money is more important than anything else to some humans.

Stones would be better than paper.

I crumple the paper, making it smaller and smaller until it's a tiny wad I hold between two fingers. After running it under the sink, I turn it into a wet ball.

Between my palms, a glow begins. I gingerly open my palms to reveal a tiny sapling, roots and all.

"Why hello there, little Maple, isn't that better?" It feels good to help this little life. Getting to create, even if only for a moment.

The three-inch sapling rests in a glass of water, soaking in the sun from a window.

"I'm afraid you'll have to wait till I'm ready to leave," I say.

After dancing yesterday and walking, this body has developed a slight funk. Rhett showed me where the shower is and all its applicable instruments. Admittedly, I've never taken one before. Nothing so primitive exists at home.

What harm could it do to try it out?

Look, Penny, I'm embracing the human experience. Showers and all.

It's not like I'm trying to impress anyone.

An image of Noah comes to mind, but I shove it away as quickly as it surfaces.

Definitely not trying to impress.

Just a customary human ritual.

It's not like I'm going to go out of my way to find Noah. Rhett is the one who should be taking advantage of a full human life.

Not me.

But a shower could still be enjoyable.

Probably.

I still don't see what all the fuss is about. There is a short fight with the nobs over the bathtub while adjusting the water temperature. I unclothe and stand in front of the mirror.

My human body reflects.

Is this how the rest of the world sees me?

Noah?

Rhett?

Penny said she stopped others from seeing me as something new every time. But I don't know if I trust that.

I should.

But I don't.

I cup my face and stroke my nose. I have high cheekbones and dark raven hair. There are various deep shades of blue, purple, and red in the waves when the light reflects off my hair. It reaches past my shoulders and reminds me of the night. Filled with color despite the absence of light.

Tracing my neckline down to my breasts, I cup one lifting it high and letting it drop—up and down. I lift the other, taking note of the strange color change. The way the nipple hardened after brushing fingers across it. So many nerve endings are seemingly alive. My hands move down this soft body to the waist and curved hip line.

I turn and look over my shoulder at her back.

At my back.

There is a birthmark just above my left hip. It appears to be a cluster of galaxies. I run a finger across it, half expecting the mark to move or grow in shape.

It doesn't.

The mirror grows challenging to see. The hot shower causes steam to roll out of the bathroom in a fog.

I gaze at my reflection once more before stepping into the shower.

Water drizzles down my naked body. I close my eyes, tilt my head back, and try to focus on how the drops of water feel running down my figure.

I shudder.

The feeling is overwhelming and better than I would allow. I'm starting to understand why humans have such an obsession with cleanliness. I don't see how showering reflects on an image, so it must be about the sensation.

I quickly remind myself that long showers aren't good for the environment, but I push the thought aside for this one time.

This first experience.

It's not like I've been showering for an entire lifetime.

Twenty minutes pass, and I'm drifting in and out of consciousness, leaning against the wall. I open my eyes and start to really take notice of the shower's contents. Rhett has all kinds of gadgets. She owns many different types of cleaners and body softeners. I open one to smell. It's fragrant, but not necessarily in a bad way. It reminds me of coconuts and fresh flowers in a spring field.

Unfortunately, the scent still contains chemical undertones. I'll need to talk with Rhett about her chemical intake. It's not good.

I opt for cleaning myself with water instead. If it works for most of the living creatures on this planet, it will work for me too.

I towel dry and borrow a knee-length black dress from Rhett. It's one of the simplest things I can find among Rhett's colorful wardrobe. It hugs me comfortably enough, and after a minor alteration, it now frays out at the waist.

It will do.

I slip on a pair of shoes and grab a light sweater from the hall closet. I'm reasonably confident Rhett won't mind. We're supposed to go shopping for clothes today. After yesterday's leaking fiasco, we put it off one more day.

Before leaving the apartment, I pick up the Maple sapling. It has grown to nearly ten times its original size in the short hour it spent on the windowsill. The poor thing is no longer contained to the glass, and there's no water to speak of. The roots of the Maple start to make their way down the wall, looking for soft ground to home in.

I'm sure to lock up as Rhett instructed and head out for the day.

"So where should I take you, dear one?" I ask the sapling in my arms.

"I feel so lucky to live three lives. Anywhere you choose would feel perfect," it replies.

I chew on this. "Are you telling me you enjoyed being paper?"

If the sapling could shrug shoulders at my question, it might have. Being just a plant, it can do no such thing. "I loved my first life, although it ended painfully and far too soon. My second was with a purpose that brought me to you. I am happy all roads lead me here, to this moment. I would not be where I am if anything had gone differently."

"You're talking in riddles. I don't know how I feel about that." I keep walking. "I thought I might plant you somewhere you can thrive. Where you can provide shade, beauty, and enjoyment to all living things who meet you."

"Yes, this sounds perfect," the sapling cheers.

I remember passing a small park where young children climbed various obscene plastics and metals. It's a depressing sight, despite the happy faces among its tiny patrons. They clearly do not understand the predicament they're in. I'm ready to rectify this human flaw.

It's the least I could do.

I arrive at the park, a semi-secluded residential corner where a chain-link fence keeps the plastics safe from wandering plastics thieves.

At least, that's what I imagine it's for.

Passing through the gate, I walk to the center of the playground. There are no children present, nor are there any passing adults.

The sapling rests on the edge of the child's play structure. Kneeling, I whisper in an old tongue, caressing and wooing Earth. My primordial words cradle the land. I place my hand on the ground, palms down, and speak softly. My hands radiate a deep golden glow. I scoop into the Earth, and the world splits open for me—large enough for the sapling. He stands more than three feet tall. Maple is situated in his new home, and I command Earth to hug him tight.

Stepping back and surveying my labor, I am confident Maple will be the perfect addition to the area. It has been lacking in flora. I am content with Maple's placement, settled between a wooden bridge and the metal structure it connects to.

I close my eyes, feel myself smile, and breathe a rush of life into the area.

The connecting planks of the bridge become part of the Maple. As though they'd been there all along. The tree becomes part of the bridge, the bridge part of the tree. A connecting structure to the other human play surfaces.

I look at my addition with pride. "Goodbye."

I hesitate.

"What is your name?"

"In my manufactured life, I was never given one," the Maple says.

"You should have one," I say.

"The woman who transplanted me in my first life was kind. She was so hopeful we'd live long lives," Maple says. "Her name was Baily."

"Then I shall call you Baily," I place my palm on Baily's trunk. "I wish you a long third life, Baily. Until we meet again."

With true satisfaction in my work, I leave.

Without much aim for my day, I head back downtown. I need to be human, avoid running into Noah again, and face the inevitable emotional upheaval this mortal life will require me to navigate.

I got this.

The smell of fresh ground coffee beans percolating wafts on a cloud of steam from a nearby café. My mouth salivates at the scent, remembering the previous morning's cup I shared with Rhett. I approach the counter, deciding to indulge in another.

"What can I get you?" The percolating coffee artist wears a green visor and an ear-to-ear smile.

"May I have coffee? Preferably the one made in Indonesia, although I'm not opposed to trying a new one."

"One drip Sumatra coming up. Any cream or sugar with that?"

"No. Why taint something so perfect already?" I say.

The artist smiles, "Can I have a name?"

"You look sort of like a Skyler to me. If you don't like that, maybe Winston is better?"

"Not for me," he says. "What's *your* name?"

"Mona," I say. "Perhaps next time, you should clarify by saying, what is *your* name?" Maybe being a percolating coffee artist doesn't require as much intelligence as I gave it credit for.

I exchange money generated with a slick flick of my fingers.

"Thanks. We'll call your name when it's ready," he says.

When my name is called, the cup is marked Ian—John—MoNa. "They let the most inexperienced of the species lead," I mutter.

"They wrote HeyZeal on mine. What did they write on yours?" The woman standing next to me says. She is quite a bit shorter than me, with long curly hair matching her gold and brown eyes.

I turn my coffee cup and show her.

"Figures. These guys get off on that sort of thing. It's Hazel, by the way." She grips her cup and smiles.

"Mona."

"Do you come here often?" Hazel asks.

"Afraid not. I was just walking by, and the smell carried me in. Do you?" I ask, proud of myself.

"Yea, I'm a writer. I've got to get my vice before the world makes sense." Hazel holds up her coffee. She points to a chair before sitting across the table.

I accept the invitation. "What do you write?"

"Fiction mostly. Right now, I'm working on a backward love story. It really gets to the heart of what it means to be human. I'd like to get into the Iowa Writer's Workshop. A girl can dream, right?" Hazel scrunched her nose, letting a smile loose. "I'm sure you don't really want to hear about that."

"Actually, I'd love to hear your thoughts. I've been working on something myself recently, more of a non-fiction piece about humanity and their effects on the world."

"Wow, that sounds intense," Hazel says.

I nod. "Yea, it's been a learning experience for sure."

"Humanity has its downsides, but also, there's a lot of good. I'd like to think we're learning and trying to change our ways."

"Really? Because I'm not so confident." I cross my arms. "Just yesterday, I was reading about the extermination of entire species because of human greed. What of the elephants? Don't even get me started on palm oil."

"You said you read it?"

I nod. "Yeah, at the library," I say.

Hazel pulls out her laptop and brings up a page listing various non-profit organizations that aim to prevent unnecessary elephant deaths.

I can't help the lingering feeling of hopelessness about the situation. "But it's still happening. People are out there killing them every day."

Hazel tells me about a video she saw online about a man who travels to foreign countries with nothing but the clothes on his back. He trades his capabilities for food, clothing, and shelter.

"What does this prove?" I ask, skeptical.

"There are many people who put their faith in humanity," Hazel says.

"So, others have done this? Trusting their lives in the hands of complete strangers?" I ask.

"Trusting strangers is deeply embedded into our genetic makeup and part of our society's social norms. Sometimes there are some shitty people," Hazel says. "But, most of us want the same things. Shelter, food, friends, family, and love."

"You didn't really answer my question."

"Back home, I met a guy traveling much like the guy in the video. This dude purchased a round-trip ticket from his home in London to the United States," Hazel says. "He said that public transportation was only allowed in emergencies but that he was supposed to rely on the kindness of strangers. This was a way of pushing his comfort levels and experiencing life instead of watching it."

I digest Hazel's words.

"He could spend money on food or souvenirs but never transportation or a place to sleep. If he failed to make a friend, then he slept on the streets. His name was Nyil. I believe he was originally from Sweden or maybe Austria?" Hazel says. "Doesn't matter. The point is people are willing to put their faith in humanity. They turn out okay."

"I can't help but think about the destructive people, polluting their kin with hate. What about all the pollution in the world? Global warming is real, humans suck, and the elephants are still dying. Even with activists."

"I acknowledge there's a problem. It's not fair. I will say this, as a species, we're learning and trying to make things right. With more advanced technology, we can track and share information. It gives us a leg up in saving the lives of elephants everywhere. But it doesn't happen overnight. It takes time," Hazel says.

She shows me more pages on her computer, demonstrating that for every large-scale poor decision someone makes, thousands of other people are trying to make things right.

"In some ways, aren't you trusting a stranger right now? You're trusting that I won't use proximity to harm you. You trusted the barista to make your drink instead of poisoning you. You trust the drivers will stay on their side of the road."

"I suppose trusting strangers sincerely is embedded into the fabric of your society. I doubt it's genetic, though. I'd have to double-check."

I finish my coffee, feeling slightly more hopeful. "This has been incredibly educational. I don't know if I feel more or less critical about the world, but I think I'm starting to understand. At any rate, I'm more open to the positive possibilities."

"Any time. I've enjoyed this a lot. It's summer so I'm here most days about this time. But, if you feel like doing it again, you know how to find me," Hazel said. "I'm always up for stimulating conversation. It makes for good nuts. I like gathering and storing them away for a rainy day."

"Where are the nuts exactly?" I ask.

"Figurative nuts, I'm a writer, remember."

Hazel hugs me. I stiffen at the contact but quickly relax.

"Have a great day," I say, leaving the coffee shop.

Hazel has given me a lot to mull over. But, the most complicated point of all, perhaps some people are even good.

There's nothing worse than when Penny is right. But I still have so many unanswered questions.

Does the negative ten percent of the world's actions lock in the fate of the other ninety? Should everyone be punished for the actions of the few? Where does the line between right and wrong lay? Who decides when that line is crossed and what the punishment is? Does ignorance equate to guilt?

Am I up for playing Warden to Humanity?

Now my head hurts.

Thank the stars above for fresh air.

35

MONA

It's damp with a light fog outside. Eventually, it burns off, brushing the clear blue sky with golden rays. I enjoy the way the sun pierces my skin and warms my core.

"Fancy seeing you here," a liquid baritone says.

I know his voice,

"Hey, Noah," I say.

I feel like I swallowed a butterfly sandwich. I didn't realize where I was walking. Right to the doorstep of Summer Grove Retirement Community.

"You never called me," Noah says.

"I lost your number?" I say, wondering if a half-truth counts as a lie.

Noah reaches out and takes my arm, examining it. "I guess you did." He lowers my hand but doesn't let go.

Awkward.

Is he going to keep it forever?

"So…" I say.

"So, I was thinking, why don't you and I go out?" Noah's eyes twinkle, and my legs go weak.

Is it neurological?

Do I have faulty wiring that causes my body to react on its own accord?

I breathe, trying to shake off whatever spell he casts on me. But my mind keeps wandering to his lips, hands and how good kissing him feels.

"Go out?" I ask.

"Yes, let me take you out somewhere. Anywhere." Noah moves closer to me; before I know it, his face is inches from mine.

My heart forms an arrhythmia. It picks up pace, and my breath comes in quick short bursts.

Noah rubs slow circles around the inside of my palm with his fingertips.

I can't focus, "I umm," I clear my throat. "What about Olli?" I hate how good his touch feels. I wish I hated it enough to ask him to stop.

But I don't.

It feels good.

What would happen if he did stop?

What else would feel this good?

"What about him?" Noah asks.

I take another breath.

Detach Mona, detach.

Dead puppies, dead puppies, dead puppies. It isn't working.

"Will he be accompanying us?" I ask.

"I usually avoid bringing my brother on dates. I'd rather have you," Noah seems to consume me with his eyes, "to myself."

"Usually? Do you go on them often?" How did I become putty in his hands? Oh, his hands…

"I didn't mean to imply I'm some sort of player. Honestly," Noah says.

I'm not sure what he means. His lips are within licking distance.

I turn away from him.

"Did I do something wrong?" Noah asks. "I'm sorry." He says, dropping my hand.

My stomach plummets. "I need to go. I'm running late for something."

"Where do you need to go? I'll take you in my truck. I'm parked right there," Noah points.

"Okay," I say.

I'm reeling as I follow Noah to his truck. Not only have I agreed to a ride to some made-up location, but I have to get inside another moving monster. Not just any moving monster, but a gas-guzzling inefficient beast.

"Where are we going?" Noah holds the passenger door open for me.

I take my time climbing into the truck. "Um, are you sure you don't have to work? Or pick up Olli?"

"No, I was just finishing up when I ran into you. Olli's at school."

"So, he's feeling better then. That's good."

"Yea, he's not diseased," Noah chuckled. "We had a very stimulating conversation about tie-dye, smallpox—the only epidemic he remembered the proper name of. Let's see, there was weasels and viral hedgehog fever. There was one more," he pauses to remember. "Oh, that's right, my-Larry-ah."

Noah isn't upset, which surprises me. I've learned a lot since that first meeting.

A smile escapes my lips. "That bad, eh?" I ask.

"Well, it took me a while to figure out what he was saying, but once I caught on," Noah chortles. "The boy is smart, sometimes too smart. He managed to google smallpox, and I caught him scouring WebMD. I'm glad Dad didn't notice, or I would have got an earful."

"When is his birthday? He mentioned it was coming up," I say.

"Yeah, we're celebrating tonight. At the park, we're doing something small, cake and ice cream. If you are free, I know Olli would love it if you came," Noah says.

"Olli would love it if I came?" I raise an eyebrow.

Noah shrugs. "Yes, he would. If you are free."

"Can we go to a place where we can find a telescope?"

"Oh, he told you about that, did he? It's all he talks about." Noah starts the truck and backs out of the parking space.

I smile. "Yeah, he mentioned he wanted one. I believe it is customary to buy a gift when Earth has done a full rotation around the sun, to the day in which one is born into the world."

"I thought you had other plans? Somewhere you had to be?" Noah asks.

"Didn't you hear? They just changed."

"Oliver was right about you."

"Oh?" I turn to face Noah.

"Nothing. He just said you were special. I can see what he likes about you," Noah says.

My cheeks suddenly feel hot. "I don't know what you're talking about," I say.

Noah insists that I don't buy Olli a telescope for his birthday. "It would be too extravagant a gift," he says. "Oliver changes his mind every few months. How about this instead?"

Noah holds up a plastic wheel, and I examine it. Seems that it helps explain the position of various stars in the night sky.

"It's more practical. The store even has a gift wrap service," Noah says.

"Seems lame," I say. Although I'm not as confident as Noah about my contribution to Olli's celebration. "But, I trust you know Olli's tastes better than I. Even though it doesn't feel quite right."

I convince Noah to take me to a store where I can find another small gift for Olli. I don't want him to see it for fear of a veto vote.

It's the first birthday gift I've ever bought, and I want it to be remarkable.

Noah takes me to a large shopping center. "Is there anything else you need while we're here?"

Apparently, there's no end to human need or extravagance.

"I did tell Rhett I would buy some more clothes and stop borrowing hers," I say.

Noah does a thing with his eyes that makes me feel hot all over again. I elbow him.

"Ouch, what was that for?" he says, rubbing his arm.

"For looking at me like chocolate," I say.

It's Noah's turn to flush pink.

I like this new color on him.

"This way," he says, leading me to a clothing store with plastic females on display. The whole thing is uncomfortable, so I quickly grab a few things I like.

"Tell me about yourself? Tell me something I don't know," Noah says.

I'm not sure what to say.

"I have a sister named Penny."

"Penny and Mona. Awe, I bet you two were a pair growing up," he says.

"You have no idea," I say. "My turn. Tell me something about yourself; I don't already know."

Noah's eyes grow in size, then he smiles, teasing me. "Something about me, hmm. I live with my dad and Olli. It's just the boys now."

"What about your mom?" I regret the words as soon as they leave my mouth. "I'm sorry. It's none of my business," I say.

"Don't be. It was bound to come up eventually. Rhi was her name. She was a good mother. The best." Noah smiles to himself. "She loved Olli and me and movies with dancing, in that order."

I feel the urge to reach out and touch his hand, but I refrain.

"Anyway, a drunk driver took her from us when I was thirteen. It's been just the three of us since."

This time I reach for his hand without fear. "Do you miss her?" I venture.

"Every single day," Noah takes my hand in return.

"My turn." Noah smiles in a way that makes me think he's overcompensating, but I'm relieved. "What is your favorite ice cream?"

"That's an easy one, chocolate. My turn. What is your favorite color?"

"Red," Noah licks his lips. "Favorite place?"

"Earth," I say.

Noah laughs, "Duh, where specifically on Earth?"

I grab a simple red dress and hold it out. Noah nods his approval, and I add it to my small stack of purchases.

"There is this small island off the coast of Fiji that's actually shaped like a dolphin. Swimming with dolphins has been, by far, one of my favorite experiences. Yes, if I had to pick, I pick there," I say. "The water is warm and crystal clear. There's nothing for miles. It's serene."

"Wow," Noah's eyes softened.

"My turn. What's your favorite thing to eat?"

Noah looks me up and down, closing the distance between us. Then, before I realize it, his mouth is on mine, and I've melted into him.

Noah pulls away, "I've been dying to do that again." He kisses the top of my nose and moves a strand of hair out of my face. "Asian of almost any kind. Pizza on the other days."

"Hmm?"

"You asked me my favorite food."

"Right. Yes," I say. Finding my footing again.

"If you could only eat and drink one thing for the rest of your life, what would it be?" Noah asks.

"Only one thing?" My jaw drops. "That seems like sheer anguish. Why would you want to do that?"

"I don't, but that's not the point. You have to pick one. There's only one thing for the rest of forever. What would it be?" a wicked grin creeps across Noah's face.

"I don't even think I can answer that. Does chocolate count?" I laugh.

"Not very sustainable. Might get tired of it eventually."

"Never," I say.

Noah grabs me at the waist. He blinks, and time slows down. My breath catches in my chest, and I lean in for another kiss.

The sweet and minty taste of Noah's tongue makes my head swirl. I reach for his neck to steady myself but only pull him closer. I steal another dragging kiss before pulling away.

I randomly turn to the clothes rack and grab two more garments, adding them to the stack.

Breathing heavily, flushed, and unable to think straight, I grab a few more items at random.

"I think I've got everything I need," I say. I'll code them to my size later.

With my quick coding fingers, I pay for my purchases.

Noah reaches for my hand, and I let him take it, enjoying the warmth and soft touch.

We walk through the mall, back to Noah's truck, hand in hand. If I had known palms, lips, and presumably every inch of my body held so many nerve endings, I would have tried out a meat suit ages ago.

It really is no wonder Penny enjoys this.

Noah waits outside Rhett's apartment while I run my new clothes upstairs. I leave Rhett a note on the bathroom mirror using lipstick left on the counter. I decide to also leave a phone number where I could be reached. I bought a cell phone after Noah asked for my phone number, and I realized I didn't have one to give.

I don't enjoy adding to human consumerism, but it seems necessary in this world. I'm only doing what Penny asked of me. I'm being human.

The red dress is so vibrant I decide to change into it. While it's not a perfect fit, a quick bit of finger magic and the dress, as well as my new wardrobe, form to my body flawlessly.

Thank the stars for sneaky programming skills.

I'm practically skipping down the stairs when I leave the apartment. I'm looking forward to the birthday party, giving Oliver his gifts, and spending time with Noah. It's a whole one-hundred-and-eighty-degree spin.

Take that, Penny.

36

MONA

As Noah pulls into the park, we are met with smiling faces. Oliver is there with a friend from school, Cora is setting out food, and several others are either mingling, blowing up balloons, or handling trays of food.

I turn to Noah, "I thought you said it was just a few people?"

He beams down at me, "Well, you know how it goes, invite a few, who bring a few more. That's the thing about a community; they all want to come out and help celebrate Oliver's birthday."

I nod, "I guess I've never experienced that. That's incredible of them."

"I told Cora I'd be by to help her finish setting up after I dropped you off. She encouraged me to take all the time in the world," Noah squeezes my hand. "That Cora is something else. And her memory has been crystal clear. You know she says that you're the reason?"

"I didn't do much," I say. "Just glad she's doing well."

"She really is."

"So ummm, who's Hazel?" I ask not that really matter who she is. But you know, curiosity and all.

"She's my best friend. She lives near here and helps with Olli when she can. I think out of sheer habit sometimes," Noah laughs to himself. "Especially since it's his birthday. She lost her sister around the same time I lost Mom. Not many people understand what it's like to feel like your whole world is falling apart. But she understood."

The thought strikes me right in the gut. An unexpected ripping of my insides. If I ever lost Penny... I can't finish the thought.

Noah and I make our way to where the others have gathered.

"Mona, I want you to meet Hazel. Hazel, this is Mona," Noah says.

Hazel turns around and licks what appears to be chocolate from her fingers. "Mona! It's so good to see you again."

Hazel hugs me before I realize she's one and the same as the girl from the coffee shop. I don't stiffen or run.

"Hazel, what are you doing here?"

"I can see my friend here doesn't speak well of me," Hazel jabs Noah in the side with her elbow. "Or at all as it would seem."

"I told her about you," Noah says, rubbing his side.

"He did, actually. I just never expected his Hazel to be mine too." I find myself smiling.

"What a small world this is," Hazel says. "I met Mona at the coffee shop this morning. She was telling me about her research paper on humanity. Such a close topic to my own writing, we hit it off right away."

"It *is* a small world," Noah says. "What kind of research?"

"Oh, don't worry, Noah, I won't say anything too mean bout you. Look at him getting all panicked," Hazel winks at him, then loops her arm in mine and drags me toward the gift table.

Secretly, I'm relieved I didn't have to answer his question.

"So, dish. Are you dating Noah?"

I shrugged, "I have no idea. We just met. I don't know the difference between what we've been doing and dating."

"But you like him, don't you? I can tell." Hazel scrunches her nose when she smiles, showing off a mouth of pearly white teeth.

I take a deep breath, unsure of how to answer her question. "I think so. If I'm honest, I'm still struggling to like humans. Of the ones I know, though, yes. I think I like him very much. I haven't wanted to delete him yet, so that's a good sign."

"I knew you were an interesting character," Hazel says, taking Oliver's gift from me and placing it on a table.

"Hey Noah, did you remember to bring a speaker for the radio?"

Noah stretches an arm into the air and holds up a finger. He jogs back to his truck. When he returns, he's got a black cylinder in his hands. "It's got a charge, but we'll probably need power eventually."

"The extension cord is over there. Your dad ran it an hour ago," Hazel says.

Noah configures something on his phone after attaching the black device to the cord. "Computer, play Oliver's Birthday Playlist," he says.

A smooth, liquid voice speaks from the box, "Playing Oliver's Birthday Playlist," and then it sings *music*.

It's a talking music box. Primitive compared to my own, but I should give humans a little more credit. Their technological development isn't as stunted as I assumed it was.

The sooner they lean into technology and less on chemicals, the sooner they can clean up the mess they've made.

"Just a little mood music." Noah winks at me and starts to shake his hips to the beat of the music box.

Noah steps toward me, each one sending warmth through my belly. I want him to grab me by the waist and spin me around.

As if he can read my thoughts, Noah's hands find my hips. One grazes my belly and rests on the small of my back. He lifts my arm with his other and spins me. He pulls me back close to him, and a giggle escapes me.

I check his hands, but there aren't flames licking my skin, only his fingers. The way he moves is animalistic. It's biological, and it ignites something in me.

We're interrupted by a young human. "Mona! I'm so happy to see you again. Thank you for coming to my birthday party," Oliver says. He grows suddenly shy.

Perfect timing, kid.

"I appreciate the invitation. I read that chocolate cake is a common tradition. Is this true?"

"Yes. Hazel made a double chocolate fudge cake. Even though she tried to convince me, red velvet was better. But she's wrong. Chocolate fudge cake is my favorite thing in the whole world."

"It sounds delicious. Since we saw each other last, I've learned how much I enjoy chocolate too. Not liquid, though. I'd rather not have a repeat experience."

Oliver's face scrunches. He looks like Noah. It's in the eyes and noise. His chin, hair, and the way he carries himself.

I don't think I've ever noticed how similar families were. The way genetics play out is admittedly fascinating.

"When do you open gifts? I brought you something I think you'll be quite excited about," I say.

"Not yet," a man interrupts. "First, he's got to mingle with the rest of his guests." He's tall and has the same dark shaggy hair as Noah, but his eyes are timeworn. "You must be Mona. Oliver won't stop talking about you."

"It's nice to meet you, Mr. Harvey," I say.

"It's a treat to meet you too. I'll let you girls talk," Mr. Harvey says before greeting other party guests.

Noah slips a hand around my stomach, enveloping me. I lean into him. The unexpected firmness sends a shiver down my back.

Oliver waves and hand at us and skips away.

"Oliver shares his birthday with approximately nineteen million other people. But it shouldn't tarnish his celebration. So why can't he do what he likes?" I ask.

"You're beaming with random knowledge, aren't you."

"Well, I did spend a day at the library, reading. I'm a quick learner."

"He'll open gifts after we've all had a chance to eat." Noah smiles softly, "Traditions and all."

I stroke my fingertips over his chin, wanting to memorize every inch of his face and bottle the feeling inside me for always.

Noah starts to sway back and forth.

"Baby, this is, hands down, one of the best dates I've had, no doubt."

My face goes hot. I look up to the sky, expecting the sun to be directly above me, but it's not.

Noah sings. His voice is warm butter in my mouth, liquid on my skin, and ecstasy to my ears.

It's only a moment before I realize he's singing along to the radio, a slow melody that lets us sway back and forth together under the trees and the open sky.

"I can die a happy man." Noah lifts my hand to his mouth, kissing it.

I want to live in this one twinkling instant, I never want him to stop.

Noah drops to the ground holding his chest and fingering the bottom of my dress. He stands up slowly, caressing my thighs. "You're a goddess."

I can't take it anymore, I grab Noah's face and pull it to mine. All my worries fade into the distance, each becoming a long-lost memory. I become the stars, the sky, the whole universe. With him in my arms, there are no limits.

Noah is the first to pull away this time. He wipes away a tear from my cheek. I reach for my face, not realizing I've begun to leak. He runs a hand through my hair, "Are you okay?"

I can't speak, I can only smile. Noah reaches for my hand, pulling it to his face and kissing the palm of my hand. He leans and whispers into my ear. "You make me a happy man."

I rest my head on his shoulder, scared of what would happen if he found out who I really am.

I'm more afraid of what it means if I stay. Emotions are running high, and I struggle to navigate my thoughts in this flesh.

It's odd how eight little emotions weigh on me so heavily.

Yet somehow, none of it matters.

Not while I'm with him.

I'll have the memory of this moment and Noah's song in my heart. I never want this day to end.

But it will end. In the same way, the body needs air to breathe. Earth's sun will set, leaving this half of the world in darkness. When it does, I'll say goodbye to Noah forever.

It's not as though this was supposed to be a permanent change. I sigh and try to stay in the moment and this twinkling evening with Noah. I'm going to enjoy every second I can, then I'll walk away and never look back.

37

PENNY

More than two hours have passed since Mona arrived at Oliver's birthday party. She's managed to hold several conversations with varying party guests. ALL HUMAN.

There was one moment when she almost blew her cover while talking to a squirrel. She got two funny looks, but not a soul noticed her having a full-on conversation with a wild bunny.

"It's so good to see that you're doing well, Cora," Mona says.

"I just wish I had better news about Agnes. She's despondent," Cora says. "She's been inconsolable. I don't know what to do, Mona. I thought it would get easier as time passed, but it's only worsened."

"I still don't understand. Isn't it better to have the memories back as opposed to none at all?" Mona asks.

"I guess that's debatable. I wouldn't trade my memories of Ralph for the world. For that matter, I wouldn't give up the rest of them either. They're everything to me," Cora smiles to herself. "But I'm pleased with the life I lived. I'm not sad about my choices or the way anything unfolded."

"You wouldn't want to spend more time with Ralph? If you were given the chance," Mona says.

"It's not that simple. I know he's not gone, here," Cora points to where her heart is housed inside her ribcage. "Deep inside, I know he's waiting for me. I'll see him in the next life. It doesn't tarnish this life's worth. Its value hasn't suddenly plummeted. I'm a strong woman who has done incredible things with her life. I'll see him again next time. But this time, this life, it wasn't our time. It's only mine."

Mona surprises me by reaching for Cora and embracing her.

"You know, Mona, I'm not sure why I thought you were so much older than you are. I must have been coming out of that fog." Cora points to her head and laughs.

Oops. My bad.

Mona smiles, but it doesn't reach her eyes.

"You are so lovely," Cora says. She runs a hand through the ends of Mona's midnight hair.

"I think you're lovely too," Mona says.

Her words say one thing, but her readouts suggest she's sad.

"I'm so happy to see you and Noah. Just be good to that one. He's not had it so easy. He deserves to be happy, just like you." Cora pats Mona's arm and walks away.

38

MONA

It's finally time to open presents. I'm more excited about the whole process than Oliver seems to be.

Presents are a novelty to me. Something humans would leave for me, but my kind never gave to one another. The whole concept has always excited me, even if some of the items gifted seem barbaric.

Everyone is gathered around Oliver for the big unveiling. The presents are piled high upon a picnic table sporting a dark blue nightscape covering.

A pigeon is trying to go after my sandwich and potato salad. It isn't even talking to me, which is just rude. Instead, I'm fending it off. I'm not sharing if it's not polite. I manage to wave it away, but not before it snags a bite.

After a bit of maneuvering, I'm in the perfect spot in the middle of the picnic table. I can enjoy the gifts' unveiling and eat some yummy-smelling substance.

When Oliver gets to my presents, it feels like it takes him a millennium to open. I start to feel a tightening in my stomach. I suddenly worry I've gotten it all wrong and Oliver will hate what I've got him.

Panic eats at my insides, they feel rotten, and I'm getting that familiar nausea feeling again.

I start to stand.

If I'm not there to watch, it won't matter if Oliver doesn't like the gifts.

"This one is from Mona!" Oliver reads the outside of the wrapping.

I hadn't given him a card. I'd only glossed over the wiki on gift giving. That particular nuance slipped past me. I pull my legs from the picnic table when Noah catches my eye.

I sit and deeply breathe, watching Oliver tear at the rainbow wrapping paper. I'd been opposed to wrapping the gifts, but the store lady insisted this was how gifts were given. Wrapping paper is my sacrifice.

For hundreds of thousands of years, sacrifices of crops, animals, and humans have been in my name.

Oliver gets to the meat of the gift, his eyes brighten, and he gives me a toothless grin.

I'm starting to find it endearing.

Of course, after I'd learned it was not a deformity.

Who knew it was a normal human growth stage? They lose all their teeth, and new ones come through. I'll have to talk with Penny about that one. I understand why animals need several sets, but humans?

Humans brush their teeth; animals can't care for their teeth the same way. It just seems like Penny is copying my designs.

Oliver pulls out a fifteen-inch wand with a unicorn core. I personally created it when Noah wasn't looking. Pulling a unicorn's hair out of thin air wasn't as challenging as I'd thought.

Since Penny seemed nowhere to be found, I could write the code without a big scene. I wanted Oliver to have the most authentic wand possible.

Reading Harry Potter was a happy accident.

"Mona! It's a wand! Oh my gosh, dad, dad! Look, it's a wand," Oliver is bouncing back and forth, showing his dad the wand. "Noah!" Oliver runs over to me and grabs me at the waist. I reach and pat his back. "It's so cool, Mona. Thank you."

The tightness in my chest eases. "Well, there is more where that came from."

Oliver's eyes grow large again, and he returns to the box. Inside are several packages of Every Flavor Jelly Beans and the star gazer Noah recommended I buy.

Noah meets my gaze, "When did you do that?"

I smile and go back to watching Oliver.

Obviously, I created it when he wasn't looking. Duh. How else was I supposed to find the perfect gift? Especially when Noah wouldn't let me buy the telescope.

Oliver was showing off the packages of jellybeans and explaining all the uncivilized flavors to anyone who would listen.

It's a perfect first gift.

Oliver was down to one gift on the table. It was from Hazel.

"Thank you, I love my new scarf," Oliver was donning a maroon and gold scarf.

"I made it myself, Olli. I'm glad you like it." Hazel's eyes dart between me and Oliver.

Weird.

Oliver looks around the table littered with wrapping paper. He seems sad.

"What's wrong, buddy?" Noah claps Oliver's shoulder. "Looks like you got some great loot here."

"Yeah, I did. I just—" He shakes his head and picks up his wand. His eyes are sad and imply things his words won't say.

"I'm sorry, Olli, I told you. Dad can't—"

I cut Noah off. "Oliver? I think you missed one." I pull my head out from under the picnic table.

Oliver jumps up and crawls under the table to find one last gift.

It's big.

"How did I miss this?" he says.

"It must have been hidden by the tablecloth. Do you need help?" I ask.

"Yea, must have. Woah!" Oliver and I maneuver the gift out from under the table. It's dressed in simple grey wrapping paper. On the top are swirly letters that read, Oliver, with love —Dad and Noah.

Oliver looks up at his father, and his eyes sparkle with hope.

Noah looks utterly shocked.

"Oh, Dad, you didn't forget," Oliver says, ripping through the paper. He unwraps a telescope.

Noah told me it was the only gift he asked for.

Oliver hugs the box tightly, then leaves and grabs his dad by the waist.

"Hey buddy, I umm," Mr. Harvey starts.

"Thank you, Dad. I knew you wouldn't forget. You're the best. I love you too."

When Oliver releases his dad, he shows anyone who will listen to his new telescope.

I don't know what this feeling is, but I like it.

"Hey, when did you buy the telescope?" Noah asks.

"Oh, you know, I wanted to surprise him. I just saw one. Oliver told me how much of a wizard fan he was, and it felt right to get him a wand. Was it a bad gift?"

"No, it's not that. The wand is beautiful. I'm still floored by the craftmanship. I'm sure it cost you a lot, which you shouldn't have. Giving a kid like twenty dollars for a birthday is far more traditional than a handcrafted wand and a telescope." Noah's gaze is piercing.

I shrug. "I don't know what you're talking about. It wasn't like I was hiding it up my skirt Noah. I assumed you bought it for him. It was what he wanted, right?"

I'm suddenly glad I didn't make Oliver a set of wizard robes too. Apparently, that would be too extravagant. Life was sacrificed for me; I don't see a telescope or a wand remotely comparable.

But what do I know?

Noah takes a step closer to me. "So, you didn't buy the telescope?"

It's not a lie, "I didn't buy the telescope. But, like I said, when would I have done that?"

I step closer to him and find his lips with my own. Pushing away any questions about the telescope.

"Ahem."

I pull away and find Hazel standing with her arms crossed.

"I thought you weren't going to get him the telescope. I said I would have gone in halves," Hazel is upset. Her face is crinkled, and her eyes are angry.

"I didn't, Hazel. I don't know where it came from," Noah says.

She points to me, "Did you buy it?"

"No, honestly. I didn't buy it. Maybe it was Cora or one of his friends? Or maybe it was your dad?" I say.

Noah shakes his head, "I don't know where it came from; I just wish someone would have asked me first."

Hazel reaches for Noah's arm. "Don't be proud, Noah; it's not a good look on you. Instead, be glad your brother is happy. Look at him; he's over the moon right now."

"You're right," he says, walking to Oliver.

"Noah is a bit too proud sometimes. He doesn't like handouts. He's always been an earn it, or you don't need it kind of person," Hazel says. "It makes him appreciate what he has, but sometimes I wonder if it's enough for Oliver. Not that Oliver needs a new telescope."

"Hazel, did you buy it?" I ask

Hazel's eyes sparkle, telling me something her lips won't. She shook her head slowly. "I don't know what you're talking about. I made Oliver a scarf."

"Of course you did. It's funny; he's such a great kid. I wouldn't have expected that from such a young human," I say.

"Do you want kids someday?" Hazel asks.

I almost laugh aloud, "Not in the conventional sense of the word. I have projects I consider very dear to me. But the idea of a human child of my own. No. Not any time in the near future."

"Maybe someday?"

"Only time will tell, I guess."

"Do you come from a big family?" Hazel asks.

"I have a sister. She's enough," I say.

Hazel falters.

"I'm sorry, I didn't mean. I don't know what I'm trying to say. I know you lost your sister. Noah told me."

"No, no. You're fine. I had a sister too. Just the one. Now it's just me. I would never have guessed how lonely it was. Being the only one. A million times, I wanted to just reach out and talk to her. I want to tell her everything. I want to text her photos or talk about our days. I want to show her all the little beautiful things in this world. I miss her." Hazel begins to leak.

She wipes away the tears.

"I don't know what to say."

"Noah is so brave. He bounced back quickly. Did what had to be done. He cares for Oliver and works at that old folk's home to help pay the bills."

"Summer Grove, the one where Cora and Agnes live?"

"Yep, the very one."

I realize I don't know what he does there.

"Rhi worked there before she died. Everyone was such a mess, including Alan," Hazel says.

"Who?" I ask.

"Alan, that's Noah's dad. He started to drink and couldn't pay the mortgage. I mean, who could blame him at first? Noah stepped up, but he shouldn't have had to. He was thirteen.

Alan should have been comforting him, not the other way around."

"Yeah," was all I could contribute. I let Hazel's story wash over me.

"The whole company pooled together and helped keep his family afloat. I know Noah's thankful for the help. He took an after-school job there a couple of years ago. He talks about staying on full time and not going to college."

"But education is important," I say.

"It is. I wonder if he stays because he feels some sort of loyalty to them. In many ways, the staff and residents became a family he didn't have." Hazel watches Noah and Oliver.

"He should go to college. He should live his life."

"Well, maybe you could talk some sense into him. Alan should be taking care of Olli and Noah. While Noah considers colleges or life after high school that doesn't involve being the substitute father to his kid brother," Hazel says. "I'm thankful for him. Losing Rhi was the worst day of his whole life. Losing Vanessa was the worst of mine. I don't know what I would have done without him. You know, Noah doesn't date. For the record."

I raise an eyebrow. "What does that mean."

Hazel chuckles. "I mean, he's not exactly celibate; look at him. He's a beautiful piece of man meat, for someone else, of course," she seems nervous. "I mean Noah and me; that's a hard pass."

Hazel has love for Ollie and love for Noah. So, that's what it looks like. A little monster stirs inside of me. Regardless of what I said earlier, I don't want to share him with anyone.

"Mona?"

"Yes?"

"I don't want you to think I have feelings for Noah," She takes a deep breath. The whole way she carries herself seems to change. "Tell me, how do I catch a man of my own? I need a good one, you know? Someone with a bit of work ethic and passion doesn't mind if I spend all my time writing. Calls me on my bullshit." She's smiling again, and I think it's real.

"Well, there are three generally accepted methods," I say.

"Oh?"

"Firstborn child sacrifice."

Hazel throws up her hands, "I don't have any kids, so that's a no-go."

"Second, building an altar and sacrificing three goats. Of course, during the ceremony, you'd have to drink the goat's blood and cover your body in ancient markings for the goddess of love."

Hazel's face crinkles again, "I can't even eat goat. What's my third option?"

"Oh, that's the easy one. Just bathe naked in salt water under the full moon, preferably on a Tuesday or a Friday night. Send your demands into the universe, and make sure they are, in fact, demands. You can't go easy on this one. Then cleanse yourself with salt water. Finally, don't forget to light a candle at true north, south, east, and west."

"I'm going to dig that kiddy pool out of my garage. Then, I better hit the store and buy a large bottle of salt; this bitch is getting naked!"

I laugh, and Hazel joins me.

It feels good to release all the built-up energy. Despite all the new experiences, I'm glad to end it all with laughter. I didn't expect it to burn my lungs or make my eyes leak, but it does, and I'm happy about it.

39

MONA

Y ou were out awfully late last night," Rhett hands me a
cup of fresh coffee.

"It was Oliver's birthday party," I say.

"I'm not judging. I gathered something was going on, considering I read your lipstick. Or should I say, my lipstick?" Rhett is giving me evil-eye vibes. "By the way, your handwriting is atrocious! Like a child's scribbles everywhere."

"I'm sorry about that. I just don't care for paper. I'm thinking about buying you a bunch of elephant poop paper. It's recycled, and the money goes toward efforts to save them."

"Ewww!! I'm not writing on elephant poop, that's gross," Rhett spills coffee on her nightgown. "Damn."

I smile and consume my entire cup quickly. "It's not like fresh poop. It's mostly dried grass processed into paper. It's a perfectly acceptable substitute."

"You know, Mona, I buy recycled paper. Which is more environmentally friendly."

This brings me up short. "Was my handwriting that bad?"

"Yes, and I loved that lipstick," Rhett says.

"I'll get you another one."

"Not the point."

I give Rhett a toothy grin.

"Now you owe me a story since you've used all my lipstick and forced me to read your shitty handwriting," Rhett pours herself and me more coffee.

So, tell her about the kissing, the shopping, and Oliver's birthday. About meeting Hazel, seeing Cora, Agnes's depression, and of course, about the cake. I could go for some more cake. Maybe next time, I can try the red velvet cake Hazel loves.

"What do you mean you don't want to see him again?" Rhett's brow is furrowed, her lips frown, and she's got the most enormous puppy dog eyes.

"He's not part of my world. I was never meant to get involved with someone. I don't live here. It shouldn't matter how I feel. I'm just…." I search for the right words but come up empty.

"Chicken shit?" Rhett offers.

"Not exactly. It's more like I was just going to observe, and I wasn't going to find myself tied to a human's life."

"You say that as though you're not human yourself. I hate to point out the obvious, Mona, but unless you're not telling me something, look in the mirror. You're allowed to let yourself feel something. There is no law against falling in love."

"Who said anything about love? I don't love him," I spit the words out like something sour, then immediately regretted my reaction. "I just mean—"

"Would it be so bad?" Rhett's words pierce my facade.

"I don't know. Maybe?" I sigh. "I don't think I even know what that means. To love someone. If you knew about some of the things I've done, you wouldn't argue with me."

"We all have a past, that's what makes us human. Nobody is perfect, in fact, that is the point of it all. There is no way to be perfect. We make mistakes, it's in our nature, and we learn from them. Or at least that's the hope. But if we were all condemned to be the person of our former selves, then I don't think anyone would like us very much," Rhett says.

I look up and find Rhett's eyes. "Hey?"

"Yeah?"

"What if I'm just disrupting his life? And really, he should be with someone else. Someone far more deserving of his attention? Someone who cares more or looks at him as though he's the only man in the world?"

"A of all, that's his decision to make. B of all, I would say that person should step up or step out."

"Thanks, Rhett."

"For what?"

"For, you know, being my friend. I've never really had one of those before. It's nice," I say.

It was Rhett's turn to return the smile. "Anytime lady face. Anytime."

There's an overwhelming concern for Agnes, nagging at my insides. It's not as though I'm close to the woman. Yet somehow, I still feel responsible. Old age brought on depression, which had nothing to do with removing the blockage in her brain.

It couldn't.

Cora is proof that removing the blockage doesn't cause depression. Which means it has to be something else.

Science says so.

The same process was completed on both women. Cora is not exhibiting symptoms of depression. Ergo, Agnes has something wrong with her.

While I don't enjoy admitting it, I could use Penny's help. I just don't see it as a viable option. Besides, if Penny was talking to me, she would have pressed pause and shown herself.

I push the thoughts away when anger and confusion bubble to the surface. I don't need anything. I'm more than capable of humanity without her.

There can't be too many emotions remaining. It's a new day, and that means a fresh round at it. Perhaps a chance to clear my conscience would be a good place to start.

Not that I feel guilty.

I don't.

But to know for sure if I'm responsible for Agnes, I'll have to go see her for myself.

I pull out my new cell phone and check it for any messages.

There's one from Noah:

Good morning beautiful. Do I get to see you today?

I don't respond. Instead, I replace the small device back into my pocket.

Duel emotions fight for control of this body. On the one hand, I'm jubilant over Noah's message. I feel attractive and wanted. Two things I've never felt before. But on the other, it makes me sad. This life would be easier if he hadn't messaged me. Why couldn't he just ignore me? Then, I could be annoyed with him and move on.

Noah dropped me off at Rhett's last night. The drive was comfortable and quiet. He held my hand the whole drive home. I didn't want to ask him anything. I didn't want to spoil the warm feeling from the afternoon. I wanted to savor it all and live in those memories for a bit longer.

He kissed me goodnight under a cloudless sky. When our lips broke apart, I walked away, never looking back.

40

MONA

D o bacon and pancakes sour? My stomach hurts. I'm standing outside the looming Summer Grove Retirement Community. My gut is doing flip flops, but they don't feel like the good kind.

I rub my stomach, but nothing helps.

The building opens to a grand foyer where several oversized leather couches rest. The ground is covered with gigantic ornate rugs in bright yellows and reds. The intricate pattern is dizzy-making. To the right is a large dining room where several residents sit at various tables eating what I can only assume is an early lunch. To the left is a separate room with a large fireplace, television, and four couches. Finally, there is a small room off the front entrance labeled manager.

Well, okay. Agnes can't be too hard to find in this place. I take a left down a hallway. Every door I pass is labeled with what I assume are residents' names. Some are formal, Mr. Anhalt, Mrs. Jackson, and Mrs. Melanie Osmer. While others are a bit more informal: Star's Room, Harry J., and Twiggle. I begin to wonder how vast this facility is.

It wasn't until I reached the third floor that I spotted a door with big block letters: Mrs. Agnes Witherbee.

I knocked.

There's rustling on the other side of the door. Someone is home. I try to remember patience while I wait for Agnes's aged body to answer the door.

The door creeks open, revealing a set of red and puffy eyes.

"Agnes? It's Mona," I say.

The door shuts, and I'm taken aback. There's a clatter, metal on metal before the door opens a second time, this time, the door opens widely.

"Mona?"

"Hi, Agnes."

"Mona. What are you doing here?" Agnes sticks her head out into the hallway and looks back and forth.

I'm not sure what for.

I clear my throat. "I just wanted to come by and visit with you. You were one of the first people I met in this town, and I just—"

Agnes doesn't say anything, she just stares at me letting my words hang in the air.

"I wanted to see how you were doing. You could invite me in and make some coffee. I hear it's customary."

Agnes sighs and steps back into her apartment. She holds the door open, and I take it as an invitation.

The room smells sharply of an astringent disinfectant. Has she learned nothing? I glance around the small space.

Agnes walks to a small coffee pot where a full carafe awaits. Agnes pulls out a cup and fills it. "Cream or sugar?" she asks.

"No, thank you," I say, reaching for the mug.

Agnes motions to a recliner and a loveseat in the modest living space. I take a seat on the small couch.

"You can't tell me you've come all this way for coffee. You could have bought a cup in town. What do you want?" Agnes is direct.

"Weird. I remember you being so much nicer the last time we met," I say. Granted, she didn't have much memory to speak of, so that could be part of it.

Agnes's eyes grow, "Rude child."

I opened my mouth several times but couldn't think of anything. Instead, I take a sip of my coffee. It's bitter, and I make a face. It's nothing like the coffee I've enjoyed with Rhett or the coffee house.

"Fine, if you won't talk, I will. What did you do to me?" Agnes asks.

And there it is. Hanging in the air between us.

I shake my head. "I didn't do anything to you. I helped clear a little blockage you had built up," I say. "I didn't do anything wrong."

"Put it back."

"Excuse me?" I say, taken aback by the request.

"I said, put it back."

"It's not that simple," I run a hand through my hair.

"Sure, it is. You removed a blockage and brought back all these memories. Now I'm asking you to put it back. Make it all go away. Put me back the way you found me," Agnes says.

"But there was something wrong with you," I say. "Surely you're not asking me to make you sick again?"

"You want me to explain to you why I miss my husband? You'd like for me to tell you why I miss my old life? Why I'd rather die than live in this place a moment longer?" Agnes's face reveals nothing to me.

I can only bob my head in response.

"It probably has something to do with the revelation that my husband died several years ago, and I had no idea. I missed everything. I missed his funeral. I never got to say goodbye." Agnes takes a shaking breath. "But maybe it's more than that. Something about being alone in the world. Not even my children come to visit me anymore. They figured I was so far gone I'd never remember them anyway. What was the point? I'm not even worth visiting."

I start to speak, but Agnes cuts me off.

"No, don't. Because it wouldn't matter if I called them now. The fact is, they don't come by. I asked to see the visitor logs, and not even my grandchildren visited. I have a new great-granddaughter. They call her Aggie. I've never even met her. Maybe I have, and it doesn't matter. None of it matters because none of them care anymore. They've left me to rot, and that's what I'm doing. Look at me," Agnes demands my attention. Her voice is tight, and she has unshed tears.

I find my voice. "I'm looking at you. I see you, Agnes. So does Cora. She sees you. She hasn't gone anywhere. I looked it up, she's been by your side for years. She loves you deeply."

Tears stream down Agnes's puffy face. She holds her head in her hands.

"She would give up the rest of her life just to be by your side. Can't you see that? You're not alone." I reach for her but stop short.

"It's not the same," Agnes says.

"Why? I don't understand why she isn't enough. Because you're enough for her."

Agnes shudders. She wipes her tears away with a lacy cream-colored handkerchief. "I didn't mean to say she's not enough," She takes a deep breath. "I miss my life."

"I miss my life too."

"What are you doing here, Mona?" Agnes tilts her head at me.

I look around the living space.

"Not here," Agnes says, pointing around her home. "Here in this world."

What? "I couldn't possibly know what you mean."

"Don't play coy with me. I know you're an alien, Mona. No human could do what you did. Are you going to probe me? I like my bottom just fine, please avoid it if possible."

A wave of relief washes over me, and I can laugh. It's deep and guttural. "I'm not going to probe you, Agnes. I'm not—" I pause. What's the harm in letting her think I'm an alien? Is it more plausible that I was alien than the creator of Earth? Humans are so weird. "I'm not going to do anything to hurt you. Who else knows?"

"Just me. Well, maybe Oliver, but Cora thinks I'm just seeing what I want to see. She thinks you're human. But I know differently. So, start talking." Agnes crosses her arms.

After weighing my options, I decide it doesn't matter much if Agnes knows. "My sister and I got into a fight. She called me unfeeling and cold-hearted. She bet me a large sum I wouldn't last as a human. I couldn't back down from the fight and took her up on it. So here I am. I'm living in this meat suit. I have no idea what I'm doing, and I can't go home until I prove to her I understand what it means to be human. Something I'm still trying to figure out."

Agnes isn't deterred by my confession. Instead, she sits up a little taller, momentarily forgetting her woes. "Where do you come from?"

"Somewhere outside of the Bio-Matrix," I say.

"Bio-Matrix?"

I didn't mean to say Bio-Matrix. Well, the damage is done. "Yea, outside of the Bio-Matrix. I helped build it. It wasn't all me, you know. There are others."

"But what is a Bio-Matrix? Am I real?" Agnes was pulling at her dress tightly. Maybe it's a nightgown. I can't tell the difference.

"Yes. You are as real as I am, sitting next to you."

"I don't know what your saying."

"Where I'm from, we built something called a Bio-Matrix. It's a computer program that creates biological matter. Think of a 3D printer but one that could print a human body or an entire world. Not quite the same as cloning because every item printed is equipped with a unique transcript, making them original. Or nearly original, but that's neither here nor there." I wave away the details. "Are you following me?"

Agnes says nothing, waiting silently for me to continue.

I take another sip of my coffee. "So, the Bio-Matrix, for simplicity's sake, is like a big computer, only it's something your species won't come close to replicating for another five hundred thousand years or so. The way it is built, my kind can upload or plug into it and live in one of your—" I only just refrained from calling this body a meat suit again. I'm trying not to come off as cold as Penny makes me seem. "Lives as a human, in a human body."

"I don't know the technology you're referencing," she shakes her head then eyes me. "Did you steal that body, Mona? Because I remember you looking different. Did you change bodies? Did you make me believe one thing and now another? Are you an illusion?"

"No," I say, stifling a laugh. "I assure you I am as real as you are. I bleed just like you do. Penny thought it would be a funny joke if people saw me in different ways. I think that's done now. The more human I become, the less people see me differently."

"Sounds like a bad joke," Agnes says.

"Tell me about it."

"Okay, so we're real but not really real. We all live in a computer?" Agnes starts to laugh.

"I don't know what you want me to say. I'm just being honest with you."

Agnes keeps laughing, "I needed a good laugh. Thank you, Mona. If you don't want to tell me, that's fine. You don't have to."

"I am telling you the truth, Agnes. I'm here because my sister is trying to save your kind. But, unfortunately, I lost a bet," I sigh.

"Oh, Mona, stop! Stop!" Agnes's laughter turns hysterical. "I'm an old woman. You don't have to convince me. I know there's something special about you. That's all I need to know."

I don't know what that means. Does Agnes believe me or not?

When Agnes could breathe normally again, she eyes me up and down. "So, tell me, my angel, what are your intentions with Noah? That boy has been through enough hardship, and if you're just playing with his heartstrings, I don't care what you think you are. I'll stomp on you."

Those were the last words I ever expected out of Agnes. I mull them over before answering her. "I don't know. I've never done this before."

Agnes raises an eyebrow.

"I mean to say, I've never been human before. I don't generally interfere with human politics or human life. I'm more of an Earthen body, if you know what I mean."

"I don't. Go on."

"I would never knowingly and intentionally hurt Noah or anyone. I'm not sure I'm going to be sticking around for long, though. I don't know if it's in the cards or not. I don't know if I should. I don't think I can be the person that he needs. Not when there are already people who would be far more suited for the job."

"Can I ask you a question?" Agnes says.

"You just did. But you may ask an additional one."

"Do you want to be human?"

I don't feel the initial recoiling reaction I have so many times before.

"Well?" Agnes says.

"I don't know anymore. It's not easy. I love my life. This one is more complicated."

"Do you have to give up one for the other?"

"Not exactly. It makes things even more complicated."

"I hate to break it to you, my dear, but life is complicated. It was never meant to be simple. We weren't put here to just eat, sleep, and shit."

I laugh so much. If Agnes only knew.

"We were put here to fight for ourselves, to love. Oh, how we were put here to love." Agnes wags her eyebrows at me.

I don't understand.

"We are here to grow and learn. Then, maybe if we're lucky, we will do it again in the next life, only better."

A shiver runs down my back sending gooseflesh to pimple my arms. I rub them.

"What are you going to do? Are you going to stick it out, or will you go back to wherever you came from?" Agnes asks.

I shrug. "Right now, I'd like to spend some time with you if that's okay."

"I guess so. I was just going to watch The Price is Right. If you want to watch it with me, I'll make us some lunch. You do eat food, don't you?"

"Yes, I eat food, just like you. However, I enjoy it far more because I understand how rare it is."

Agnes smiles at me, "You remember when you look back on all this. When you're old and grey, and the world is sad and lonely. When you think back on this later, just remember, it was a really big deal."

41

MONA

It feels like Agnes and I have a certain amount of understanding. However, I'm more confident that Agnes won't let her memories prevent her from living. Agnes has lived a beautiful life; giving up now would be a waste.

It's simply not an option.

While I don't think I fully grasp the why, I feel better knowing that Agnes is a fighter. The achy, itchy feeling burrowing under my skin has begun to ease.

Turning the corner as I leave Agnes's room, I nearly run into Noah. He's leaning against the wall, hands in his pockets.

My heart beats out of my chest. "What are you doing here?"

Noah captures my eyes, "Cora mentioned she saw you. So I thought I'd stop by. Check and see if everything is okay."

A question, but I'm not sure about what.

"You know," Noah says. "With Agnes, she's been upset."

"I just spoke with her. She's doing better, I think. But, since her memory's come back, she's had to confront the loss of her husband all over again." I can't meet his eyes.

Noah seems to weigh my words. "How do you know her memory is back?"

"Well, I mean—Cora's did. So…" I trail off.

"I was hoping to talk to you about that. Can we go for a walk?" Noah asks.

"Sure, I was headed out anyway."

I follow Noah down the stairs and out the doors of Summer Grove. I wait for him to talk, afraid of what I might say if I break the silence. Anxiety settles in the air. I breathe it in, and it burrows its way into my bone marrow. With every breath, I overthink things with Noah. I think about telling him who I am, figuring out what this is between us, and wondering if I still want to delete these humans. These people have become friends.

Would it be so bad if I told Noah the truth? Would he still want to be my friend, or would he think I was making it up the way Agnes did?

Noah keeps his hands in his pockets while we stroll on the sidewalk. I find myself wishing he'd pull them out. Wishing he'd he would grab my own. Wishing he would hold me.

Why can't things be simple?

Which moment did it all become so complicated?

Time froze.

42

PENNY

The world stands still. Noah is mid-stride, a bird mid-flight, and Mona is left at a loss for words.

"You can't tell him," I say.

"You don't get to tell me what to do," Mona says, spinning around, ready for another fight.

My arms hang at my sides. I'm not here to argue. "It doesn't work this way, Mona. You don't get to have it both ways. You can choose to be human, or you can choose to be Mother Nature, but you can't live both lives anymore."

"What is that supposed to mean? You can't just dictate my life. I'm doing what you asked of me," Mona's heart races.

I sigh and walk around Noah, appraising him, looking for the words that won't set Mona off again. "He's a nice person. Do you wonder what might have happened if you hadn't intervened in his life?"

I won't pretend to know what Mona is thinking. I may have the ability to read her bio-readouts, but her thoughts are still private. However, I'd guess that Hazel and Noah play at the surface, and just as quickly, she pushes them away before giving them room to breathe life into her mind.

"I don't know what you mean," Mona says.

"He would have met someone else. Maybe fallen in love. That person might encourage him to do more with his life. He could do good things, become a man who impacts the lives around him in great ways," I say.

"I'm Mother Nature, that's just who I am. Why can't I be his girlfriend too?"

"You can, but you can't be both. Humans catch on to inconsistencies. You saw Agnes, she thinks you're an alien. How long do you think it's going to last? How long will it take Noah to notice you're not human?" I place my hands on my hips.

"Who says he will?" Mona glances at Noah.

"He'll notice. Are you going to stop him? Are you going to just code his memory away?"

"I wouldn't do that," Mona says.

Hurt and guilt register.

"But you don't hesitate to work a little finger magic to get your dress to fit right or to craft wands for Oliver's birthday party.

"It was one wand," she says.

"Look, I don't care about that. It's harmless, but what will you do when he falls in love? What will you do when you move in together? That's what humans do. They cohabitate. Are you going to get a job? Are you going to give up what it means to be who you are?"

When Mona doesn't answer, I crouch to Earth and lie back in a grass patch. I soak up the sun rays peeking through the trees.

"What are you doing?" Mona asks.

I peek up at her, but I don't speak. I can stall all day if necessary. I'm far more patient than Mona gives me credit for.

"Fine. If that's how you're going to be, you win," Mona says.

"I'm not trying to win anything. I'm just trying to get you to listen," I say.

"I'll stay," Mona says.

I perk up at this.

"But this doesn't negate our bet," Mona raises a finger. "We're still on. I get to decide what happens in the end."

"Providing you complete all eight emotions, yes. You get to make the decision," I say. "But you can't do that while living both lives. When you're done on Earth, I'll hand over the reins. Willingly. That was always the deal."

Mona takes a long, slow breath. She closes her eyes for a moment before answering. "I'll stay."

"You're choosing to live as a human?" I stand up. "Giving up everything it means to be you?"

Mona glances at Noah, and I wish I could know what she is thinking right now.

"Yes, if that's what it means, I'll do it," Mona says.

"You can't tell him. You need to keep the façade up. No one else can know who you really are," I say.

Mona only blinks at me.

I take it as my sign to go.

Mona gives me a terse bow before I press play.

The world spins again, and Mona is left human.

Mother Nature no more.

43

MONA

Noah looks at me and does a double-take. "Weren't you just?" he points to where I am not.

Damn the stars above and damn Penny. I can't tell him, but she can be sloppy?

"Are you okay?" I ask, knowing that gaslighting him is the last thing I want to do.

"Yea, I—never mind," Noah says, shaking his head. "How is Agnes doing?"

"I thought we talked about this already?" I say before I realize he's trying to fill the space between us.

"Right," Noah says.

"I think she's going to be okay. She just needed a friend to take her mind off things. Someone to remind her that life has meaning and that although she lost her husband, it doesn't negate the rest of this life here on Earth. There are people and things worth being here for," as the words escape my mouth, my throat tightens, and suddenly I understand.

"Cora told me you had something to do with her memory. She said you—" Noah's eyebrows crease. "She said you made her spit out black gunk that was poisoning her mind." His voice is thick with skepticism.

For once, I'm thankful I don't have to lie. I reach for Noah's hand feeling emboldened. "I am as human as you are. I'm not a doctor."

Noah's eyes search my own. He blows out a breath he was holding, runs a hand through his hair, and pulls me closer. "I don't know what I was thinking. Of course, you couldn't have had anything to do with her memory. It was silly."

"Silly," I parrot, feeling a pang of guilt.

Noah cups my cheek and moves a strand of hair out of my eyes.

I smile, and for the first time, I feel okay about the decision to stay human. I lean in, and his mouth meets mine. He tastes of warmth and cinnamon. I let my worries fall away and melt into Noah.

I'll figure it out.

I'll figure it all out.

I will be human.

I am human.

The afternoon moves into evening, and Noah and I have spent the entire day talking before I realize it.

"Macaroni and cheese with peas, ground turkey, and crushed red chili flakes. Stir in mozzarella till it's warm, then bake the whole dish off with cheddar, Parmigiano-Reggiano, and Dubliner," Noah has an ear-to-ear grin.

"You'd eat that for the rest of forever?" I ask.

"Damn straight. Did you decide yet?" Noah asks me.

"I still don't understand why chocolate isn't a viable option. I could do a vitamin drink or whatever," I say.

Noah laughs at me, "I think you'd get sick of it real quick."

"Okay, then maybe pancakes, bacon, eggs, sausage, and fresh fruit," I say.

"I think that's cheating. That's a lot of different things, not one," Noah smirks.

"But I ate it all for breakfast. I think it should count. Yours is several things too. You just layered it."

"Whatever," Noah laughs.

"I also reserve the right to change my mind."

"If you could have dinner with anyone, alive or dead, who would it be?" Noah says.

He's thumbing circles around my palm, and it's incredibly distracting. "I think I'd like to have met Rhi," I say.

Noah stops walking and turns to face me.

"Was that a bad answer? It's just that I think I'd enjoy having dinner with her. We'd have a lot to talk about. I don't have a lot in common with most people and—"

Noah tilts his head, searching my eyes.

"I'm sorry?"

"Don't be. I'd like to have one more dinner with her as well. I'd talk about life and Oliver. I'd like to show her what an amazing kid he's turned into," he says.

"And what an amazing man you're turning into. She'd be proud, you know?"

"You think?"

"I know," I say, taking Noah's other hand and kissing it.

We walk for a few more minutes before I break the silence. "My turn?"

"Yes, it is."

"Would you ever wish for fame?" I ask.

"Fame, fortune, and rock and roll?" Noah asks.

I don't know what that means, but I don't say it.

"Nah, I don't think that fame is really in the cards for me. Besides, fame usually implies you're a people person, and I'm not really."

"Me either. Besides, fame isn't all it's cut out to be," I say.

I don't tell him that I've seen it destroy people. Although, on the other hand, I could always... the thought stops in its tracks. I can't program anything.

Human.

Noah gazes at me quizzically.

"From what I hear," I add.

"Right. Of course. Me next, then." Noah says.

"Yes, my favorite part."

"If you could change one thing about yourself, what would it be?"

Oof.

I blow out a breath, "That I wouldn't be so afraid all the time."

"Really?"

"I don't know if it's a bad thing to want to change or not, but yes."

"I guess I'm surprised that you feel afraid all the time. You seem so confident," Noah sneaks a peek at me.

"I don't really see how the two correlate. You can be terrified and head into battle at full speed, leading the cavalry. Fear does not denote a lack of courage."

"Well spoken, my dear." Noah kisses the back of my hand this time.

"You?"

"Same, I think."

"Really?" I'm in disbelief.

Noah doesn't say anything at first. We walk in silence. I let him take all the time he needs.

"I'm afraid I'm not doing Oliver justice. I'm afraid I'm going to let him down somehow. I don't want to fail him as a brother. Am I giving him enough? Should I go to school somewhere and leave him? He can't lose me too. What if I never amount to anything? I—" Noah's voice hitches, and he quiets.

I don't know what to say. He always seems so together.

We stop walking, and I envelop him in my arms. I take his mouth with mine and let my kiss say everything I can't with words.

Noah still holds me close when we pull apart, searching my eyes.

"You are worthy," I say.

His brows crease.

"I don't have all the answers, but I know you are worthy of a good life and of following your dreams. You are enough just the way you are." I'm unsure where the words come from, but they feel right.

Noah kisses me again, deep and slow. Perhaps he's telling me everything he doesn't have words for.

He strokes my cheek and kisses my forehead before we walk again.

"You know what really gets under my skin?" I say.

"Hmm?"

"Sisters."

"I bet they're a lot like brothers," Noah laughs.

"I don't have one, so I'll have to take your word on it," I say.

"I mean, I don't have a sister, so I could be wrong," he says.

"Penny always has to be right. It doesn't help that folks have always liked her best."

"I find that hard to believe. I think you're wonderful. I can't imagine that your sister is half the woman you are."

"You're biased. She's prettier and more creative. She takes risks. She's brave."

"Perhaps, you're too hard on yourself? I can't imagine that anyone is prettier than you," Noah says.

My cheeks grow warm, and I shake away his words. "There is a certain kindness about her. It's unmatched by anyone I've ever met. I'm not surprised that people have always liked her more. I get it. I'm not the easiest person to get along with. Sometimes she still annoys the ever-living rivers out of me. I think she presses my buttons just because she can. What are sisters for and all that," I say.

Noah chuckles, "That's a sibling thing for sure. They have the ability to press just the right combination of hot spots to send you derailing, doing, and saying things you wouldn't normally."

I'm nodding along, he's so right.

"They can make you feel like you're twelve all over again, and they've just broken a favorite toy. It can be insufferable. Then there are these moments where you think, no one in this world could possibly understand me better than they just did."

"Don't I know it. She makes me commit to doing things I don't know I would have ever done on my own. Penny is the social butterfly. Whereas I have always been on the nerdy side. I got called a brainiac a lot. But it was always as if I didn't work my butt off for it. I spent far too much time on my—" I barely catch myself, "—computer. I've always been a wiz at that stuff. Building, creating, designing, it's all come naturally. I've always preferred the company of my creations to actual people."

"You're cute when you talk about yourself," Noah winks at me.

"It's not cute. It's powerful! I'm gifted and all-knowing," I say, puffing out my chest. I can't keep a straight face, and the laughter bubbles out.

"I'm sure you're all of those things. So, does that mean you can help me with mine? I can do a lot, but computers have never been one of my strong suits," Noah says.

"Not a gamer boy? I thought it was all the rage," I tease.

"Ha! Nah, I'm more of a bookworm," Noah smiles. "Dumb, I know."

"Not dumb at all," I say.

"But honest, I could use a few pointers if you had the time."

"Yes, of course. I'm happy to help."

I wonder briefly if this means I have a purpose here. Other than finding emotions to feel. Maybe I could be good at something on Earth after all. I know I can show Penny I'm more than just Mother Nature. I'm Mona. I can live a full human experience.

I'll make it work.

Walking the urban trail is maybe the highlight of this life thus far. Noah wraps me in his arms at every opportunity. He tickles my arms, stomach, and neck, leaving a trail of fiery kisses on my body. I want to drink him in completely.

If I'd known it could be like this, I might have come more willingly.

It's not like this at home.

Limbs don't intertwine so effortlessly.

A stumbling man interrupts my thoughts. He pushes into Noah and almost lands on me before Noah catches him. The man secretes vomitus fluid all over my shoes.

"What in the stars of Apollo are you doing?" I step back.

Noah stabilizes the man when I want to push him down.

"Whoa, man, are you okay?"

The man grunts before flipping Noah the middle finger and stumbling off the trail.

My insides boil, and my heart raises. "Am I going to die?" Instant panic has set in. I don't want to die. I want to live. "I mean, I know I'm not going to die, probably. Yet. Right? Oh, man."

I pull at my top and puff out my chest. It's like I can't get enough air. I suck in a full breath, but nothing hits my lungs.

A million thoughts race through my brain. Every possible way to die as a human. My vision starts to blur. I suck in more air, but it's like breathing through a straw.

"Am I going to catch something? He gave me dysentery, didn't he? I'm going to die of dysentery, and I haven't even really started to live yet."

My face is leaking fluid, my throat is tight, and I think I might be having a syncopal episode.

Noah is talking, but his words don't register. He smiles, reaches down, and removes my footwear. He's careful not to get anything on himself.

Once I'm able to get enough distance between me and the death of me, my hearing slowly comes back.

"It's going to be okay," Noah says.

"I don't want to die," I say.

Noah cracks a smile, his lips saying one thing while his words say another.

"Perfect," I say. "Will you still be laughing when you visit me at the hospital? It won't be so funny when I'm frothing at the mouth, and you're the one with body fluids on your shoes."

"He was probably just drunk. I'm sure he had one too many Mickeys, and well," Noah points to my shoes. "I'm sorry for laughing. You're just so cute when you're being a germaphobe."

"My shoes, my feet," I sniffled. "This is so gross. Should I get a shot or something? Is there a treatment process?"

Noah lifts my chin with a single finger. His lips find mine and press the softest kiss. He wipes my tears away. Noah leads me to a nearby bench. He slips off his own boots and socks. He uses one sock to wipe down my bare feet and then slips his much larger shoes onto my bare feet.

Noah stands, gathers the dirty shoes and socks, then walks away.

"I don't understand. You gave up your shoes for me? Why?"

Noah looks down at his feet and reaches for my hand.

I've never felt so awkward. Every step is effort, keeping his monster steel-toed boots on. "Thank you," I say.

Noah leans down to kiss me. "You're going to be one of those high-maintenance girls, aren't you?"

I stop walking. Penny is high maintenance.

I am anything but.

I remove Noah's shoes and set them in front of him.

"Stubborn as well, I see," Noah gently jabs me with his elbow. "I'll tell you what, why don't I let you win every other time. We can take turns. Yea?"

I lower my eyes at him, then stick out a hand.

Noah grabs it and pulls me close. "Now, will you put the damn shoes back on?"

"Only if you kiss me."

44

MONA

Blinking back sleep, I momentarily forget where I am. I sit up. My heart is racing.

"You were dozing pretty hard there. I didn't want to wake you," Rhett says. She's curled up on the loveseat holding a book. "Are you okay? You're looking sort of pale."

My bones ache, and a shiver runs from my head to my toes. I reach for a nearby blanket and crawl under it. "I'm a little chilled, is all." I've never needed to acclimate to the weather before.

"Are you sure? I could turn up the heater." Rhett stands.

"No, no. It's fine. Really, I'm fine. I just had a weird vision or memory?"

"A dream?"

Understanding hits. "Right. I guess I've never remembered one of those before. It was horrible."

"You had a nightmare?" Rhett adjust the thermostat and tucks back under a blanket of her own.

"Yeah, I guess it was." I can't shake the lingering feeling. The realness of it all.

"Do you want to talk about it?"

Talk about it?

Maybe.

Telling Rhett everything is a risk I've considered. She's been a confidant, a friend. She's been so kind to me.

Loneliness creeps in, and I instinctually reach for the pause button. Just a few minutes without a watchful eye. Time to feel like myself again.

Even just one minute.

Thirty seconds.

Not much time.

Just a moment.

The pause button doesn't work.

Nothing happens.

My heart tries to crawl out of my throat.

"Are you okay, Mona? Do you need help with something?" Rhett asks.

My body is on fire.

Not the good kind of fire, the way Noah makes me feel.

It's itchy, unstable, and makes me want to crawl out of this skin.

I bolt upright. "I'm fine. Do you mind if I take a shower? I think it would help clear my mind."

"Of course. I was thinking of ordering a pizza. Would you like some?" Rhett asks.

"Yea, that would be fine." I reach into my pockets for money but find them empty. I try to write simple code, and nothing happens.

Penny said, human. I just didn't think it meant without resources. "Of all the planets circling Zazerbolk. You've got to be kidding me."

Rhett's sudden hand on my shoulder startles me. "Why don't you just take a shower. I've got the pizza. You look a bit haggard," Rhett says. "Your smile doesn't reach your eyes, honey. Go take time for yourself. We can talk later."

So I do.

Stepping out of the bathroom after a hot shower, I find Rhett with a freshly delivered pizza. Oliver mentioned the delicacy to me, but I have yet to try it. I'm pleasantly surprised by its warm hearty aroma. The grease on my fingers and the way the hot cheese seems to pull forever are delightful. Rhett even ordered a chocolate brownie pie that nearly sent me into ecstasy-filled oblivion.

"Whenever I feel like the world is working against me, pizza and chocolate do the trick. Doesn't always pull the world back together, but it eases the pain. If only momentarily," Rhett says. "Do you want to talk about whatever is bothering you?"

I take another bite of brownie, biding myself a bit more time.

Rhett raises an eyebrow at me.

"My sister came to see me," I say.

Rhett searches my eyes, "I didn't know she was in town."

"Yeah, well, me either. It was a brief visit. I had to make a tough choice, and I don't know if it was the right one." I pick at the brownie.

Admitting it aloud hurts.

"Why don't you call her?" Rhett says. "Can't you talk it out?"

"It's not that simple."

"May I pry a bit?" Rhett waits a beat for my protest before continuing. "What did she say that put you in this funk? If you think you chose wrong, call her and tell her you have changed your mind. Don't let her win if she's just being mean to make you feel guilty."

My eyes prick, and my throat has gone tight. "She told me," I start, but my voice breaks. Tears fall, and I need a moment to find my breath. "She told me if I continued down this path to prove her wrong, I'd have to make a choice."

Rhett doesn't interrupt. Instead, she listens and nods along.

"I don't know if I'm cut out for this, Rhett. I don't know if I can make it work. I don't know if it's what I wanted but I stayed. I told her I wanted to stay."

"Do you? Want to stay, that is?"

I meet Rhett's dark eyes. "I don't know. I would have jumped at the opportunity to leave a few days ago. But things change. I've changed."

"Noah?"

I shake my head no. "Maybe." I take a quivering breath. "No. I don't know. I am not one of those people who falls for someone and gives up her life. It's more than that. It's the food. My stars above the food here is so good. But it's also how he makes me feel and being here with you." A smile escapes. "I like the way he touches me, the way he looks at me like I'm the only woman in the world. Every small problem fades into the background when he's near. Kissing him makes my mind go blank. And my stars above, he smells so good. I just want to lick him."

Rhett giggles, and it makes me chuckle too. The laughter eases some of the internal pain.

"You know," Rhett says. "It doesn't have to be all or nothing. You can have feelings for someone and still be you."

"I don't know what that means. How do I have feelings for someone if I barely know how to navigate my own thoughts?"

"Welcome to womanhood, Mona. You're allowed to have as simple or as complicated of emotions as you need to have. You can hate something and change your mind the next day, deciding it's not so bad after all. Chocolate three meals a day is acceptable one week out of the month, and lastly, you never have to justify your feelings about someone, who you are, and what you want in life."

"Is there a book where I can learn all these rules? Please don't say the library."

"Don't let your sister get you down. It's not the end all be all, is it?"

I take a sip of water and put off answering.

"Will the world end tomorrow if you don't change your mind right now?" Rhett asks.

I nearly choked on my drink at her words but managed to shake my head no.

"Well then, belly breathe, and tackle it all one step at a time," Rhett says.

I nod, "I've been cut off. I don't know what to do. I have no means of supporting myself." I look away, embarrassed at the confession.

"So then, you'll look for a job first thing in the morning. One step at a time, lady, one step at a time."

The following day, Rhett let me borrow her computer, so I hunt the internet for a job.

But what type of job do I search for?

I thought about my skills and what I could bring to the proverbial table. Initially, I thought about something to do with technology. I would naturally excel at it. I'm a programming queen; I create life, and writing code comes as easy as breathing.

Only, this was all true back home. Here on Earth, it took me more than five solid minutes to figure out how to turn it on. Forget navigating the screens. It was like trying to understand hieroglyphs. In theory, I understand these ancient texts, but in actuality, it's a nightmare.

I went for the old failsafe, "Computer, bring up the admin window."

Nothing happened.

"Computer, bring up a search window."

Again, nothing happened.

"Computer, access the mainframe."

I can't even get the machine to talk to me. How in the world would I manage anything else?

Rhett saves the day. "You press this button here to get to the internet."

"I feel so lost; I don't know if I can do this," I lean back on the couch. "If I can't figure the internet out, how the heck am I going to find a job?"

"Breathe. Why don't you start by getting to the heart of who you are? What makes you happy? What do you live for?" Rhett asks.

The pounding in my head eases, and the caffeine kicks in. "Flora and Fauna."

"Plants?"

"Yes, plants. I know everything there is to know about them. Plants, animals, why didn't this occur to me before?" It's like blinders being removed. I almost forgot what it was I loved the most about being me.

I love my creations.

"Okay then, I don't have a green thumb; it's quite the opposite. I have a black thumb. You'll notice not a solitary shrub in the vicinity."

"You're thumbs look normal to me," I say.

Rhett laughs, "What about working for a florist? You could create beautiful arraignments for anniversaries, birthdays, and weddings. Maybe work as an assistant or something to start?"

"Are you talking about murder?"

"Scratch that." Rhett thinks for a moment. "What about landscaping? Or gardener? There's always the local zoo, they might be hiring for a pooper scooper."

"Sure," is all I can manage. It's not Rhett's fault she's a human. She can't help the hideous error of her human ways.

I'm going to have to learn to make a sacrifice.

"Are you sure?" Rhett asks.

I manage a tight nod. "Yep. I'm sure. Let's do this. I can pick up poop."

Rhett types up a quick resume, fudging some of my previous work histories. When she asks where I last lived, I thought back to the last place I lived on Earth.

"New Zealand?" Rhett asks.

"Yea, in Auckland. Auckland, New Zealand," I say.

"I didn't know you lived there. For how long?"

"Well, I traveled those parts, but that's where I always—" I fake a cough. I shouldn't say sawm home, breeding grounds, or anything that might indicate my past. "—went back to live."

"How long did you say?"

"Fort—" I clear my throat. "—for four years."

Lying is hard.

Rhett looks doubtful. "And before that?"

"Antarctica."

"You lived in Antarctica? Where?"

I frowned, "Does it matter? I've traveled a lot. I've never gotten on well with other humans, so I always prefer to do my own thing. It's never bothered me. I like being far, far away from prying eyes."

"So what brought you to Washington, of all places?"

"Penny."

"Ahh, family."

"Tell me about it."

45

MONA

With a stack of resumes in my bag, I leave Rhett's with the confidence of a human. Rhett assures me that the bag is only pleather and is made to look like leather, but no animal was harmed in the making. Of course, this led to a long discussion about the ethics of eating animals. I'm pretty sure Rhett was quite uncomfortable.

She didn't know how to explain that meat was on our pizza last night and half the other meals she shared with me. While I'm the first to understand the circle of life, creator and all, I'm glad I didn't have to bear witness to the deaths of my food.

Rhett explained that most of the time, all animal parts are repurposed. This time I was uncomfortable. I tried to show her the truth about the leather industry, but the conversation annoyed me. I may disagree with her choices, but the least I can do is try to understand them.

Even if she's wrong.

Ultimately, Rhett carefully skirted the dark topic as quickly as possible. We moved on to another conversation where animal maiming wasn't the headliner.

Rhett dressed me head to toe in black. Not my first choice. She pulled my long mane up and out of my face, calling the whole ordeal professional.

I beg to differ.

As luck would have it, I was offered a job from the first place I went.

Well, sort of.

While my exemplary skills wooed the manager at the local shelter on paper, I was told I'd be given a trial run. I'd be offered the job if the first few days worked out. If not, I'll be hitting the pavement again.

The manager says she's looking for someone to walk the dogs, clean the cages, and care for the various animals in the shelter.

Easy enough.

After all the emotional energy I expelled, I thought finding a job would be much more complicated.

This would be the easiest job in the world. Taking care of my creations sounds like something I'll excel at.

Swinging the apartment door open, I announce, "I got a job!"

"Oh my gosh, really? That's wonderful! Where? Oh, I'm so excited for you," Rhett's words come quickly.

I plop onto the couch and tell Rhett all about my new job. Every word is filled with satisfaction.

Validation never felt so good.

"I'm so proud of you. You're absolutely glowing right now," Rhett seems genuinely happy for me.

"I start tomorrow. They're going to pay me to walk dogs. Like, does it get any better?"

"That sounds amazing. See," Rhett gives me a toothy grin. "I knew you could do it. Should we celebrate? What time do you work tomorrow?"

"I have to be there at nine in jeans and a T-shirt," I say.

"Perfect. Let's celebrate. We'll go to the Horsehide. Poutine and drinks on me."

While Rhett gets her keys, I change into something a little less black. Then the two of us leave with a kick in our step.

When we arrive at the restaurant, we're the only two customers. So we sit at the counter and wait for Shae to return to the front. "Hey, Miss Margrhett, how's life getting on?"

"You're lucky a bar separates us, or I'd turn you into lunch." Rhett pounds a fist into the palm of her hand.

Shea laughs with his whole body. "Oh, you're too cute, Margrhett. Such big words for such a little girl." Shea nods at me, "Who's your friend?"

Rhett examines me with her eyes. "I know she was a bit toasted the last time we were here, but you've met Mona before."

I'm eavesdropping on this conversation, but I'm not about to enter it. Instead, I pretend to examine the various bottles behind the bar instead of explaining why Shae remembers a different me.

"Sure, Mona. But—" Shae scratches his head, leans closer to Rhett, and whispers conspiratorially, "Wasn't Mona Japanese? Cute, with the bangs? I even asked how long she'd been stateside, and she said, just that day."

Rhett glances at me.

"So her name is also Mona?" Shae says.

"Are you drunk? Been smooching the hooch? Battered? Wellied? You can tell me. Do you need me to cover for you if Dom comes around?"

"What? No! What are you talking about?" Shae throws his hands in the air. "None of the above, I swear. Wait, what's battered?"

"You know, like a fish, hiding the good stuff inside. Come on, I expect better of you," Rhett says.

"You're setting your standards too high," Shae winks at Rhett.

Rhett rolls her eyes, unimpressed.

"I'm sorry, Mona," Shae says. "I wish I could remember you. It was a busy night. My bad."

"Don't think twice about it. It happens more often than you'd guess," I say—only a half-truth. If Penny hadn't messed with me, Shae would have remembered me. But alas.

"Can I get you, ladies, a drink?" Shae asks.

"We're celebrating. Mona just got a new job," Rhett beams.

Her pride in me warms my insides.

"Congratulations are in order. Your first drink is on me." Shae turns to Rhett, "You still have to pay." He sticks his tongue out at her.

Rhett copies him, and the two giggle.

"Your usual?" Shae asks.

Rhett nods.

Shae deposits two liquid chocolate drinks in front of us. I hesitate, remembering how sour my stomach and head were the next day. But when the chocolate bouquet hit my nose, I took a sip.

Everything is in moderation.

Two drinks later, Rhett, Shae, and I are in the midst of a giggle fit when Dom walks in. He pulls up a stool next to Rhett.

"Hey beautiful, not that I'm complaining, but you're in here awfully early," Dom pats Rhett's hand.

"Day off, plus," Rhett makes drum noises on the bar, "Mona got a job! So, we're celebrating."

"Congrats to Mona. Where is that sexy cup of hot chocolate hiding?" Dom licks his lips.

"How's it going, Murder Card?" Two martinis in, and I'm feeling wobbly.

"Murder card?" Dom is confused.

"Mona has a weird sense of humor," Rhett says.

"That's Mona? What happened to the other girl?" Dom asks.

"I am the other girl," I blurt.

Dom smiles at me, "Well, I'm happy to have you here. Again. Mona. The next round is on me." Dom winks at Rhett and kisses her on the head before leaving.

"I guess you have one more," Shae starts to make us a third.

"I'm going to step outside and make a phone call," I say. I manage to get off the stool without falling over this time. I even skipped to the front door!

Why do people love these little bricks so much? I pull out the phone, poking me in the side all day.

Noah picks up on the first ring. "You are just the person I was hoping to talk to."

"Yeah?" I say.

"Oh yeah," Noah's voice grows husky.

"I don't know how it's possible, but you just became even more attractive," I say.

I swear I can hear Noah smile. "What are you doing right now?" he asks.

"I'm celebrating with Rhett. We're at the Horsehide."

"What are you celebrating?"

"Didn't you hear? I got a job," I'm practically singing into the phone.

"That's wonderful."

"What time are you off?"

"Well, I'll be done with Mrs. Amy soon. Then I'm free for the afternoon."

"Do you want to come over? Meet me here?"

"Sure, I'll see you soon."

My whole body is smiling. "Good, sooner is better."

Forty minutes later, Noah walks into the restaurant. His presence alone sends my mind whirling. Heat and adrenalin rush through me in waves.

Can things change since the last time we saw one another?

Will he look at me like I'm the only living being in his world?

Is it possible his kisses will still ignite a fire in me?

With shoulders back, Noah strides right up to me. He's wearing two things. A tight gray shirt shows off what's hidden beneath and the confidence of a man who knows exactly what he wants.

My knees part, and Noah's body fills the space between them.

When his mouth finds mine, all of my human anxiety melts away. When he starts to pull away, I kiss him deeper. Holding him to me, wrapping my legs around him. He cups my face, and we break to breathe. I don't let him go.

"I want to devour you right here," Noah whispers.

"I want to let you," I say.

Hungry eyes stare back at me. I release him, but he never stops touching me.

"Why, hello. Mona failed to mention she was dating Construction Worker Ken," Rhett says.

"Who's Ken?" I ask.

Noah laughs, "I'm not in construction, but I think there was a compliment in there?"

Rhett smiles.

"I'm Shae, how's it going, man?"

"Noah."

The two shake hands.

"Can I get you something?"

"Soda?" Noah asks.

"Sure thing."

This time it wasn't the liquid chocolate thawing my insides. I suppose it could be the chocolate. But it's also more than that. It's these people.

These friends.

I roll the word over in my mind like a foreign object.

Friends.

The closest thing to a friend back home is Penny. But, even then, we're at each other's throats most of the time. I didn't know it could feel like this.

Safe.

Noah interrupts my thoughts. "What's on your mind?"

"Hmm?"

"You seem pensive. Like you've slipped into a bubble of your own thoughts," Noah says.

I can't help but grin. "So much excitement. I just—" My eyes are leaking. I wipe the tears away. "I'm happy. I feel so thankful right now."

"Is that what we are? Friends?" Noah's voice drops an octave. It's the same one that made my knees wobble.

"Are we? I like the word, friend. I don't have many of them," I say.

"I'd like to do things to you I wouldn't do to my friends," Noah says.

"Yeah?"

"Oh, hell yeah."

"Can we still be friends and do those things?"

Noah thinks momentarily, "What if I want to be more than friends?"

I kiss him.

Noah catches Shae's attention when we part and pays his tab and mine.

"Want to get out of here?" Noah asks.

I nod.

A faded red double-decker bus with washed-out yellow trim sits on the street corner. Forever pointing to the order window is the statue of an aged fisherman wearing a long blue jacket.

Walking off the wobbles was a good idea.

"This is the best fish n' chips in the whole state," Noah says.

"Oh, Rhett likes chips. They come in so many flavors. I think I'm partial to the jalapeño flavors."

"I wouldn't have pegged you for a spicy gal," Noah says.

"There's a lot you don't know about me."

"I enjoy learning the ins and outs of you."

My face grows hot.

"Also, I hate to break it to you, but this isn't that kind of chip. It's battered fish and French fries. But trust me on this one. It's delicious. And if you don't like it, more for me," Noah smirks.

"Bring it on, Mr. Harvey."

"So formal. I like it," Noah's eyes twinkle, and I wonder briefly if swooning is only something you read about.

It's our turn. Noah orders and then pays for our food. Instead of sitting on white plastic chairs in front of the bus, we walked around a bit.

The fish smells savory, and while I hesitate to consume this, I breathe out my judgments and take a bite. Flavor explodes in my mouth and stops me dead in my tracks.

"It's good, right?" Noah says.

"Oh my gosh. This might be the best thing I've ever had." I take another bite.

"High praise from you," Noah says.

"To be fair, I've really enjoyed most things I've had, so there's quite a bit of competition," I say.

"Why doesn't this surprise me?" Noah licks his lips and steals a salty kiss between bites.

Every bite was deliriously delightful.

Every time I think I can't be any more surprised by this world, someone comes along and proves me wrong.

We finish our food and wander into a large shop. It's deceitfully tiny on the outside. I pause when Noah opens the door for me, unable to step inside.

"What's up? Please don't tell me you hate books," Noah says.

"It's not that. We'll not, really." I can't exactly tell him that the last time I was around books, I deleted his existence. Instead, I reason out the negative from the library experience. "I've always been an avid supporter of forests. I struggle walking into places where trees are sacrificed in great numbers. I'm working through it," I fake a smile.

"Then you'll appreciate the sheer number of books made from recyclables. Especially here of all places. Plus, the stories. They outweigh so much," Noah was really trying.

I shrug.

"I guess you don't read much?" he asks.

"No, I guess not. What I have read wasn't too," I find his eyes "uplifting."

Noah frowns, "I'm sorry.

"Don't be."

"But it breaks my heart. Books are amazing. When I read, I'm no longer wherever this body is. I'm somewhere new, experiencing things I never imagined. Which I know is cliché, but it's a cliché for a reason."

"Overuse?"

"Because it's real. As long as there is imagination, the opportunities are endless." Noah sighs, "Oliver loves to read too. He's always begging for new books. I can't even keep up. As quickly as I bring them home, he seems ready for something new. He's a book monger."

The way Noah talks about books reminds me of how I feel about coding worlds. Uploading is unlike anything I can experience at home. This time, my smile is genuine. "Then we should find him one."

"He'd like that."

Noah takes my hand, and we go in.

46

MONA

We pull up to an older house atop a steeply sloped driveway. Hand in hand, we walk on stones to the front door.

"It's beautiful," I say, utterly enamored with the architecture of Noah's home.

"Thanks, don't let the exterior impress you too much, it's falling apart quicker than Dad can fix it," Noah says.

"You're probably too hard on yourself, I bet it's not as bad as you think it is," I say.

"That's flattering, but the list of issues could wrap around this house twice if I had to write them out. It's easier to list what works than what doesn't." Noah holds the door open to the two-story blue and white Victorian.

The warmth of colors fills the room, softening the house's feel and bringing out its cozy qualities. The entryway opens to the right, where three walls lined with bookcases. They are overflowing with books. Deep maroon peeks through the cracks of years of reading material, hinting at a wall.

I step fully into the space and take in the new smell. This wasn't the same aroma as the library and not quite the bouquet of the bookstore. Instead, Noah's home smelled of fresh laundry, cedar trees, and dusty books. Simply put, it was heavenly. I wander into Noah's office, running my fingers over the titles, walking the room slowly.

When I turn back to the door, Noah is leaning there, one leg crossed over the other, arms overlapped loosely, watching me. A smile plays on his lips.

"You're welcome to read whatever tickles your fancy."

"I'm sorry, I umm—"

"Don't be. I thought you weren't really a fan of books," He says.

"I'm coming around to the idea." I spot a copy of Harry Potter and its subsequent six books. Six? I have the sudden urge to sit and read them.

"Do you want to see the rest of the house?" Noah asks.

"Sure, I'd like that." I take one last look at the collection, then take Noah's hand.

"So you've seen the library, it's my favorite. And down here," Noah holds the swinging door open to the kitchen. "This is the kitchen. Pretty standard, except for the leaking faucet. I like to call him Bart."

"You've named the faucet Bart?"

"Yes. You see Bart here, he never shuts up. Listen." Noah leans his head toward the damp sink. "You hear him saying hello?"

My heart beats twice.

Thump, thump.

It starts double time, trying to leap out of my chest.

Noah, smiles.

I breathe out my disappointment. For a moment, I thought Noah could talk to the water. My heart falters when I realize it's a joke.

"What's through there?" I ask.

"That's the dining room, where Olli and I eat at least one meal a day together. I think it's important to have regular time together. When he's at school or with Hazel, then this is where the magic happens. Homework, eating, he used to play with his trains in the corner there," Noah points, "after school. I'd pick him up from daycare, and Dad would still be at work."

"Are you good at school? What do you want to be?"

"I think about being a teacher someday. I want to go to school and get an English degree. Maybe I will write a book myself or become an editor. I don't know yet. I just know I love to read. Maybe it's the escapism." Noah shrugs.

"I can see you as a teacher. Oliver is brilliant for such a young one. He must get it from you."

"Well, I don't know about that," Noah smiles softly. "But thank you."

Noah and I continue to walk through the house. He points out various items that need attention. He was right, the home is far from perfect, but somehow it feels perfect to me. It's a home.

It's Noah and Oliver's home. It's where they live and make memories. It feels like part of the existence in a way. I never thought I'd find a house so emotionally moving. This place breathes life the same way I do.

Noah leads me upstairs, each creaking under our weight. The banister is loose.

"It's on my list of things to fix," he says.

"I think it's all wonderful. I can feel you in this house."

Noah's eyebrows raise.

I continue to follow him.

"This here is Oliver's room," Noah opens the door.

Oliver has long curtains pulled back, and his telescope aims out the window, spying on the cosmos. The ceiling of his bedroom was covered in small green glowing stars. I can make out familiar constellations in the sky of his bedroom. Orion, Cassiopeia, and the Big Dipper were most prominent.

Noah shows me the bathroom, his dad's room, and the spare bedroom. Then he stops in front of the last door upstairs.

"This one," he points to it with his thumb, "Is mine."

My insides begin doing summersaults. Being human is filled with all kinds of unexpected surprises. The biggest one for me is what lies beyond this door. I think of touching Noah. My mouth goes dry.

I lick my lips.

Noah waits for me to open the door.

So, I do.

It's a modest room, with a bed centering one wall. There was nothing special about the space. Except it was Noah's. That makes it special to me. I reach for Noah, pulling him closer to me by the hem of his shirt.

He takes a step, "Can I kiss you?"

"Yes please."

Noah leans in and his lips meet my own.

Fire.

I slip my hands under his shirt and onto the small of his back.

Noah pulls away. "We don't have to do anything you're not ready for."

I drop my hands from his body and close the door, affording us privacy.

I turn to him and pull his shirt off, "Is this, okay?"

Noah nods and finds my lips again.

A warming sensation moves through my body, flames licking my insides. The only way to quell it is to be closer to him. I want my skin on his. I want him.

Kissing Noah's neck, produces a moan I wasn't expecting. I slowly make my way up to his ear and suck on it.

Noah shudders. "May I?" he tugs at my top, hands on my belly.

I help him remove it.

Noah leaves a trail of kisses from my neck to my stomach.

My head is fuzzy. I am a fusion of nerve endings and desire. I pull him up and find his eyes. "Noah?"

Noah kisses my neck softly. "Yes?"

"I've never done this before."

He removes his lips from my body, and a throbbing tingle remains where he's touched me. "We can stop. I don't want to do anything that you're not comfortable with," Noah says caressing my cheek.

"I've never done this before," I hold up a finger so he won't interrupt me. "I'd like to have sex with you."

Noah's brows shoot up. "You do?" Noah's voice trembles.

I nod, "Very much."

"Are you sure?" Noah's voice is husky.

I find his eyes, and my legs wobble. Heat pulsing off us. "I've never been surer of anything in my life," I slowly crawl backward onto his bed and entice him to come join me.

Noah removes his pants. He grabs a small square foiled thing from his bedside table, and holds it up, "Condom." Noah lays next to me, our body overlapping. Legs intertwined.

Kissing and tasting on one another, leaving no skin untouched.

Noah is fire, and I melt.

His touch sends warmth between my legs and suddenly I understand what all the fuss is about. I breath him in, feeling electricity running through my limbs.

I'm ready for this.

I want this.

I want him.

I rouse, nestled into Noah's side. My arm is draped across his chest, his is wrapped around my body.

"Mmm…" is all I manage.

Noah kisses the top of my head ever so gently. "I didn't want to wake you."

"I don't mind. I know you have things you need to do." I don't want to move. I want to lay here in Noah's arms forever. "I can go. I have to work in the morning. Oh, stars above." I sit up. "Is it morning? Did I sleep all night?"

"You don't have to leave. Please, my love, lay back down. I'm not ready to let you go yet." Noah tenderly tugs at my arm, and I melt into him again. "That's better. We have a bit of time before Hazel drops Oliver off and Dad gets home."

I stiffen, "Oh?" There is a pang of—jealousy?

"It's not morning. It's only six-thirty. I'm not ready to leave this moment yet. I," Noah exhales and smiles down at me. "I want to be here with you a while longer."

"When will he be home?"

"Around seven or seven thirty." Noah glances at the clock on his nightstand.

"So we have a bit of time?" I flash him a wicked grin.

Noah's eyes smolder as I move on top of him.

Noah changes into a fresh shirt, and I watch him through the bathroom mirror. I comb out my hair and wash up in the sink. The doorbell rings, echoing through the house, breaking the spell cast upon me.

Noah jogs downstairs ahead of me. By the time I finish, he's holding a bag and wearing an ear-to-ear grin.

"I ordered some food. Thought you might be hungry," Noah says.

"What would ever give you that idea? And when did you find the time?"

Noah steals a kiss before leading me to the kitchen. He produces several boxes of takeout. Before either of us can get a proper mouthful, the front door opens.

"We're home. Noah?" a woman's sing-song voice rings through the home.

"Hey, Noah, it was amazing," Oliver says.

"Of course, it was." Noah goes to the cupboard and pulls out another plate. "Hazel, you staying for dinner? There's plenty."

"Uh," Hazel hesitates when she spots me.

"Please stay," I say. "I'd love to hear all about your day."

Hazel physically relaxes. "Okay, sure. Grab me a plate."

Noah gets two plates, passing one to Oliver and Hazel. "So Olli, tell me all about it. I'm dying to hear the play-by-play."

"It was amazing! We saw Venus and the moon. Did you know it has a face? There's a man in the moon, Noah. How crazy is that?" Oliver continues to regale us with his adventure at the university. Hazel has a friend in the science department who has the same telescope as Oliver. She took Oliver to see the stars and get a quick hands-on lesson for his new telescope. He also got to use the much bigger and more impressive university telescope. He even came home with printed photos of the constellations they saw.

Looking over the pictures, I feel a sense of pride. My obsession with planets, with stars fills Oliver with such joy. Of course, it was inadvertent, but it still makes me beam. "It sounds like you two had an amazing time," I winked at Oliver. "I'm so happy for you. Hazel is so kind to show you off to her friend."

"Thanks again," Oliver smiles shyly. "Hey, Mona, did Noah show you my telescope?"

I smile, "No, I was waiting for you to show me, duh."

Oliver throws his head back with an exaggerated sigh. He jumps up and runs upstairs. I follow.

"Professor X," Oliver tilts his head, "okay, that's not his real name, but he said I could call him Professor X."

"I don't know what that means. Were A, B, and C taken?"

"As in X-Men?"

"Still drawing a blank, kid."

Oliver shrugs. "Never mind. Anyway, he showed me how to set up my telescope. The right and proper way. Hold on a second, I'll get the moon."

"Do you keep him safe somewhere?" I ask.

"What?"

"The moon. Is he in your pocket?"

Oliver laughs, "No, the moon," he points outside. "Up there."

"Ahh, well, let's have it then. I'm dying to see all you've learned."

Oliver fiddles with the telescope, "Look, there he is."

"The moon?"

"No, the man."

"Oh, let me see," I say, swapping places with Oliver and gazing at my creation. "I bet it's a clear enough night, we could probably find Venus."

"I don't remember how to find her," Oliver says with a tinge of sadness.

"That's okay, Olli, I know exactly where she's at." I moved the eyepiece, and within a few moments, we were gazing at the bright planet.

A pang of longing pulls at my insides. Homesickness washes over me.

"What's wrong, Mona?" Oliver asks.

I shrug. "I miss my home."

"Out there?" Oliver points to the sky.

I could only nod with a tinge of fear that Penny would take Oliver away from me too. "I get a little homesick from time to time. But I'm okay."

"Your home isn't like this one, is it?" Oliver is watching me closely.

I think about how to answer. "Well, I have a sister and a job. But you're right, it's a lot different than here."

"Can you go back?"

I nod. "Yes, but I can never return here when I go home."

"Why?"

"It's just the way it has to be."

"I don't want you to go anywhere, Mona. I like you too much."

"I like you too much, too, Oliver."

There's a shared silence.

Oliver breaks it. "Mona?"

"Yeah?"

"If you do have to go home," he sighs, "I would understand. I'd miss my dad and brother too much if I left. I would understand if you missed your sister too much and wanted to go back."

I reach out and envelop Oliver in a hug. My throat grew tight at the idea of leaving. I take a breath and let it out, then let him go. "You're an amazing little person. Do you know that?"

Oliver rolls his eyes at me. "Yeah, yeah. Noah says the same thing."

"What do I say?" Noah is standing at the door.

How long has he been there? I feel the blood drain from my face. I've never outright lied to Noah, but I haven't been too honest about my situation.

Noah's smile doesn't reach his eyes. Instead, his arms are crossed at his chest, and I feel distant.

"You always say how amazing I am," Oliver says.

"That's because you are," Noah says.

Noah looks just like Oliver. I suppose it's probably the other way around. Doesn't matter. I just want to capture those similarities forever. Bottle them away so I can look at them later, long after they're gone, and nothing more than a fading memory.

The sudden realization that I would outlive them into infinity sends a chill down my back and deep into my bones.

"Maybe Penny will have to come for a visit, then she will see how amazing you are, too," Noah says.

"I'd like nothing more," I say. "I don't know if it's possible. We've had a bit of a row. I don't know if I can fix it. But I'm hopeful in time."

"I'm sure you'll find a way to fix it. Family is important," Oliver says.

"I know. I don't know if things are so easily fixed. It might take a sacrifice on my part. I'm just not sure how to give that up just yet." I smile. "I thought I'd see how it went for a while before I made any drastic decisions. I want to make things right, but I can't give up my end of this fight just yet."

"Noah says life is too short to have regrets," Oliver says, glancing between Noah and myself.

"I couldn't agree more." I pull Oliver in for a side hug. "Your brother is a smart man. Just don't tell him. It might go straight to his head."

Noah chuckles, easing the tension I felt pulsing off of him.

We head back downstairs, and Hazel is at the door. "I was just going to head home. Have a good night, Olli. I'll see you tomorrow."

"Hazel, can I get a ride home? I have to work early. I should probably head out."

"Uhh, sure." Hazel glances at Noah.

Noah gives me a kiss goodbye.

"I had a wonderful afternoon. Thank you," I say.

Noah strokes my face. "I'll call you later."

To say that the car ride home is awkward would be an understatement. There is no radio and the pressure to say something grows heavy. It pulses in the air until I can't take it anymore.

"I don't think I had the chance to tell you how much I appreciate your kindness."

Hazel glances at me.

"You're an amazing aunt," I clear my throat. "Oliver speaks the world of you."

Hazel only stares straight ahead.

Being uncomfortable is putting things kindly.

"I saw your name on a book back at the house," I was careful not to mention Noah by name. "You said you wanted to be a writer. I didn't realize you'd already published something."

"Would you stop?" Hazel's words are ice.

"What?"

"Would you please stop trying to be my friend? You know I have feelings for him. I know, you know. I'm the one who told you. I'm not dumb."

I let Hazel's words tumble around in my head.

"Look, I know I'm the one who made it weird, okay. But if you are sticking around, please don't make it worse. We don't have to be friends. More importantly, please don't tell Noah about any of this." Hazel's words are sharp and unexpected. "I don't know what your plans are, but don't hurt him."

It's this moment when everything comes together. "You don't want me to tell Noah you've bottled your feelings about him. You're afraid that it would ruin the balance of things? Do you feel small? I don't want that."

Hazel breaks the car suddenly, and I'm jolted forward. She stares at me with anger and fear.

"Hazel, I would never do anything to hurt you."

"You've already done that."

"I would never intentionally go out of my way to bring you unease. I don't want to hurt anyone. I'd like to be your friend."

"You don't get it." Hazel slams her hands on the wheel. "Oliver told me about you."

My heart pounds into my throat. My pulse rings loudly in my ears. I close my eyes, trying not to pass out. "I hope it was only good things," I manage.

"We were looking at the constellation Orion. Oliver says, *Mona knew it would be worshiped by the Egyptians before she created them.*"

I don't speak.

"I told him that was a funny thing to say. Why would he say that about you? I said Mona didn't create Egyptians, and she didn't create Orion." Hazel waits for a beat before continuing. "Do you want to know what Oliver said next?"

I look away, not sure if I do.

"Oliver says, *you know that's true. Humans were more of Penny's doing, but Mona helped. And mostly, she created the planets anyway. But she knew it would be special. Mona knows a lot.*"

"Kids say the funniest things don't they," I say.

It's about all I can manage.

"I thought the same thing, you know. Until I saw you today. Sitting in the kitchen chair."

I racked my brain. Had I said anything weird? What had I done?

"Noah and Oliver didn't notice the difference, but I did. I see you for what you really are, Mona. Ha! Mona. Mona what? Do you even have a last name? Is *Mona* even your real name?"

"I'm not sure what you're talking about."

Hazel starts to drive again. She's picking up speed. Erratic at best. "Don't lie to me. Are you here to hurt us?"

"I don't know what you're talking about. I'm not trying to hurt anyone."

"Stop lying!"

Hazel jerks the wheel, and I snap against the belt. She takes a corner sharply, and I hold to the side of the car. My head thrums with the speed of my pulse.

Never in my life have I wished to press pause more than this moment. I don't want to die at the hands of this woman. I'd been so sure it would have been a human malady, murder never even crossed my mind.

"Tell me how you did it?"

"Will you please slow down?" I say.

Hazel speeds up.

"Okay, okay. But you'll need to explain what you're talking about. I don't understand."

"This! All of this, how did you change it? Which is the fake? Is your British accent or the American one? The short red hair and the bluest eyes I've ever seen. Now look at you. Your hair is long and black as coal. Your voice is different, even your eyes changed to green, and no one seems the wiser. It's more than that, though. Your nose was long before, and you were stumpy looking. Where did your freckles go?" Hazel jumps a curb on our next turn. "I was ready to brush off Oliver's comments until I saw you sitting at the kitchen table."

I can't find words.

My mind is in full panic.

"At first, I was convinced Noah had moved on again. I felt sorry for myself, like he could take notice of every other damn girl in the world, but he couldn't see me. I've been here the whole time. I cradled him when he lost Rhi. I'm the one who cares for his brother. It doesn't matter how much I love him, he'll never see me as anything more. But it wasn't that at all. It was you. You changed."

I suck in air, but it goes nowhere. Instead, it dissipates and never reaches my lungs.

Didn't Shae and Dom both mention something about my appearance? They'd let it go so quickly that I didn't give it much thought.

"Hazel," I say, but it comes out weaker than I intended. Barely an audible whisper.

"What? What can you say that would possibly explain any of this?"

Stars above Penny. "I can't. There's nothing I can say. Please just trust I only have the best of intentions."

"Why should I trust you? You've lied to all of us."

"No. I have never lied to you, Noah, or Oliver. I've always been honest. I've just left a few details out. Details that don't matter."

"They matter to me. I'm betting they matter to Noah too."

Hazel grows quiet. Her threat lingers in the air as she pulls into Rhett's apartment.

I'm too afraid to move.

Afraid of what she'll say.

Do.

"If you hurt Noah or Oliver, I will hunt you down. I will make your life a living hell. I will personally see to it that you can never hurt another person again," Hazel's words are laced with venom. "Do you understand? I will never rest until you've paid interest on your actions."

A chill shoots down my back and reaches every nerve in my body. "You have my word."

"Prove to me your word means more than just empty promises. Because right now, it's as good as shit."

I glance at Hazel one last time before quietly slipping out of the car. I watch as she drives into darkness.

47

MONA

It was a sleepless night. The kind of night where time is nothing but a plague, trapping its prey inside a hunting eternity.

The alarm goes off, alerting me that it's an acceptable hour to rise. I paced the apartment for forty minutes until Rhett hurled a pillow at me and told me to go back to bed.

Hazel knew the truth.

There's no denying it.

Penny warned me what might happen if I was caught as anything more than human.

I want Penny to be wrong.

I want to wake up from this nightmare like it never happened.

Rewind the clock and do things differently.

I shower and try to find comfort in the hot water. It's become a favorite pastime of mine. After I slipped on the only pair of jeans I owned, thankful I'd already coded all my clothes to fit properly.

Rhett is curled up on the couch with her pillow. "So, you were in a mood last night. Everything okay with Noah?"

"I don't know," I say, shaking my head.

"That's it? That's all you're giving me? What don't you know?" Indignance thick in her tone.

I half smile, "I just don't know. Things with Noah were," I can feel my face go red, "perfect."

"And?"

"Then Hazel showed up. I thought things were going fine, but then she made it clear she didn't like me. It was just weird. I felt this shift between Noah and me, and I can't explain any of it. I'm so confused."

"This is what kept you clucking around the apartment like an elephant all night?"

"Elephants don't cluck."

Rhett rolls her eyes at me.

"Sorry."

"You're just lucky I don't work this morning."

I plop down next to Rhett. She moves her arms and allows me to lay on her lap. She plays with my hair, and the unexpected intimacy brings tears to my eyes.

If I leave Earth, I'd say goodbye to more than Noah.

"Do you love him?"

My chest tightens. "I like him. I think I could maybe even feel love for him one day. But I don't think I understand what love is. My understanding of this complex emotion is limited in comparison to its vastness. What is love anyway?" I bury my face into Rhett's lap.

"Love can be complex. It can be intimate or friendly. Unconditional love for someone means that no matter what they do, you care for them without conditions. Despite their greatest flaws, that love doesn't waver. You might not always like them, but you love them just the same. Despite your differences, I imagine Penny loves you this way," Rhett strokes my head and kisses my temple.

I sigh.

"It doesn't have to be complex, though. Love is how the sun feels on your skin after a cold day. It's the smell that rouses happy memories long forgotten. Love is the feeling you get when you see your favorite person. Love is feeling safe. It can be complicated, Mona, but it doesn't have to be."

"Thank you. For everything you've been to me. I never expected to come here and meet so many amazing people. Thank you for being my friend." I kiss Rhett on the cheek before leaving the apartment for work.

Could love be so simple?

I wish I could be more sure.

Deb, my new boss, welcomes me in the door with a smile and bubbly personality. "You made it! I was hoping you wouldn't bail on me and decide you'd agreed to only the worst possible job like the last two people I hired," a flash of anger crosses her eyes, but it leaves as quickly as it arrives.

"The worst job?" I ask, suddenly unsure of what I'd agreed to.

"Worst. Best. It's all subjective now, isn't it? The point is that you're doing something positive for the community and these animals. You get a paycheck and leave work feeling accomplished and like your actions make a difference every day."

I paste on a smile to match Deb's energy. "I'm happy to be here. I want nothing more than to help."

"I'd give you a tour, but it will have to wait a while. I have potential adoptees waiting for me. For now, why don't you wander a little and familiarize yourself with the pooches. Don't open their cages until someone can show you how we do things.

"Cages?"

"Yes, there should be some treats against the wall just as you walk in. Sometimes buying their love with food is how to ease into the job. No more than one each, though. I shouldn't be too long.

"I'm confident making friends with all animals will be the one thing I'll excel at," I say, waving as I head toward the door labeled dogs.

I enter the room and am bombarded with barking, growling, and one howling dog. The noise was overwhelming at first. Forgetting about the treats, I walk down the corridor of dogs. I stop at one and read the sign on her door.

Hi, I'm Doris. I'm nine years young. I'm a Pitbull mix, and my favorite thing to do is play fetch. I'm good with children but bad with cats. So you should have a cat-free environment for me to call home. I really just want to snuggle and find my forever home.

Why do I get the feeling Doris didn't write this.

I squat to see the dog behind the metal contraptions. The room is pungent with urine, feces, and an overwhelming wet dog smell. It is something I'd noted humans didn't understand. If they'd only let the dogs roll in the Earth when wet, that smell would disappear, replaced with a more natural aroma.

"Are you okay, Doris? What have they done to you? I thought this was a rescue clinic."

I wait for Doris to communicate her feelings, to tell me it's not so bad or that she enjoyed the cement floor and rag she had to sleep on.

Doris is silent.

I reach through the cage, trying to drown out the noise, smell, and devastating sense of confusion that crashes down around me. No amount of coaxing would make Doris budge.

I move to the next cage, where two smaller pooches yipp incessantly.

Neither spoke.

"My name is Mona. Do you recognize me?"

Their signs read Eyven and Grace.

I crossed the narrow hallway to a rottweiler who wasn't barking. I approached the cage. But nothing.

Was it me?

Does a lack of human sleep prevent me from talking to animals?

Like an ice water bath, I realized it was me.

I'm human.

"It's me, isn't it?" deflated, I hang my head.

The rottweiler's eyes conveyed the sadness I felt.

"I hear you, girl," I say.

"Please," I beg, "Even just one of you? I made you. I gave you life. Speak to me!" I'm crying. "PENNY," I'm on my knees, pleading. Every silent moment rips further into my heart.

The sound of mixed cries echo in the cold chamber.

"Mona, are you okay?"

I look up and find Deb with two eager women close behind her.

"I'm," but I can't finish my thought. My voice is shaking.

"You've been crying." Deb reaches a hand out and helps me up. "Did one of them bite you? Are you hurt? Should I grab the first aid kit?" Deb frantically looks for signs of aggression.

"I'm not hurt. I'm sorry. I don't know what's wrong with me. I think," I say, trying to stall. "I don't want to lose this job. But I have to go."

Staying here would taunt me.

These are my babies.

Caged.

Silent.

"I have to go."

48

MONA

When I started running, I couldn't stop. I ran until I found myself outside of Summer Grove Retirement Community. I stood there, tears staining my face, gasping for air, and a sharp, excruciating pain in my side. I push through the ache, wipe my face, and go inside. I climb three floors to Agnes's apartment.

I take three calming breaths, then knock.

There's a muffled sound coming from inside.

I knock again.

Agnes opens the door an inch, peeking through the chain. She huffs, then shuts the door. I hear the sound of metal unhooking, and the door opens wide.

"Can I come in?"

"I don't know. Can you?" Agnes seems better.

"Yes, thank you." I walk in and find a seat on the small couch.

"Would you like a cup of tea or coffee?"

"I've never had tea. May I try one, please?"

Agnes makes us two cups of herbal tea and sits across from me. Waiting.

"Thanks for the infusion. It's lovely. It's spicy. No, not hot spicy but filled with spices spicy," I stumble over my words.

"It's pumpkin spice with a dollop of pumpkin creamer. I know a guy," she waves away her words. "Why are you sitting here in my apartment?"

The pros and cons of telling Agnes weigh on me.

What could Penny do?

She could pause the world. Maybe I would pause with it. Perhaps I wouldn't. I feel desperation bursting inside of me.

Agnes already knew too much.

"Well?"

"I was hoping that we could talk. Openly?"

Agnes tilts her head. "I'm listening."

When I open my mouth, the story inside of me vomits into existence. Once the words start, they don't stop. I told Agnes about my encounter with Penny and what Hazel said about Oliver. I told her about how Hazel noticed the physical changes. And worst of all, I can't hear the animals anymore.

"Did you tell Oliver about your—uniqueness?" Agnes asks.

"No, that's just it. I never told him anything. I don't believe in this human thing called lying. Telling such stories never proves to be anything but bigger problems down the road. I've omitted parts of my life, but I've never lied about myself.

"Could he have gathered that you're an alien from your non-omissions?"

A wave of shame engulfed me, leaving my cheeks ablaze with embarrassment. I'd chosen not to correct Agnes's assumptions. It wasn't lying if I didn't correct her.

Right?

It's saving Agnes from an even bigger, potentially life-threatening truth. Could Agnes's heart handle that? I refuse to be the cause of her death.

"I have never led Oliver to believe anything. In fact," instantly, a flash of inspiration struck me, a lightbulb switching on. "He's tapped into the glitch."

I know it like I know my own name.

"What's the glitch?"

"It's a break in our software coding. At first, we thought about fixing it. Ultimately we decided it wasn't hurting anyone, so we left well enough alone. Oliver is tapping into the glitch. It's how he knows about me," I say.

Agnes stares at me, her eyes devoid of understanding.

"Think of it like a pair of magic sunglasses. Oliver looks normal, but his sunglasses are magic. They let him see the world for what it truly is."

"Well, I'll be," Agnes says. "Are you talking about computer glasses? What did you do?"

I shake my head, pressing on with this revelation. "I bet that's why I looked the same to him. He saw me the way I always was instead. But—"

"But what?" Agnes asks.

"I can't remember if our findings said anything about the human ability to tap into the glitch, having genetic markers."

"I'm sorry dear, but you had me up until you started talking computers. It was never something I cared to learn much about."

"I think Oliver has always seen me. But I just wonder if Noah has seen me too?"

"Noah has eyes for only you. I'm not sure how he could see you any other way."

Agnes's words are kind, and yet they still rip at me.

"I don't know why. What makes me any more special than—Hazel? Or anyone else, for that matter? My old life aside. He doesn't know about it. Why does he make me feel both at ease and like I'm wound up tight? And what if I can't stay? What then? What is the point of any of it?" I blow out a breath, deflated.

Agnes is laughing. "How can you love the taste of one coffee and despise another? That's all we are, honey. Sometimes we're exactly what another person needs at that point in their life, or vice versa. Even their whole life, and you get lucky. And sometimes, we're just blowing in the wind, tasting life as we go. Leaving little bits of ourselves along the way. It's not always about longevity, but more about how it all tasted while we were there."

Agnes pats my hand and holds my eyes with her own. "My dear one, the point is that we learn to love; we learn to experience this life, to take it all in. We embrace the idea that we only get to live this life once. Whatever you believe comes after this is up to you. But there is no doubt you only get to live this life one time. So quit fussing about all the what-ifs. Either do or do not. But get off the pot. No point in fussing around. You love him, or you don't. You can love him and go home. Or love him and stay. These choices are independent of one another. So you go home, say goodbye, or stick around and see how it plays out. Doesn't matter to me much either way."

"I like you too," I say with a smile.

"I've been around long enough to know getting rid of you won't be easy. I have a feeling even when I kick the bucket, you'll be haunting me for lifetimes to come."

I stiffen.

"Thought so," Agnes says.

"I can't hear them anymore," my words are a whisper in the wind.

"The voices?"

"They're gone."

"The voices in your head are gone? I don't think that's a reason to complain, honey," Agnes chuckles heartily, unable to contain her amusement.

"That's not what I mean."

"What *did* you mean?"

"I used to hear them all. The trees and blades of grass, squirrels, and elephants. All of Earth's inhabitants."

"You can—" Agnes glances around the apartment and pointes to a Ficus in the corner. "—talk to that?"

I take in the plant. "She's not getting enough water or sunlight. You should move her to that corner," I point at a window, "and you probably need to double the water you're feeding her. She would love some fresh mulch as well."

"The plant told you all that?" A look of complete shock crosses Agnes's face, her jaw slackening.

"I can't hear them anymore. She didn't say anything. I'm just really good at knowing what plants need to thrive. I've lost my ability to communicate with this whole part of me. It's like losing a limb."

"If you're crazy, that's okay with me. Healing someone with magic? Sure. I'll bite. Even changing your physical appearance, why not. But you talk to plants and animals? I thought you said you don't lie," Agnes says crossly.

"I could do more than talk to them, Agnes. I could heal your plant before," I look at my hands, limp and lacking. "Before I became one of you."

"Human?"

"Human."

"So why did you do it?" she asks.

"I told you why."

"No, you told me you weren't ready to leave. I'm asking you why you gave it all up. Why did you choose to live as a human when you had all the theoretical abilities of a god?"

I couldn't answer.

"What is it, Mona? Spit it out already. Why did you decide to become a human? Was it to study us?"

"No," I shake my head firmly.

"Was it for Noah?"

"I don't know. Maybe?"

"Maybe isn't good enough. Why did you do it? Was it to prove something to your sister?"

"I don't have to prove anything to her. I'm more than capable alone," I lean back in my seat.

"Oh, so that's it then, eh? She got under your skin," Agnes smirks.

"What?"

"Penny got under your skin, and you couldn't back down from a fight. Let me guess, you never back down from a challenge. I bet the only reason you're here is that you were too damn bullheaded to say no," Agnes spat her words.

"I'm not a bull. I can say no to her. I have said no to her. Plenty of times."

"Really?" Agnes says, full of skepticism. "Like when?"

"Like, when she asked about—or when I—like," I trail off. "You know what, Agnes?"

Agnes fixed her gaze on me, her expression void of any emotion.

"I don't have to explain myself to you."

"You're the one who came here seeking answers from an old woman who's got one leg in the grave. You're only here because you can't tell a secret to someone who already knows. I'm no spring chicken."

"No, you're a hell of a lot punchier than you were the first time I met you."

"Oh, you mean when I had the memory of a goldfish?"

"Sorry," I try not to laugh.

"Don't be sorry. I still don't know how I feel about it. I mean, reruns were much more interesting before."

My face crumples.

"I'm kidding. Mostly," Agnes relaxes. "Look, here's the thing, darling. You can sit here and fret about all of it. You can cry, and you can be sad. I'm with you. That's a human reaction. But then, when you're done eating your bag of wallow, you need to pull up your big girl panties and put yourself back out there. Either you decide you can live without your abilities, as a human. Or you go back. Maybe try again when you're better prepared for this sort of thing. When you're a little older and have more life experience.

"Is there such a thing as being more prepared?"

"No, of course not. That's not the way life works."

"Yeah, I was afraid you'd say that."

"Well, there's one good thing that comes from this mess you've created," Agnes says.

I perk up, "Oh?"

"Yes. Apparently, I got a knee replacement. If I get caught in the woods, the timber limbs can tickle my butt."

This makes me laugh a lot.

Agnes has a spark.

"I'd like to see that," I say.

Agnes stood up, tugged up her pant legs, and squatted.

49

MONA

Walking was always an enjoyable venture. It never felt lonely. Earth had started to remember what it means to be in harmony with living things. Trees spoke of their fondness, and I would send them energy to brighten their day and prolong their lives. Passing wildlife whispered their good mornings and well wishes. They spoke of their homes, the sky above, and the humans in their stratosphere.

The only sound that echoes in my mind is the pounding of my beating heart. Thoughts haunt me, and I can't escape myself for even a moment.

Penny is nowhere to be found while I'm left swinging between rage and anguish.

The mere idea of never experiencing the sound of my creations again feels almost too heavy a burden. Should I interpret this feeling as a sign that I should go?

Say goodbye?

The playground where Maple lives is bereft of life. No one comes or goes. No sounds of the living and breathing that surround me.

I brush my palm upon its bark. The world gradually fades into a blur as more tears fall to my cheeks.

I'm so tired of crying.

The world is silent.

Maple is silent.

I wipe away my tears and reach for the tree, climbing the bark and using the knots to push myself up. Inch by inch, I pull myself up into the heart of the Maple's branches.

Panting.

Nearly falling twice.

But when I reach that spot, I look out onto the small park, curled against the trunk.

The most miraculous thing happened. The Maple tree's branches coil around me in a slow, comforting embrace, creating a soothing cradle for my body. I lean back, reassured by her silent care.

Somehow, I know everything will be okay.

50

PENNY

My gaze remains fixed on Mona, who slumbers quietly within the embrace of the Maple tree. I pause to prevent neighboring humans from stumbling across Mona in this abnormal state. After all, Mona didn't force the tree to hold her. Instead, the Maple loves her so much that she holds Mona on her own.

After our fight, I couldn't stomach the thought of facing Mona. To tell the truth, I still don't know how Mona would react. Sometimes it's better to put some distance between us.

Settling down on a bench nearby, I fix my gaze on the tree. I am engrossed in the reflections about the profound effect on lives while navigating the human realm.

Somehow, I convinced myself that what Mona was doing was different than anything I'd ever done.

Only it isn't.

Anguish and agony drove me with fear, leading the charge to hide a human child.

My human child, in the belly of another.

My love child, my daughter, was born six months later. She lived a life free of me.

Free of Mona.

Free of all pain I could have inflicted, however, unknowingly.

Free of any happiness she could have brought to my life.

Earth forever provides my family shelter.

At first, it pained me to find her. To know such a beautiful, wonderful, kind child and remember, I walked away from her out of fear. It simultaneously tore at me while bringing tears of joy to see Kalidasha in her eyes, her soft smile, and her quick replies. She was full of wonder, and her laugh pierced my soul a thousand times over. My heart ripped from my chest, bled into infinity.

I know sorrow intimately.

As time passed, I found comfort in knowing I'd left my mark on the world. Without knowing such sorrow, I would have never appreciated the kindness that came forth from generation after generation. One child at a time, my ancestry was easier to follow than I ever anticipated.

After Kalidasha passed, I went back, searching for his soul. I was determined to reunite with the celestial body his soul would inhabit next. This man changed my world for the better. It was, is, my greatest dream.

Only I failed.

I didn't have the technique or tools to scout a person after life. I was too afraid to tell Mona, to own my mistakes, and risk humanity along the way.

To risk my family.

I'm haunted by the knowledge that Kalidasha's life would have been different without me. Would he have lived if I walked away and let humans live their lives without interference? What would he say?

I wish I could hear his voice one last time.

Every morning I learned to let the loss go. Little by little, the weight of my loss became easier to bear. Every time I saved Earth from Mona, I did it for my daughter. For my daughter's daughter and the generations that came after. I did it for the love I carry for Kalidasha.

I saved Earth for Mona too. My sister may never appreciate what humanity could bring her if she fails to open her heart to them.

Mona deserves love.

She deserves a world of love. I'm just afraid she'll never truly know what it means.

Taking away Mona's abilities as the creator of life was not done lightly. It was a decision made from a profound love for my sister. Her abilities manifested in ways I never anticipated. I'd deduced that humans saw her differently based on their ancestry and innermost desires. By the time I figured out how to remove her abilities, she'd made several friends.

Kalidasha was the greatest love of my life. I only wished even a fragment of that for Mona. I wanted to give my family a fighting chance.

They make mistakes, that's what humans do. But they adapt, and I live in awe of them.

Hours pass, and I watch Mona sleep. She has no haunting dreams or worries of her existence as a human. She has no fears about the passing of friends or the shortness of their lives. Mona thinks nothing of how long her human life would feel or if she'd choose to leave and live on without them.

While Mona sleeps, I can't help but think about all the mistakes I've made.

My biggest mistakes brought my most profound sorrow. But generations later, a piece of my past befriended Mona with open arms. She took her in and cared for her like one of her own.

Margrhett Mati is the direct descendant of my love affair with Kalidasha.

51

MONA

When I rouse from my tree branch cocoon, I am released to the ground as gently as I'd given life to my resting place. I pull out my phone and am surprised to see so little time has passed. Yet I feel rested.

Have I slept more than a day?

I brush the sleep from my eyes, stretch to the sky, and wrap my arms around the tree. "I can't hear you but know I'm still here. Thank you, friend."

I let her go and walk away.

Eventually, I'm back at the animal shelter, ready to give it another try. I can only hope Deb is in a forgiving mood. If I'm going to stay on Earth for any length of time, I need a job.

"You're back?" Deb says.

"I'm sorry. I don't deserve a second chance, but I'm asking for one. Do you still need a canine caregiver?"

Deb looks me up and down. "Are you okay? You're rumpled, and are there leaves in your hair?"

I shrug and brush my hair with my fingers. "I don't know. But I won't let it get in the way of doing my job. I hope for a chance to start over."

Deb seems to weigh her options before answering. "Get the mop, we'll start with grunt work. If you last the day, we can talk about tomorrow."

"Yes, ma'am," I start to the back room but pause. "Thank you," I say. I remember where the mop is and get to scrubbing the floors. I will take every moment one at a time.

I will get through this day.

I am strong, and more importantly, I won't give up without a fight.

The end of the work day cannot come quick enough. When I get home, I go straight to the bathroom. I strip off my urine and mud-stained clothes and walk straight into the shower. It was not an easy day, but I powered through every disgusting and torturous minute.

The hot water releases tension, and I feel almost normal again when I leave the shower.

"Tough day?" Rhett is at the stove, browning meat.

"You have no idea," I say.

"Try me?"

I sigh, "Are you cooking dinner?"

Rhett smirks, "I am if you spill."

"Fine." I pull up a barstool, unsure of where to begin. "I couldn't sleep last night."

"No shit," Rhett glares. "Continue."

"Hazel confronted me about Noah last night."

Rhett's eyes grew big. "As in, there was something to confront? Did you two have a little bedroom rodeo? Were you boppin' squiddles? Playing a little dungeons and dragons?"

"I don't understand."

"Come on, were you pondering the unicorn? Slaying the vadragon? Twirling the Dum-Dum, using the telescope to explore the black hole? A little bow-chick-a-wow-wow," Rhett sings out.

"I still don't know what you're trying to say."

"We're you taking the magic bus to Manchester?"

"I'm not sure where Manchester is. Should I take a bus there?"

Rhett laughs. Tears fall as she says, "Yes, you should."

"I don't understand. What's so funny?"

Rhett hoots louder. She puts a hand on my shoulder and gasps. "Do we need to talk about the birds and the bees?"

"Why? Do you have any questions? I actually know a lot about both birds and bees," I say.

"Oh, I can't. Stop," Rhett can hardly breathe. She's holding her side. "My cheeks hurt from laughing, Mona. Did you two do it or what?"

"Do what? We had sex twice. Then Hazel and Oliver showed up. We were done at that point, of course."

"Of course," Rhett purses her lips. "So you had sex twice? How was it?"

A flood of feelings fills me. "It was lovely."

"Lovely?"

"Yeah. It was hot and sticky and romantic, and my whole body convulsed multiple times. I could feel it behind my eyes, down to the tips of my toes. It was gratifying."

"You're such a trip. But it sounds like you had a good time. Just remember, no glove, no love. So tell me, what happened after you rode the bony express?"

What does she keep talking about? "Noah ordered dinner, and Hazel and Oliver showed up. Hazel stayed for dinner. I thought things were going okay. Oliver showed me his telescope, and I told him I might be unable to stay in town. I think Noah overheard us."

This news sobers Rhett right up. "Why would you have to leave?"

"I don't, but my sister made it clear if I stayed, I could no longer see her. I was just being honest, but I think Noah thought I was hiding things from him."

Rhett chews on her lip. "Go on."

"Hazel gave me a ride home, and she told me she knew something, and if I wasn't careful, she'd tell Noah."

Rhett takes a moment before responding. "Are you hiding something?"

I can't answer.

Rhett lets out a breath. "Is it bad?"

I still can't answer.

"Can you tell me?"

"Penny swore me to secrecy."

"Are you breaking the law?" Concern billows off Rhett.

"No. It's not like that. I've never lied to you, Rhett." This seems to ease some of her attention. "There's part of my past I can't talk about. But it's in the past, and if I open that door, there's no coming back. It's been made clear that I can't have everything. So, until I'm ready to leave and never see anyone again, I'd rather not say."

"I trust you. I would never have invited you into my home if I didn't. From the first time we met, I knew we'd be friends. You're like a small puzzle piece that was missing in my life. I can't explain it. But I trust you. So if you can't talk about it, then so be it. But if you are too afraid to talk about it or you need an ear, ever, I'm here. I'm a good listener. The non-judgmental kind," Rhett says.

I give Rhett a long hug. "Thank you for being you."

Rhett smiles, "Anytime, lady face. But next time you're out playing a game of Tetris, I want to be the first to hear about it."

"What's Tetris?"

"Oh gosh, there's no helping you, is there?"

I shrug.

"How did your first day go at the shelter?"

"It could have been worse. I wasn't expecting it to be so rough."

Rhett's face drops. "That bad?"

"Nah. It wasn't so bad. Just a learning curve is all. Nothing I couldn't handle," I force a smile.

"I'm sure it will get easier." Rhett's smile is hopeful. "How do you feel about chicken and red curry for dinner?

"Sounds perfect."

Just as Rhett and I were cleaning up dinner, a knock on the door caused both of us to jump.

Rhett turns and shuts the dishwasher. "Are you expecting anyone?"

"Nope. But I also don't really know anyone," I say.

Rhett peeps at a hole in the door. "Mona, it's for you."

"Who is it?" I whisper.

"Your tango partner," she says.

Embarrassment stains my cheeks. I brush off my clothes and smile.

Rhett gives me a nod and then opens the door.

Noah is just standing there, eyes averted. He sucks in the air and finds my eyes. "Can we talk?"

My stomach drops out from inside of me and lands somewhere among my feet. I check to see but find it's just nerves. "Sure. Let me grab a jacket."

I pass Rhett in the hall. "I'll be back. Wish me luck?"

"You don't need luck. And if he can't see how wonderful you are, then he's the one missing out."

I mirror Rhett's hopeful smile and make my exit.

"Should we walk?" I ask, hesitant to reach for Noah's hand.

"Sure," Noah says, but his smile fails to reach his eyes.

"I feel like we've been here before," I say.

"I don't know how to say this," Noah reaches for my hand and brings it to his mouth for a kiss.

"Be honest with me. It's okay," I say.

We round the corner of the property where a gazebo lay hidden by crawling and budding grape vines.

"Should we," I say, pointing to a double-sided swing in the middle of the gazebo.

Noah nods and sits across from me. My heart thuds in my ears. The mere idea of Noah ending things churns my stomach. Butterflies become carnivores, maggots rotting my intestines and souring my belly.

"Do you remember when we first met?" Noah asks. "It was like the celestial realm revealed itself to me, bringing you straight to me. Lightning struck my palm, and I captured it in your eyes."

I wasn't sure if I should cry or smile. "I didn't like you much at first," I admit.

"I know."

"You did?"

"It's like I've known you my whole life. Besides, you didn't like anyone much," Noah says.

"True," I can't help but smile. "I don't like most people much at all. But I'm learning, and I'm trying."

"I knew I wanted you in my life before you spoke two words. You were standing next to my brother, and he had an ear-to-ear grin. He doesn't make friends easily."

"He's not like other boys," I say. "He's a special person."

"Before he or I ever met you, he told me about a dream he had."

I feel the blood leave my body. Chills move from head to toe, and I shiver.

"He said in this dream was a woman who had many faces. I asked if he meant masks. He said, no, that she had many faces, and it was because she did not like what the world had become," Noah pauses to gather words. "This woman was singularly beautiful, and Oliver struggled to describe her. His eyes teared up, and he told me, it's like she fell from the sky and wears the perfume of every flower. Eventually, he told me she made the world a better place. He said she saved mankind from their destructive ways, but they saved her too. He said humanity shows her there's good to be found among the chaos."

Tremors course through me.

Noah moves to sit next to me. He holds my shaking hands between his own. "Oliver saw you coming into our lives before you ever stepped out of the world you've hidden away in. He saw you coming, and I didn't believe him. Not till I saw you for myself. Not till we danced under the stars, and maybe not even then."

I can't speak.

I can't find words.

"Mona, be honest with me, the way you've asked me to be honest with you."

There are no signs of life outside of the gazebo. I listen for the sounds of footsteps or the breaking of leaves.

"I know we've only known each other briefly, and I sound crazy for saying this so soon. I love you, Mona," Noah holds my gaze.

Noah's eyes softened.

"When? How?" I say.

"When did I know I loved you? I'm not sure. I think I was lost somewhere in the middle of this," Noah points between him and myself. "Before I realized I'd even begin falling."

"How could you love someone who's been so careless with your heart? I don't even think I know how to love," I look away, my words so quiet I'm not sure he hears me at first.

I won't cry.

"Sure, you do. Love is found in our actions Mona. Sometimes it's not our words but in what we do. It's in how we are with those around us. It's found in the way someone laughs and the way they light up a room. Love doesn't have to move mountains. It can be as small as moving a man to his knees."

"Noah, there's something you don't know about me. Something I don't know how to explain."

"Try me."

"I can't."

"Don't hide behind your fear. Don't build walls to keep me out," Noah's voice is sharper than I expected.

"What if telling you means never having the chance to love you?"

"What if not telling me keeps you from loving me for always?"

The silence between us echoes and takes on a life of its own.

Noah is hurt.

But I can't.

Telling him could mean losing him forever. And the fear of never seeing this beautiful, kind, brave man is enough to keep me quiet.

Noah drops my hand. "I should go."

"I'm sorry. I don't want you to leave. I—I don't know how to do this."

"You have to trust me. You have to put a little faith in us. Only a little."

"Please don't go."

Noah turns away. "Mona, I just bared my soul to you. I told you I love you. I'll tell you anything you want to know. I want to share myself with you. I—I want this." Noah looks up, "Can you say the same?"

"Noah, I want you, but I can't…."

"I have to be enough. I need honesty. I don't know how to make this work if you can't do that. I'm not just looking at today or tomorrow. I'm looking to forever."

My heart shatters.

Noah brushes a kiss on my lips and leaves.

I'm entirely alone.

52

PENNY

Mona weeps as though the sea has opened, and in one gulp, she is gone. Snot runs down her face, and by all accounts, she's brought forth a new definition of ugly crying to this world.

Bottling emotions has never been healthy for humans. And whether she's ready to admit it or not, Mona is human. Emotions have been eating at her slowly. She's falling apart in spurts and gasps.

I want to reach out and hold her. Instead, I watch as sobs rock her body. I want to tell her everything will be okay. This is not the end of life. It will go on regardless of if she fixes things or not. Mona could still fix things. She could learn to open up; even if it never worked out, this world is worth living in.

I watch Mona from a distance.

I don't approach her.

No one but Mona can make things better.

No one can push her to feel if she's unwilling.

So I listen to my sister cry into the night.

53

MONA

P enny! Damn you. Damn, you for leaving me here. Damn, you for taking away the only thing I know. Damn you, Penny," I hiccup and cough on my tears. I wipe my face with the sleeve of my shirt.

"Do you really think so little of me to damn my name?" Penny asks.

"Yes."

"That's your prerogative, I guess." Penny steps into the gazebo and sits across from me. "Have you decided to delete Earth? Or are you dying? Which is it? Because I should know if I'm losing my sister to a human disease or saying goodbye to my great-granddaughter because you're deleting her home.

Suddenly sobered, I wipe my face clear of snot. "What do you mean? You don't have children, Penny."

"You're right, I never gave birth to a child, but I felt her move inside me. I fed and housed her in my womb until I could not take it anymore. I could not deal with being human and placed her inside another. That woman cared for her none the wiser of my interference," Penny says.

Like a punch to the gut, I can't breathe. "What are you saying? Where was I? How were you pregnant on Earth? Where was I? Don't answer that," I wave my words away. "Who? How?"

"The usual way, which from what I can tell, you're plenty versed in the art of squishin' the gibly bits."

"For the love of Saturn. Rhett was talking about sex?" I break a smile.

Penny chuckles, and the tension between us eases. She scoots next to me.

"I miss you."

"I miss you too," I say.

"You're not fat. You're really quite beautiful," Penny says, leaning her head on my shoulder.

"Thanks. You're lovely too, you know. I'm not surprised someone squished your bits."

Penny squeezes me tightly, and I hold her until my fingers hurt.

"So tell me about this child you didn't have," I say.

"It's a long story, and I want to tell you every last detail. But in the end, it won't matter right now. It's in the past. It was my story, and this is yours. This is your time, Mona."

I know my sister well enough not to pry at her innermost secrets. But curiosity gnaws at me. "Give me at least a name? Tell me you loved him or her? Can you tell me something that makes this pain worth living?"

"I will provide you with the archives. I'll share it all under one condition," Penny says.

I raise an inquisitive eyebrow.

"You have to be honest with Noah."

"But you said—"

"I know what I said," Penny sighs. "Maybe I was wrong."

"I don't understand," I say.

"Look, here's the thing. I don't want you to stay for love. I don't want you to stay on Earth to spite me. I want you to stay here because you can't imagine leaving any of it yet. I want you to stay here because you want to, not because you feel forced into it out of obligation."

"I don't know if I can do this. I don't know if I have it in me to keep going on like this," I say. "I'm not human. I haven't had as much practice at this as you."

"That is what practice is for, silly. The act of doing something over and over until you become versed at it," Penny says.

"I thought that was insanity."

A gentle warmth fills Penny's gaze. "only if you don't make changes."

"What if I'm not good at it?"

"You're Mother Fucking Nature," Penny says. "What do you mean you won't be good at it?"

I smile and wipe away the tears I didn't realize persisted. "I don't know how to be anything other than who I am. How do you do all this?"

"That's the beautiful thing about being human, Mona. You don't have to know how to do it. Every one of them learns along the way. Do you think they were born knowing all there is? They all make mistakes, and they all have regrets," Penny says. "But they have the chance to turn it around, fix those mistakes and make a change for the better. Make new mistakes. So do you, sis. You don't have to give up."

"And my abilities? Will you prevent me from coding and using my gifts as Mother Fucking Nature?" I say and giggle. "It does have a ring to it, doesn't it."

"I didn't want you to have the easy way out. I didn't back you into a corner intentionally. I only wanted you to experience all those human emotions. You couldn't do it if you had your gifts. You would have never known sorrow."

"You did this to me on purpose?" Hurt and anger wash over me. "You wanted me to feel like this?"

"Yes. Get angry. Get mad at me. Feel all those emotions. I've been sitting right over there," Penny says, pointing outside the gazebo, "watching you, wanting nothing more than to comfort you. You're my sister. I don't want you to ever hurt like this. But how could you learn what it was until you felt it too? I didn't do this to you, Mona. I just didn't stop it."

Unsure of how to shift through these emotions, I ask, "Was it worth it?"

"Do you know what it means to hurt?" Penny asks.

"What do you think?" I avert my eyes.

"Yes. Yes, it was worth it, and I think you know what it means to feel that emotional stab to the chest."

"I could be bleeding right now."

"But you're not."

"Then why does it feel like I am?" I say.

"Because that's what we created. We did this. Both of us. Not just me," Penny rests a palm on my leg.

Accepting my part in things isn't easy. Because it means accepting all the bad that happened too. "They are pretty great sometimes. But it doesn't change the fact that they are hurting my planet. They bury the garbage in my land and dump plastic in my oceans. They've killed thousands of species. Humans are reckless, Penny."

"I've never disagreed with you on those points," Penny says.

"I can feel a *but* coming."

"But, does that mean they all deserve deleting?"

I can only shrug. "No. Maybe? Probably not. But I'm not sure where that line is. I can't pick and choose this human or that one to delete. They all have so many ties. I never wanted to be a dictator. I'm an artist, Penny. All I wanted to do was make more art."

"I know. I'm not asking you to be a dictator. I'm not asking you to change things. In fact, I'm not asking anything I want you to leave them. I want you to stay. For one life, is all," Penny raises her hands. "They aren't all bad, you know."

"I know."

"Will you consider it?" Penny pleads.

I shake my head. "Why? What more is there to learn?"

"So much." Penny closes her eyes, lost in a far-off moment. "Let's do something."

"Okay? What are we going to do?"

"Trust me? Okay?" Penny says.

I blow out a breath. "Fine."

Penny leaves the gazebo, and I follow on her heels. I hadn't realized Penny paused until she pressed play, and the world moved around us. The wind rustled the trees, and birds took to the sky. The sounds of the living could be heard in all directions.

"It's over here," Penny says, pointing to a small hole-in-the-wall shop off Hawley Street.

"Tattoos? You can't be serious," I say. "You want a tattoo?"

"Well, it's not my first. Who do you think made tattoos cool again?" Penny smirks.

"Well, I'll be. Ms. Penny, I had no idea you were so scandalous. What else are you holding back?"

"Oh, the things you don't know about me could fill books," Penny says, her voice a song.

"How?"

"How what?"

"How can you be the same sister I've known my whole life?" I say. "It's like you've been hiding so much of yourself from me. I don't know how."

"Do you mean, why?"

"No," I can feel my face growing hot. "I don't wonder why. I haven't been a good sister. I've tried to delete your creations every chance I get. I don't wonder why you've hidden things from me. I just, I'm not sure how."

"Less concerned with why, but the thought of someone having a one up on you bothers you, doesn't it?" Penny says.

"How?" I say again.

"You can't be everywhere at once. You're not that talented. Besides, when you get to building things, you go into a deep focus. Nothing else seems to matter. The worlds could collapse all around you, and you'd be none the wiser till you stopped."

"I'm not dense, Penny."

"I never called you dense. I just said that sometimes you're a bit unobservant."

"Whatever," I say, wanting to end this conversation. "So, you still want to get a tattoo?"

"I want you to get one with me," Penny says, grabbing my hand and dragging me into the shop.

The small parlor is dimly lit. Posters of skulls, Harley Davidson, and artwork fill the walls. A small barrier exists between the front desk and the rest of the shop. Behind the barrier are three leather recline chairs and several tables.

"It looks a bit like a medieval mad scientist's lab," I say.

"Nah, I was there, and they were much grimier than this."

No words.

A woman approaches the counter with long emerald hair, dark eyeliner, and red lipstick. "Hey ladies, can I help you with anything today?"

The woman has a naked mermaid on her left arm, and the detail is absolutely breathtaking. "Did you do that? It's stunning."

"Thanks? Jeff did my mermaid, but we worked on her art together," says the woman pointing a finger over her shoulder at a man.

"My sister here thinks we should get tattoos," I say. "What did you have in mind, Pen?"

"That is some wicked ink. Could you draw up a unicorn bust using a watercolor design?"

The woman smiles for the first time. "I'm Zoe. Yeah, that sounds rad. You looking big or small?"

I can't help but watch Penny in fascination. I'd never seen my sister so...human. She fits here. Penny's one of them. There's no hesitation in her body, no question in her voice. Penny knows who she is, and I envy her.

"What about you?" Jeff came to the desk with a couple of books filled with examples of his work. "Do you know what you want?"

I hadn't given it much thought, but I told Jeff my idea. It feels right. Besides, if I don't like it, it's not like a tattoo means forever.

"Sounds simple enough. I can do it," Jeff says.

"Wonderful."

I cringe under the gun. That's what Jeff called his handheld torture machine, a tattoo gun. No one told me it would feel like the fires of Reyon. I risk a glance at Penny, and she's stoic. Her skirt is pulled up, and Zoe works on Penny's thigh. She's proving to be a different person than I believed her to be in my head.

Penny catches me flinching and smiles. "The last one I got was on my chest, I almost did another there, but this seemed much more—sexy."

"Stop making me laugh. It hurts more than I thought it would, and I'd rather it hurt less," I say.

"Baby."

"Whatever, Penn-neeee."

"Sure, sure, Mon-naaa," Penny smiles.

All might not be right with the world, but I never felt more sure of my footing with my sister.

Would you look at that? "You did a beautiful job. Thank you,"

I say.

"It wasn't too difficult. Do you think the paint stroke has enough color?" the tattooist asks.

"Yes, it's perfect. I love the way the purple fades to pink and then to yellow. It's exactly as I pictured it," I say, admiring the infinity sign on my wrist.

I hid my new tattoo from Penny, wanting it to be a surprise. By the time Penny was finally done, I'd already paid and enjoyed a coffee from next door.

"What do you think?" Penny raised her skirt showing off her unicorn bust, sporting pinks, purples, and blues dripping down the side of her leg.

It kind of looks like someone dribbled paint on her. "It's exactly you. It's colorful, romantic, and filled with magic."

Penny's eyes water, "That's so sweet."

"Oh, don't start crying just yet. I haven't shown you mine." I hold out my arm for her.

"Mona…"

"I got it for you, Penny. It's a reminder that my love for you goes on forever. Even when I want to push you off the cliffs of Sion, I still love you. It's a paintbrush stroke because I'm an artist too, and sometimes I need a reminder of that."

Tears fall onto Penny's rosy cheeks. "Mona, I—" she wraps her arms around me. "I knew you had it in you all along. I love you too, sister. I love you too."

I hold Penny at arm's length and feel a tingling sensation start at the base of my neck. It spreads down the tips of my fingers. "Did you?"

"I promised you the reins if you managed all eight tiny, little human emotions," Penny winks.

For the first time in days, I press pause.

"What are you going to do with them?" Concern flashes in Penny's eyes.

"I'm going to do what I should have done all along," I say. "I just wish it hadn't taken me this long to figure it all out."

"Whatever you decide, a promise is a promise. I love you either way."

I stretch my fingers, take a deep breath, and start writing code.

54

MONA

This is the same coffee shop where I first met Hazel. It feels as though years have passed since that day. I get in line behind Hazel without being noticed.

Hazel orders, "Can I get a sixteen-ounce drip with steamed soy milk, please?" After she pays, she makes her way to the pickup counter.

"What can I get you?" the barista asks.

"I'll have a cup of coffee. Can you add the chocolate sauce to it?" I smile.

"Sure thing. Anything else?"

"Nope, that's all," I say, handing the barista a ten-dollar bill I coded a moment before, placing the change into the tip jar.

"Can I get a name?"

"Mona."

"Alright, Mona, that will be right up."

"Thanks."

"So you think they'll get your name right this time?" I ask.

Hazel picks up her drink, and the side reads, *Hayzeal soy drip*. "I've read worse before."

"Can we talk?"

"Sure," she says.

I grab my cup before leading Hazel outside to a table, which afforded us slightly more privacy than the inside of the noisy café.

"Do you ever put chocolate in your coffee?" I sip my drink and ride the chocolate train to cloud bliss.

Hazel shakes her head.

"Well, you should try it next time. It's really quite a treat. They don't have chocolate where I'm from. In fact, the food is a source of energy, not made to tickle and delight the taste buds. Here though," I close my eyes. "You have such treats. I don't know if I'll ever get used to it. I don't want to think about life without tasting such divine treats again."

"What do you want, Mona? This small talk is nice and all, but I'm sure you didn't ask me here to talk about chocolate."

"No, you're right. I didn't," I smile, but Hazel doesn't waver. "I wanted to talk to you about the other night."

"What about it?"

"You know, as well as I do, I'm not from around here," I say, twirling a finger around in the air.

Hazel doesn't speak.

"I didn't lie to you when I said I meant no harm to you or Noah. I really care about him. I would never do anything to deliberately hurt him."

"I've heard this speech before. Tell me something new because this one is getting old," Hazel crosses her arms.

"My name isn't Mona."

Hazel sips her coffee. "I'm listening."

"I've had many names. Several of them even I struggle to pronounce. Most recently, I've been called Mother Nature. I shortened it to Mona because I didn't want to appear overly egotistical. There's a fine line between narcissism and egomaniacal. I enjoy riding that line, but I don't like to cross it."

"What makes you think I'm going to believe some cocked-up story you've pulled out of your ass?" Hazel sets both hands on the table.

"I didn't make it up."

"Prove it then."

"I thought you might say that." I reach for the sleeve on Hazel's coffee, remove it, and fold it up smaller and smaller. I hold it out to her when it's as small as I can make it.

"So?"

I hold Hazel's gaze while squishing the cardboard between her palms until there is nothing but ash between her hands.

"I've seen Chris Angel. You're not pulling one over on me."

"Who do you think taught him?" I have no idea who Chris Angel is.

I close her hands again, only focusing my energy on the ash this time. Our hands grow brighter. Light emanates from the inside out.

Hazel starts to stand, I'm sure wanting to distance herself from the human glow worm.

I release Hazel's hands slowly. She thumps back down in her seat, transfixed.

In the center of her palm sits a rosebud. It slowly grows in her hand, transforming from a bud to a full-fledged flower, deep purple in color.

Hazel lifts the blossom, mesmerized as it turns from plum to snow white. She takes a deep breath inhaling the sweet aroma.

"How?"

"I told you, I'm Mona."

"But how? Why? Help me understand."

"My sister and I played our part in building this world," I say, carefully leaving out the part about being the creator of Earth. The last thing I need is another god complex. "Well, we fight. Like all sisters do. One thing led to another, and I was sent here. On Earth. I needed to prove to her and myself that I could live here and belong in the human world."

"So you're not…." Hazel trails off.

"Human? Not exactly. No," I say.

"But you look human."

I smile, "This body is human, Hazel. I am as human as you are. Only I can tap into the Bio-Matrix system. It's what allows me to create that flower you're holding."

"Are you god?"

I nearly choke at this, "Not hardly. I'm just Mona."

"What about Noah and Oliver?"

"What about them?"

"I'm trying to wrap my head around all of this."

"Oliver is a gifted young man. I adore him. There are glitches in the system we built. Oliver has an innate genetic ability to tap into the glitch," I say.

"The glitch? You're making it sound like we're all a computer program or something."

"Or something," I look away, uneasy. "Oliver is able to know some things before other people, or sometimes instead of other people. He is special. There's nothing wrong with him. There's nothing wrong with you either."

"And Noah? What do you want with him?"

"I don't want anything from him. I just want to continue getting to know him better. I have feelings for Noah, and I want the opportunity to explore what he could mean to me."

Hazel casts her eyes down. "So, you and Noah?"

I breathe in air and find courage. "Yes, me and Noah. If he doesn't hate me, that is."

"Why would he hate you? You're perfect."

"I'm not perfect, Hazel. I'm far from it. I'm just as flawed as you. Probably more so because I'm still learning how everything works. I don't know how to navigate these emotions or this human life any better than you do."

Hazel harrumphs.

"I was jealous of you when I learned you have feelings for Noah. Still am."

"Jealous of me?" Hazel throws her head back, laughing. "Don't lie to me."

"I will never lie to you," I say with utter conviction. "Ever."

"But then why?"

"Look at you. You're smart, funny, and caring. You know what you want. You move through this life with grace and confidence. You are kind to strangers who are having a bad day. You take care of Olli when no obligations are forcing you. Why wouldn't I be jealous of you?"

Hazel's eyes prick with tears. "Thanks—but I'm the one who should be sorry."

"No. You don't get to be sorry. I wasn't upfront with you when I should have been. I can't tell the world who I am. It would cause chaos. But I should have told the ones I care about. I want you to be in my life. Can you forgive me?"

Hazel looks from me to the white rose in her hand. "I guess that depends."

"I understand." I take my coffee, prepared to walk away.

"Will you teach me how to do this?" Hazel rests the rose in the palm of my hand.

I breathe a sigh of relief. "I'd love nothing more."

55

MONA

Rhett was on a mission to save the world. After I came clean about everything, she was set on helping me and some person named Prithvi.

"Can I get you anything?" Rhett says.

"Who's Prithvi?" I ask for the third time.

Rhett gives me a coy smile. "You can't fool me, Prithvi. Play dumb all you want. I still know who you really are."

I sigh, "I didn't tell you I was Mother Nature, so you could worship me like one of your deities. I'm simply Mona, okay?"

"Prithvi *is* Mother Nature. I'm just trying to show you the respect my mother beat into me. She'd freak if I told her I was living with Prithvi without any sort of ritual."

"It's a good thing you've just been living with Mona then, right?"

Rhett rolls her eyes.

"How dare you roll your eyes at me, child," my voice booms.

Rhett pales.

"Only kidding!" My whole body shakes with amusement.

"You're an asshole," Rhett says.

"Nope. I'm just Mona."

"Okay, *just Mona*. What's your plan?"

"I don't have one," I say.

"What about Noah?" Rhett asks.

"What about him?"

"You have to tell him."

I look away. "I don't know how yet."

"One word at a time," Rhett says.

"You make it sound so simple."

"It doesn't have to be hard," Rhet says.

"Everything you humans do is hard," I counter.

"So you're just going to do the human thing and see how it goes?"

"I'm not ready to leave yet. I'm not ready to say goodbye. Besides, Prithvi has many lives, and this is just one of them," I smirk.

"See, I knew it!" Rhett says, and we both break out into giggles.

Rhett streams music to her stereo. "Okay, so let's do this. You'll never survive being human if you can't learn to cook."

"Sure, I can." I reach for my phone. "I have the pizza guy's number right here."

"Ha. I don't know how long that will last. You'll burn out on it eventually."

"As if."

"You have to learn like the rest of us, lady," Rhett says.

When she's not looking, I code my parts of the recipe to completion. I want to be human, but what's the point in having supercomputer powers if I don't use them occasionally?

"It's been three days. You have to get up," Rhett says, picking up an empty pint. "No more Chunky Monkey? Did you eat all the red velvet cake too?"

"No, I think there's one slice left," I mutter.

"You think? You don't know?" Rhett says. "Just go talk to him."

"I can't. Look at me." I pull at my ice cream-stained shirt. "I'm a mess. He's probably already forgotten my name."

"Prithvi, no one could forget you." Rhett clears away an empty pizza box from the couch and sits.

"They can if they don't know who I am. Remember, he just thinks I'm the girl who broke his heart."

"No way. I've seen the way he looks at you."

I reach under the couch, sliding out a cake box. "You didn't see how things ended. He doesn't want me." Inside the box is the last piece of red velvet cake.

"Give me that," Rhett says, stealing my fork. She takes a bite. "Mmm—we should get another one of these."

"It's so good," I agree.

"Yeah, but after you've fixed things, or I might not get any."

I snag the fork back.

"Don't pretend you can't just snap yourself clean. I know better," Rhett says, giving me a dubious look.

"But I'm trying to be human."

Rhett snickers. "I'm sure. Like I didn't see you code those dishes clean last night."

"I—Oh, fine."

Rhett points a finger at me. "Caught! See, nothing gets past me."

"I wasn't trying to hide anything," I say, knowing my face

turned three shades pinker.

"I know, you're just being mopey. Do something about it already. You've made up with Hazel and your sister, but you can't fix things with Noah? Please." Rhett waves me away. "I don't want to hear it." Rhett takes the cake with her to the kitchen.

"I wasn't done with that," I say.

"I don't care. Take a shower and get out of here."

"What?"

"Did I stutter? Take. A. Shower. And. Get. Out. Of. Here. Don't come back till you've fixed things."

"What do I wear?" sudden panic taking over.

"Go naked."

"As if," I say, appalled at the suggestion.

"You could just open a jacket and show him the goods. Wouldn't have to say much at that point," Rhett says.

"Be serious."

"I just don't think it matters. What matters is that you're honest. I know you're not ready to lose him. The two pints of Chocolate Cherry Garcia told me so yesterday. Are you prepared to walk away? Be done?

I play with my shirt, avoiding Rhett's watchful eye.

"I didn't think so."

Thirty minutes later, I was stopping by the coffee shop, procrastinating every last moment I could.

"Half-caf mocha with almond milk, please." I pay the barista and spot Hazel furiously typing away on her laptop.

"Hey lady, how's it going?"

Hazel glanced up and offered a seat. "Great, actually. I'm trying to meet a deadline, and I think I've about got it."

"What's this one about?"

"Same as yesterday, I'm afraid," she says.

"Right, that makes sense. You're not a book-authoring savant," I say.

"Nope. I'm the normal kind of book writer. One word at a time."

The sounds of coffee shop traffic fill the air, and I find it oddly comforting.

"Did you get the email I sent you?" Hazel asks.

"Yes, thank you. I appreciate the information. If I can't delete the world, I'll have to take it one person at a time." My smile falters thinking of Noah. The one person I'm still afraid to take on.

"Have you talked to him yet?"

"No." I run my fingers through my hair.

"Just talk to him," Hazel says.

"You sound like Rhett."

"Trust me on this one. Okay? It's going to be fine," Hazel's eyes sparkle like her name.

I want to believe her.

"You can't know that," I say in a futile attempt not to shed more tears.

"I know Noah."

An uncomfortable churning begins in my stomach. "I was heading his way before I stopped here."

"Well, don't let me be the reason you don't go," Hazel makes a shooing motion at me.

"Yeah, I guess." I take a long slow drag of my coffee. "Wish me luck?"

"You don't need it."

Changing the world didn't scare me. Changing someone's heart, however, is terrifying.

When I walked up to Noah's house, my feet cemented to the sidewalk. I try to take a step, but my feet are Osmium weights holding me to the spot. I quickly check my system and am disappointed to learn I'm not actually stuck. It's in my mind.

My nerves settle, and I ring the doorbell.

The door opens before I've gotten my finger off the button.

"I wondered how long you were going to stand out there," Noah says, holding the door open.

"You knew I was out here?"

Noah steps to the side, tempting me in.

"Thanks," I smile and curse the moths hatching in my stomach.

"Told you she'd come today," Oliver says, skipping down the stairs. "Hi, Mona!"

I open my arms, and Oliver lands in them. I wrap him in a tight squeeze. "I missed you too, kid."

"Yeah, I know. You missed Noah too, didn't you."

I glance at Noah. "Yes, I missed him too."

"Hey, Olli, why don't you run and check on our hot cocoa," Noah says.

"I don't think that the hot cocoa needs supervision. It's not going to run away," Oliver says.

"Oliver," Noah says through gritted teeth.

"Yeah, yeah. I can take a hint. I'll see you soon, Mona. I've got to check and see if the hot cocoa spawned legs recently." Oliver trots off to the kitchen.

"Kids," Noah says, running a hand through his tussled hair.

I walk into the library, sit down, and pat the seat next to me. "Can we talk?"

Noah sits.

I reach for his hand. "I've only loved one person in my whole life. My sister. I've never done this before, and I don't know how. But I want to try. With you," I say. "I promise to always be here, to never run away again. I promise to always hold your hand and dance under every star-filled night we can. I don't want this," I point between him and I, "to ever end."

"You had me at the doorbell," Noah leans in to kiss me, but I pull back.

"No, not yet. I'm not finished."

Noah forced a laugh. "Should I be worried?"

I breathe out my fear and remember I'm *Mother Fucking Nature*. "I'm not who you think I am."

Noah's eyes smolder. "I don't care."

Noah tries to kiss me again, but I place a hand on his chest. "What do you mean you don't care?"

"Do you want to be with me, Mona?"

"Yes."

"Do you want to be in Oliver's life?"

"Yes."

"Are you Cthulhu? I think I'd have seen tentacles if you were," Noah says in jest.

Waves of heat roll across my skin. "Nope. I'm not Cthulhu."

"Oliver is convinced you're here to help humans, not hurt them."

"Ha! Yes. Well, your brother is correct. I'm here to help them…now."

"Then there's nothing you could say that would scare me away. May I please kiss you now?"

I put up a hand. "You don't make this easy on a girl."

"You don't make it easy for me either," Noah says.

"You good?" I ask.

Noah laughs, "Baby, I've never been better than when you're nearby."

"You see, the thing is, I'm—" I search for the words. "I'm not like other women. The thing is—"

Noah cuts me off, "Hazel told me."

"What?"

"She told me everything after you had coffee with her," Noah says.

I feel stunned. "Why didn't she say anything last I saw her?"

"I'm not going to lie. I was a little taken aback by the whole Mother Nature thing, but once Oliver explained," Noah moves a piece of my hair behind my ear. "It didn't seem to matter. I love you, Mona. That hasn't changed. Maybe it means you can get my garden looking good," Noah chuckles.

"I don't care about any of it. Not if you still want this with me."

My eyes sting, and my chest inflates with so much warmth I think I might float away. I take Noah's head and pull his mouth to mine. He tastes sweet and warm. I let all the anxiety roll off my shoulders and melt into the moment.

Noah pulls back. "So, I'll take that as a yes?"

"You can take that as hell, yes."

56

MONA

Spinning around barefoot in my new apartment, my heart is full. "It's exactly how I imagined it would be."

"I'm still not sure why you didn't opt for some land. Wouldn't that be, you know, more your style?" Hazel says walking around the open space.

"I want to spend my days influencing those around me in positive ways. Not tending to my own garden." For the first time, I feel like I belong.

"Think of the whole world as her garden," Rhett says.

Noah wraps an arm around my waist and kisses my neck. "Besides, if she was going to move into some big house on land, then I want to be part of the decision. But for now, this isn't too bad, I guess. As long as you're still not reconsidering moving in with me?"

I playfully pinch at Noah's arm. "I can't just move in with you. I need to stand on my own legs first. Plus, you're going to college. You'll need the quiet study time. We've talked about this."

"I know, I know. I'm only teasing. I support your decision. As long as I get to keep you, you can take all the time in the world. You're worth the wait." Noah kisses me sweetly.

"Oh, you haven't seen the best part yet," I say, dancing my way to the open window. I climb out onto the fire escape.

On the roof of my apartment building is a secret garden. Three archways stand in the center, covered in grapes. Flower beds line the entire roofline, blossoming out of their boxes. I grew vegetables in one corner and there are full grown fruit bearing trees that give this rooftop a true forest feel.

"Did you?" Hazel was the first to speak.

"I gave it all new life, but the framework was already here."

"How are the trees rooted?" Noah asks.

I give him a sly smile.

Oliver was the last to climb up the ladder and the only one who wasn't fazed by the wonder. "Can I have an apple?"

I point to a ripe one for him. Oliver ate half the apple before the others recovered.

"This is amazing Prithvi. I mean, I knew you were gifted but this is something else," Rhett says.

"I asked you to stop calling me that." I narrow my eyes at Rhett. "This is because I moved out, isn't it? I couldn't live with you forever. What would you do if you needed to squish your gibly bits?"

Rhett claps her mouth and glances around. "Oh yeah, I'm going to get on that real soon," she giggles. "But I can't help who you are no more than you can."

"Does Penny know?" Hazel asks.

"Penny doesn't have to approve of every aspect of my life. I made sure I'm the only one with access to the roof," I say then immediately go crimson. "I mean, besides you all."

Noah's hand finds my own, slipping his fingers into mine. "I think it's spectacular. Just like you."

"Good apples Mona," Oliver says.

"Thanks Olli, I'm glad you liked it."

"It was like eating candy. You guys should try one," Oliver

says.

I sit down on a bench. For the first time in the history of Earth I'm excited about what being a human could bring into my life. It hasn't been easy, even with my coding abilities. I hear it's not supposed to be. I might grow right alongside them.

I'm human, and I wouldn't have it any other way.

Acknowledgments

For better or worse, I haven't always had a lot of women in my life. But I have sisters. When I wanted to explore the depths of female relationships in my writing, drawing on the women in my life became not just a choice but a necessity. Over the years, I've been blessed with the privilege of knowing some truly remarkable women. Their strength, resilience, and compassion have left an indelible mark on my heart. This book is a tribute to them, a celebration of the profound impact they've had on me and my writing journey.

In no particular order, this is to Melanie, Angie, Lindsey, Betty, Tomoko, Devri, Emily, the real Hazel, Natalie, Nhi, Torrieann, Kathy, Sky, Heidi, Heather, Sophie, Adelaide, Penny, Beabo, Candice, Melissa, Janet, Grace, Eyvyn, Charline, Nat, Kaytie, Donna, Sarah, Deb, Sonia, Brandie, and Jo. Even though time or distance may have created gaps in our communication, I want you all to know that each these beautiful women has left a permanent impact on my life. Your presence, friendship, and support have been nothing short of extraordinary, and I'm forever grateful for the memories we've shared. Each of you has enriched my life in unique and meaningful ways, and I hold you all close to my heart. I love you all so much.

Thank you to Liam for inspiring Oliver. I love you forever, kiddo.

This book has had three full iterations, and I'm thankful to my beta readers for sticking it out. Justin, Peter, Hazel, Angie, Deb, Pattie, Melanie, Ron, Denver, Brandy, Sam, Moe, Kathryn, Rowan, David, Sara, Michelle, and whomever else

I'm foolishly forgetting. Your insightful feedback and unwavering support have been invaluable in shaping this story. Your encouragement kept me going during the toughest moments of doubt. For believing in me and my work, I am eternally grateful.

Writing this book has been a labor of love from beginning to end. I'm deeply indebted to everyone who has been a part of this journey. Your presence has filled it with warmth and purpose.

To my family and friends, your love and understanding during my countless hours of writing and editing have meant the world to me. Your belief in my abilities has been a constant source of motivation.

A special thank you goes to my editor, whose expertise and guidance have been instrumental in refining this novel and making it the best it could be.

To all the writers and creators who have inspired me, thank you for showing me the limitless possibilities of storytelling.

Last but not least, I want to express my gratitude to the readers. Your interest and support make this endeavor worthwhile. It's my greatest hope that this book will touch your hearts and minds in some meaningful way.

With heartfelt appreciation,

Miranda

About the Author

Miranda Levi is the award winning author of "A Tear In Time" and "From A Youth A Fountain Did Flow." She is an accomplished fiction writer and poet hailing from the Pacific Northwest. Her writing is known for captivating readers with her evocative storytelling and lyrical prose, which transport readers into other worlds and perspectives. With a passion for exploring the human experience, Levi's works delve into the complexities of life, love, and loss and offer a glimpse into the human soul.

Miranda lives in Seattle with her husband Peter, their demon cat Hamilton, and a taxidermy raccoon named Vincent Cheese.

You can visit her at https://mirandalevi.com